KRISSY DANIELS

Published by Kiss Me Dizzy Books
Edited by Corinne DeMaagd
cmdediting.com
Formatting by Elaine York
allusiongraphics.com
Cover Design by Okay Creations
okaycreations.com

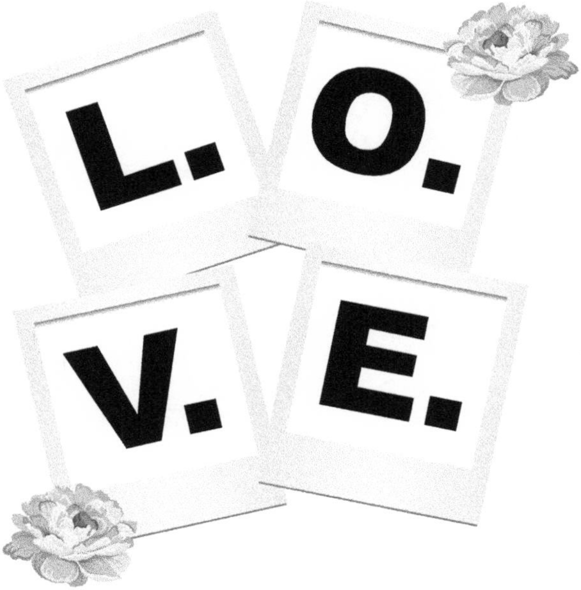
L. O.
V. E.

For those who fight with their heart
and cling to integrity, despite knowing
they'll be left broken.

PART ONE

Look Away

Natalie

My coffee was hot. My speech well-practiced. Nat King Cole's "When I Fall In Love" played in the background. Not the ideal soundtrack for a public breakup, but I could use the sentiment to my advantage.

Gathering courage in one deep inhale, I opened my mouth to speak.

Holden beat me to the punch, belting, "Who are you looking at?"

"What?" I snapped my gaze from the swirling liquid in my mug to the man sitting across from me, who as it turned out, wasn't paying me any attention at all.

Face red, chest inflated, body vibrating with unbridled energy, Holden glared hellfire at someone at the counter. I risked a quick perusal at the poor soul, and dear, sweet Jesus, no wonder my hotheaded, soon-to-be ex-boyfriend, was ready to blow. The target of Holden's outrage was handsome, the kind of pretty that made you do a double take, but his obvious beauty wasn't the issue. The problem was the beautiful stranger seemed to be frozen in time, coat in one hand, phone in the other, dreamy eyes aimed my direction with laser focus.

My stomach flipped, then warmed, the heat spreading from gut to limbs like a shot of Dad's expensive whiskey. I had never felt more coveted. Ever. Not through words, touch, actions. Especially not from the way someone looked at me. And that man studied me like I was the answer to all his questions.

Oh, shitty, shit, shittard.

Look away, I mentally urged the clueless stranger. *For the love of God, look away.*

Holden shifted, readying to stand, a move I knew too well.

Predicting the outcome, I slammed a hand around his thick wrist, my grip tight but slight compared to his bulk. "Holden, please. Not today. Just ignore the guy."

"Ignore him?" he seethed. "He's eye-fucking my woman."

He wasn't.

Admiring. Appreciating, maybe. Regardless, I kept those thoughts to myself.

Holden ran hot one hundred percent of the time, and the slightest spark could cause a devastating explosion. Great quality in bed, not so much in public.

"Please." I summoned my frail voice, knowing he couldn't resist vulnerability in any woman, but especially, *his* woman. "I need to talk to you." Then, because Holden loved an ego stroke, I threw in, "He's probably one of your fans and recognizes me from your posts."

Holden vibrated, his leg bouncing under the table. He gnawed on his bottom lip, that vein in his left temple protruding. Finally, a dramatic exhale signaled a shift from his rage haze, and he turned to face me once again.

"Yeah, baby, you're probably right. What do you need to talk about?" His steely, blue eyes searched mine, but never landed, never focused.

Palms sweaty, I released his arm and opened my mouth to speak. "I think—"

"I wish you'd wear contacts when we're out together," he interrupted. "Those glasses hide your gorgeous face." Leaning closer, he reclaimed my hand and rubbed a small circle in my palm, as if to soothe the sting of his words. "And those lenses always ruin our pictures."

I choked down my retort because his comment was only one of the many reasons our relationship was over.

In my periphery, a tall figure drew near, his presence a pulsing, radiant force. My body hummed, attuned to his frequency. With every bit of willpower I possessed, I refrained from straying my focus.

I pushed my glasses higher on my nose, sucked in a breath, and started again the speech I'd practiced for days. "Listen, Ho—"

The stranger, now mere steps from our table, cleared his throat, drawing Holden's attention, and mine, in his direction.

I was met with a soft, inquisitive gaze, and my insides shifted, tightening and tingling and, dammit, I heated from the inside out, my cheeks burning something fierce. The man was dressed for a day at the office but carried himself like a prize fighter about to enter the ring, confident, focused, ready to conquer.

As if Holden was nothing but air, the clueless patron offered me a nod and added a cocky, sideways grin before moving past.

Dimples.

Sweet Lord, he had dimples.

My kryptonite.

If the man's presence was a spark, his blatant flirt was a barrel of gasoline with a lit bundle of TNT thrown into the mix.

Holden exploded from his chair, knocking the table, me, and my coffee off balance. Hot liquid scorched my chest. "Goddammit, Holden!" I cried, stumbling to my feet. A woman screamed. Men shouted from behind the counter.

Someone hooked an arm around my waist, pulling me to safety before our table flew. Behind me carried on the unmistakable grunts, huffs, and all-too-familiar smacks of a fight well under way.

Just another day in the life of Holden Oswald Travers the Third.

My vision blurred, rage washing away the humiliation.

One and a half years had been five hundred forty days too long to be acquainted with the fitness model/personal trainer/self-proclaimed media superstar, despite his boyish blue eyes, well-conditioned body, or his giant...ahem, never mind. For the record, size did not matter when attached to a narcissistic gym rat.

Without a second thought, or running to the aid of the innocent victim who'd done nothing but look at me, I stormed out the back exit.

Fuck Holden. He didn't deserve the courtesy of a mature breakup.

And fuck that beautiful stranger and his mesmerizing stare.

Cole

Mesmerizing. Sweet Jesus, that woman knocked me for a loop, and then some. Right before her bulldog attacked.

Been a long time since anyone had gotten the jump on me. Too bad that silver-eyed angel hadn't stuck around to watch me wipe the floor with her boyfriend.

The guy was all brawn and bravado. No brain. The type I was all too familiar with. A runaway train with faulty brakes. Only way to stop that path of destruction was by way of decommission. A few jabs for warm-up, then one strike to that square jaw, and the hot-head had dropped like a fly.

Even unconscious, the guy looked angry. Made no sense, that matchup. She was sunshine, and he was gloomier than the fall drizzle outside.

Not my problem, I reminded myself.

The police were called. An ambulance, too.

Witnesses confirmed my story. I'd been jumped and acting solely in self-defense. I wouldn't press charges. Not worth my time.

The kicker? The woman had disappeared. I didn't get a chance to make sure she was okay, and that bothered me more than losing thirty minutes of my morning.

Ellis waited outside, arms crossed over his massive chest, hip against my Roadster. "How is it you manage to destroy a cafe, but don't get a speck of dust on your silk shirt?"

"Thanks for your help, asshole." I bumped his arm as I passed.

"You had it handled. Besides"—he tapped on the door—"someone had to guard your shiny new car."

I'd recently ditched my gas-guzzler for electric and, damn, she was a beauty. Quick, too. God bless Elon Musk. Ellis, two sizes too large for the vegan leather seat, never wasted a chance to be seen standing next to, or sitting inside, my sporty black Tesla. Always with the window down. Always with a cheesy grin on his face. Didn't take much to keep my friend happy and, damn, I liked him happy.

I made my way to the driver's side and told him over the roof, "Some over-juiced pretty boy didn't like me looking at his girl."

"What girl? And why the hell were you looking?"

"God's honest?" I settled into the driver's seat, waited for Ellis to tuck in. "I don't fucking know."

I knew. Didn't like what had come over me. A strange sense of kismet, an unexplainable familiarity, an unholy attraction.

"Spell it out for me." The skin between his thick brows wrinkled.

I merged into traffic. "I was minding my own business, waiting for our coffee, and I heard her voice. She sounded like Cadence." I swallowed the lump in my throat. God, I missed my sister. "That's what made me look. And, damn, the woman was beautiful. Had this aura. She glowed. Stopped me dead." I refrained from waxing poetic about her silky blond hair, her pink, full lips, or eyes the color of cold steel.

"Aura?" Ellis laughed. "C'mon man. That's bullshit, and you know it."

"Yeah, I fucking know. Doesn't change the fact it happened. Swear to Christ, when she looked at me, my brain short-circuited."

"You're lucky her boyfriend didn't make a meal outta your skinny ass."

Ellis stood an inch taller than me, had me by a good fifty pounds, but where I was turkey breast, my friend was more prime rib, and he never let an opportunity slip to remind me he was bigger, despite the fact he'd never taken me down on the mat.

Our trip to the gym passed in silence. Ellis only zipped his lips when he had something epic to say, a think before you speak kind of guy, so I parked, cut the engine, and said, "Spit it out, bud," then made myself comfortable, settling into the seat and buckling down for an earful.

After a deep rise and fall of his chest, he blurted, "I'm worried about you."

"Okay." So was I, but that was between me and my weathered spirit.

"Seriously. What's up? You've been off lately. You're always on edge. You spend all your free time at the gym. And what was that scuffle really about this morning?"

"He attacked me," I reminded him. "And you know damn well why I'm at the gym."

Holden rolled his eyes. "Yeah, I know. You're on a mission. Noble, yes, but nobody gets the jump on you unless you wanna fight."

Fuck. True. First glance I'd known that, if provoked, the guy at the coffee shop would react, and maybe I'd needed the release. But that wasn't what'd made me look in the first place. That woman's presence had drawn me in. Siren enchanting the sailor. Seeing her sitting next to that Mike O'Hearn wannabe had summoned my primal urges.

"Not sure what came over me. It was crazy like I knew her, but on a whole different level. God." I scratched my aching temple. "This is hard to explain. There was a connection. Just...something. That ever happen to you?"

The left side of his mouth twitched. He tried and failed to hide his grin. "Yeah, when I met Darlene."

Darlene, the woman who'd broken his heart more than once before skipping town with Eva, his one-eyed Yorkie.

"So you get it?"

"No, dipshit." He flicked the side of my head. "I don't get it."

"But you just said—"

His thick finger jabbed my chest, silencing me. "Not the same."

"How's it different?"

With a huff, he jerked the door handle and dropped one foot to the asphalt, then paused. "When I met Darlene, I was single." Before closing the door, he turned and asked, "And where the hell is my coffee?"

2

Natalie

"**S**o, how'd he take it?" Mom asked over her shoulder, working the buttons on the Keurig. She wore her favorite cardigan, the violet highlighting her ice-blue eyes.

I slammed my handbag down next to a stack of mail on the dining table. "I didn't get a chance to do the deed." I huffed, then plopped my rear onto a stool at the kitchen island.

Mom slid a fresh cup of coffee my way. "Why not? Did you change your mind?"

"Oh, hell no. We're over." I chugged, suffering through the burn, because Mom's coffee was the bomb. "But that bulldozer will have to figure it out on his own. I'm done."

I relayed the details of my horrid morning. The fight. The humiliation. My ruined blouse. The stranger with the dreamy eyes who did nothing but look at me like I was everything he'd ever wanted in the world... And wow, thinking back, I'd suffer again to bear the weight of that gaze.

"What happened to the guy?"

I looked up from my drink to find Mom leaned over the counter, chin resting in the palm of her left hand, a knowing smirk twisting her pink-tinged lips.

"I didn't stick around to find out."

She blew a raspberry. "Too bad. Sounds like a keeper, to risk life and limb over a woman he's never met."

"Yeah, too bad. The man might've been my soulmate. Now he's possibly dead, or at the very least, pulverized because of my embarrassing lapse in judgement when it comes to dating." Dropping my face to my hands, I shook off the funky vibes and laughed. What else could I do?

Mom raised her mug. "Good riddance, Holden Oswald Travers the Third."

I lifted my cup to hers. "Damn straight."

Mom mumbled, "I always hated that name."

I tapped her mug again. "Amen to that."

Dad strode into the room, his thick gray hair wet from his shower, his shirt unbuttoned, his belt buckle undone. "What are we celebrating?" he asked, sleepy eyes brightening when he looked at Mom.

He slid a weathered hand over her hip, up her spine, then settled on the nape of her neck before pulling her close. A kiss on her forehead. Next, her nose. Then downward to devour her lips. He pulled back, whispered, "Yummy," making Mom giggle. He then topped off his assault with a sharp smack to her ass. Same routine, every morning, for as long as I could remember. Swear to the good Lord above, Charles and Linda King fell more in love every passing day.

"Mornin', Nugget." Dad kissed the top of my head, grabbed the drink out of my hand, and took a long swig.

Holding my coffee hostage, he stared at me long and hard. "Well?"

"I'm happy to report that Holden will not be the father of your grandchildren. It's over."

"That's my girl." He ruffled my hair. "I always hated his name. Besides," Dad continued, "he wasn't your soulmate." Dad wiggled his eyebrows and turned to the sink before I could shoot him a glare.

"He's right." Mom never wasted an opportunity to remind me I'd met my soulmate in the hospital on the day I was born. "You're going to marry a man named Caleb."

"Yeah. Yeah. Well, when will I meet this Caleb? I'm gonna be an old maid soon."

"I wish I knew, baby." Mom held a palm to her heart. "Fate works on its own top secret schedule." She bent to pull something out of the cupboard and said while out of sight, "I wish I wouldn't have lost that woman's number. I just know we could've been great friends."

Legend had it my mother and my soulmate's mother had met in the maternity ward while walking the hallways late at night in hopes of speeding up their labor.

I'd heard the story countless times but never tired of the way Mom's eyes glazed over when she relived that memory.

"Was the funniest thing." Her voice now muffled, she continued. "You cried and cried. And the second I held you next to that little baby boy, you stopped and smiled. At barely two days old, you smiled."

Unlikely, I know, but there was no convincing Mom otherwise. Not for lack of trying.

On and on, she went. Dad, still at the sink but now facing me, finished my mug of coffee while he brewed another cup, this time in a travel mug, his gaze glued to Mom's ass while she dug through the cupboard.

When she surfaced with an ancient brown-tinted glass cake pan, I gasped. "Oh. My. God. You're making Auntie Mercy's Mud Cake?"

"For dinner this weekend." She blew a lock of dirty blond hair out of her face.

"Lacey's gonna weep with joy when I tell her." The chocolate gooey concoction had been the star attraction at every family gathering since I was in diapers and had nursed Lacey and I through many adolescent dramas.

Mom winked, her smile triumphant. "Well, an epic breakup deserves epic cake."

"You're the best mom ever."

"I know."

I hopped off the stool. "I gotta get to work." I kissed my mother, then Dad, snatching the travel mug from his fingers.

He chuckled. "Love ya, Nugget."

"Love you guys. See you Sunday."

"Go ahead and say it." I stopped outside the painted brick building and pulled Lacey clear of a hurried delivery woman.

My best friend batted her thick, dark lashes, smirked, and then said, "I told you so."

"You so did."

"So, you just walked away. You don't know if he's alive or dead?"

"Oh, he's alive. Blowing up my phone. Mad I'm not pining over him at the hospital." I slapped a hand over my forehead. "God, what was I thinking with that guy?"

"You were thinking with your vagina, Nat Brat. It's okay. We've all been there. What's important is that we learn from our mistakes." She shot me a playful wink and tugged me toward the heavy wooden door. "Have you lost weight? You look about a hundred and eighty pounds lighter."

"Ha. Ha. And correction, he weighed a hundred ninety-five pounds, according to his Instagram feed last week."

"Must've been a bad fight if he's in the hospital."

"Don't care. He got what was coming." Lacey and I weaved through the tables until we found a booth in the back corner of the club, our favorite spot to people-watch.

The after-work crowd dwindled while the college kids slowly filled the dark space. Lacey and I sipped our first drinks, Barolo, of course, ordered another, caught up on our week's events, and as per our girl-night protocol, we headed for the dance floor to work off our frustrations, celebrate our wins, and let loose—no men allowed.

We danced. We laughed. We teased. We flirted. We never left each other's side, and when we'd exhausted our energy, we called it a night.

The Rusty Ram was a popular bar in our Belltown neighborhood that served the best pizza, had the dirtiest bathrooms, the friendliest bartenders, happened to be just around the corner from our apartment building, and the go-to for our girls' nights because we didn't have to drive.

We could let loose and walk home. Perfect set up.

"Lordy, that was fun." I stepped out of my heels and scooped them off the ground, the cold cement soothing my aching feet.

"Hey." Lacey nudged me. "Have you checked out that new gym on Blanchard?"

"What gym?" I had an unfortunate weakness for muscle men.

"Come here." She hooked her arm through mine and dragged me around the corner. One more block, and we

L.O.V.E.

stood in front of a window that stretched the entire length of the refurbished brick building. The bottom floor appeared to be a gym. Above, floor after floor of matching windows. Apartments or condos, maybe.

The front door read *Cadence Fight Club,* and the gold logo was a simple circle with CFC in the middle. Inside, several people of varying shapes, sizes, and genders gathered around a large mat. In the center of the mat, two men circled each other, fists wrapped, bodies glistening with sweat.

One man, blond and beefy, landed a strike to his opponent, whose back was to me. And what a glorious back. Broad shoulders, slim waist, muscles that rolled and bunched with every move. He bounced from foot to foot, his calves taut and strained. His dark hair curled at the ends in a cute little flip, its boyish charm at odds with the brute force he possessed.

While the blond was larger, his muscles thick, the dark-haired man dominated the space, moving with the grace of a dancer, taunting his opponent.

I slipped my phone out of my pocket and snapped a picture because the scene was surreal. Such beauty amidst the violence.

Blondie swung again. Dark and Dangerous ducked and then struck Blondie in the gut, making me wince. As Blondie doubled over, Dark and Dangerous backed away, still bouncing. He danced around the other side of Blondie, grace, rhythm, and raw sex appeal, his face finally coming into view.

My gut clenched. My heart raced. My lungs ceased to work. I gripped Lacey's arm for balance.

The man was fit, his sweaty skin stretched over finely honed muscle. Dark chestnut-colored hair. Regal nose. Full lips. But those eyes. Dark with thick lashes. Sweet baby Jesus.

He shot a glance our way, rolled his shoulders, and dropped his gaze back to Blondie on the ground, then his head jerked up. His arms fell to his sides and those mesmerizing eyes locked with mine.

For the second time that day, the man stared at me like I was the light at the end of his tunnel, his sunrise and sunset, his morning bacon, his nightcap, his *precious*. My insides warmed, cheeks blazed.

"Ooh, girl." Lacey blew a low whistle.

What luck. Twice in one day. That man. The way he looked at me. Had to be fate. Right?

I froze in place. Mere seconds passed, yet an eternity stretched between us, my future revealed, the stars spreading their arms and pointing to my destiny, toward the man behind the glass, the dimpled Adonis.

He was the *one*.

He told me so with the heat of his gaze.

Just as I found the courage to smile, he was tackled from behind and thrown to the ground, our connection lost. My lust haze lifted and, without looking back, I shoved Lacey forward and left that gym behind, hurrying my pace.

"Oh, my," my best friend squealed. "Did you see that guy?"

"Which one?"

"The big one with all that sexy blond hair. *Dios Mio*. Did you see those biceps?" Lacey fanned herself with her free hand. "We need to join that gym."

I'm not sure why I refrained from telling her that Dark and Dangerous was the man Holden had scuffled with during my attempted breakup speech. Maybe I got a certain thrill from keeping that little secret to myself. "Looks like a fight gym."

"So? I've always wanted to give boxing a try." Moving in front of me, she raised delicate hands and threw a fake punch, bouncing on her feet, her ample bosoms nearly shaking free of her push-up bra.

We were polar opposites in shape and size. Lacey stood four inches taller than my five-foot-three, had curves that conjured fantasies, and silky raven hair that hung to her small waist and seemed immune to common annoyances such as frizz or split ends.

"I hate fighting." I dropped my shoes to the ground and wiggled my feet back into the leather sling-backs.

Lacey grabbed my arm to steady me. "But you've got a thing for gyms and the men who frequent them."

"Not after today," I assured her, finding my balance and continuing toward home.

"Oh, come on," she pleaded, hands steepled. "I have to meet that guy. He was gorgeous."

"I'm not spending money on a new gym when I'm perfectly happy at the gym I've been going to for over two years now."

"Might I remind you that Holden spends fifteen hours a day at that gym?"

"Good point."

We reached the entrance to our apartment building and giggled our way up the stairs, shushing each other, then laughing harder. I hugged her goodnight at her second floor apartment, then made my way up to the fourth where I resided.

A large, unconscious lump of drunken testosterone sat slumped against my door, his face a mangled mess, lip cut and swollen, both eyes boasting varying shades of bruising, and a ridiculous bandage wrapped around his head and under his chin. Thank God, I'd never given him a key to my place.

Funny, the man he'd attacked hadn't a mark on him that I could tell. Maybe I should've stuck around to watch the scuffle.

I rolled my eyes and considered calling security. Instead, I grabbed the half-empty bottle of Jack out of Holden's fingers. He wasn't a drinker. If he woke up and finished that fifth, there was a good chance he'd choke to death on his own vomit, or walk in front of a moving bus. Couldn't have that on my conscience. "Sleep it off, you big lug," I whispered, then turned around, headed back downstairs, and spent the night on my best friend's couch.

"You actually joined that gym?" I grabbed the pink bakery box out of Lacey's hand and closed the door behind her, inhaling the sinful chocolate aroma.

Mom butchered the lyrics to "Gooba" from the laundry room. I rolled my eyes. Lacey laughed.

She still wore her workout clothes, but somehow looked fresh as a daisy, hair piled on her head in a perfect messy knot, red lipstick, eyes bright. "Of course, I did."

Lacey James. Hopeless romantic. Nobody deserved an epic love affair more than my bestie. At age ten, she lost her mother to a tragic train accident. Her father fell ill shortly after. Lacey, the most selfless person I'd ever met, had spent her late teens and all her college years taking care of her ailing father. Mr. James had done his best to raise Lacey right. He'd never remarried and spoke of his wife daily. The doctors had never been able to diagnose his illness, but as the years passed, he withdrew more and more until eventually he died of what I believed to be a broken heart.

"Good for you. Did you meet Blondie yet?"

She followed me into the kitchen. "No. But he's there every day. I've caught him staring at me, and he's smiled at me three times."

"So, go talk to him."

"I've tried." She huffed, dropping her keys on the counter. "I just don't know how to do this." Lacey rarely dated. First her father, and now her job as an HR Assistant took most of her time.

"Just do you. You are the most compassionate, funny, gracious person I know. Be yourself, and you'll be swatting men away like flies."

"You should come with me. I'm always braver when you're by my side." She threw an arm around my shoulders, giving me a hip bump. "Come. Just once. There are hotties everywhere."

"I'm on a hottie hiatus," I reminded her, before kissing her cheek and ducking free of her hug. "But I do need to get back into the gym."

I'd avoided my daily workouts for one reason and one reason only—Holden.

Two weeks had passed since our breakup. Twice he'd shown up at the bank, and I had pretended to be in a meeting. After day three, I'd blocked his number and changed the security code to my apartment building.

I considered accepting Lacey's offer to join CFC, but Mr. Dark and Dangerous used that gym, and I wasn't sure I would survive another encounter with his smolder.

Ugh. My body tingled in all the wrong places just thinking about that stranger.

No, I would not join CFC and further humiliate myself. And even if the guy was interested, my plate was full. I had a corporate ladder to climb. I was currently a junior associate, the best at crunching numbers, and had a sharp eye when it came to assessing risk management, but what I wanted and where I thrived was landing the clients, sealing the deals on corporate accounts. Not an easy feat considering I was a young female in the banking industry. Work was my priority.

Avoiding any commitment to the gym, I changed the subject. "You're late." I glanced at the clock. "You're never late."

Sunday dinner with my parents was a longstanding tradition. Lacey had only missed one dinner in four years, and only because she'd had a bad flu.

"Yeah. Sorry." Her doe eyes widened. "You'll never guess who I ran into."

Mom came around the corner, carrying a bottle of wine, then stopped short when she spied Lacey. "Who'd you run into?" She pulled both of us into a hug. "Do tell."

Dad called from the dining room, "Gossip after grace. I'm hungry."

We joined Dad at the table. We prayed. Before my knife hit the steak, Mom said, "The suspense is killing me. Who'd you run into?"

"Victoria Ford," Lacey blurted.

Dad cleared his throat. Mom choked on her merlot.

"Oh." Last name I'd expected to hear. My gut twisted into painful knots. "I thought she moved across the country." My fork suddenly weighed a thousand pounds, and I lowered it to my plate.

"Get this." Lacy wiggled in her chair and leaned closer to me. "She's engaged to some uber rich guy, an heir to some real estate or retail fortune or something like that. She couldn't stop flashing her ring."

The room darkened and my stomach sank, but I blinked my best friend back into focus. Victoria Ford.

Beautiful, sociopathic bully. The girl who had tormented me for years. Grade school through graduation. Memories pelted my psyche, a cold chill prickling my skin. She could only continue to taunt if I gave her the power. I would not concede my power ever again.

"Well. Good for Victoria. Hope she gets all the happiness she deserves." I studied my steak, the crust of caramelized spices, the juices dripping down the sides.

One deep breath. Release the negative energy in a slow exhale.

Time to steer the conversation elsewhere. "Tell Mom and Dad about your new love interest."

Mom jumped all over the subject change. "Who? What? What? What? Did you have a date?"

Lacey gave Mom the lowdown on her gym crush. I chewed my sirloin with gusto. Dad eyed me warily but kept his mouth shut. Good man.

Lacey drove me home since I'd helped Mom polish off the second bottle of wine. At my door, she said, "Are you okay? I'm sorry I brought up *She Who Shall Not Be Named.*"

That made me laugh. "It's okay. I just haven't thought about Victoria for a long time." I tried, and failed, to get my key into the lock.

"Well, Seattle's a big city. Chances are we'll never run into her again."

"Yeah. You're probably right. And if I do, well? I don't know what will happen, but we're adults now. I'll be an adult." After six years of therapy, I could survive an encounter with Victoria. Life would be peachier, though, if I never had to look at that face again.

After the third attempt at my lock, I managed to open my door.

"Do you need me to help you get in bed?"

"Naw, I'm good."

Hands to hips, Lacey stared at me.

"What?"

"I just love you so much, Nat Brat." She pulled me in for a squeeze.

"Love you more, Lacey Lulu."

"Shit. Shit. Shit. Shit. Shit." I repeated my morning mantra as I jogged down the stairwell, my Free People booties making a terrible racket on the cement steps, an ungodly echo ringing my ears.

I'd overslept. *Thanks, Mom, for the wine.*

The elevator was under repair, hence my morning jog down four flights of stairs. My head buzzed, pounding something fierce, and my stomach threatened punishment. I pushed through the nausea, adrenaline kicking in.

If I skipped my morning coffee and cut through two alleys, I could still make it to work on time. Although, starting work without my coffee would not be a good idea.

Shit. Shit. Shit. Shit. Shit.

I slammed through the back exit of my apartment building. Speed-walked down the brick alley while breathing through my mouth to avoid the urine stench. Narrowly missed a head-on with a produce delivery truck, then turned on the next corner and waited impatiently for the crosswalk light to allow me safe passage.

I'd made it across the busy street and was two buildings from the bank when a large figure caught my eye. I stopped dead, my heart racing.

Holden stood on the sidewalk, leaning against the bike rack, arms crossed, head down. Chin-length hair tucked behind his ear. Thank the good Lord, he hadn't seen me. I turned on my heel and raced around the corner, running smack dab into a steel-hard figure.

"Oh, shit. I'm so sorry." I rubbed my nose, my eyes watering something fierce.

The deep voice penetrated my body like a possession. "Whoa. Sorry." A long pause, then his chest rose and fell. A smudge of my lipstick marred his blue and silver medallion tie. "Are you okay? Wait...you?"

Righting my glasses, I lifted my chin to see the face of the man that held me steady. Confusion, or maybe curiosity, knitted his brows. Thick dark lashes almost overshadowed his piercing eyes, more gold than brown. Then I looked at my arms, because where he gripped my biceps, his thumbs rubbed slow circles, as though he'd soothed me a thousand times before. Like we were familiar. Like I was his and he was mine.

The suit under his wool coat was crisp and clean, and he smelled like expensive cologne, citrusy and sensual. I braved another gander at his face and, *dammit*, there it was again, that beautiful, wanting, knowing, needing gaze.

I was hungover, out of breath and, *oh, God*, lighter than air in the man's grip.

His Adam's apple bobbed up and down. "Do I know you from somewhere? I mean, other than the coffee shop?"

Speechless, I moved my head back and forth. He had a lovely mouth. Full lips, the bottom slightly larger than the top. Would he taste as good as he smelled?

"Are you okay?" he asked, his fingers curling into the soft wool of my blazer, his voice calm, warm, and alluring.

Chalk it up to insanity, lack of sleep, lust, or destiny— but most likely insanity—I rose high on my toes, slapped a hand around his neck, and pulled that man in for kiss. I couldn't *not* kiss him. We were brought together that very moment in time for one purpose and one purpose only. A kiss. I knew it in my soul.

His lips were soft and smooth. He tasted like mint and coffee, his flavor registering at the same time I realized he'd stiffened, dropped his arms, and wasn't returning the affection, but pushing me away.

Stumbling back a step, I brought a finger to my lips. "I'm— Oh, God, I'm so sorry."

I turned on a dime and dashed back the way I'd come.

"Wait!" he called.

Appalled, I moved forward, my lips singed, my ego bruised.

Holden came my way the moment he spotted me. I shoved right past the crazy brute and had made it to the front door when he grabbed my shoulder and swung me to face him.

"Baby, please, let—"

My palm met his cheek with a loud crack. Every bone in my hand protested, white-hot pain jetting up my arm. Holden didn't budge, but he did let go of my bicep.

"Leave me alone," I whisper-shouted.

I turned and left him to stew.

I made it to work with one minute to spare and one hundred percent of my spirit drained.

Cole

"You gonna talk to her, or what?" I slapped Ellis on his back and nodded toward the hot little number who'd joined CFC a few weeks ago. The woman obviously had a thing for Ellis, sneaking glances, turning down the horde of men who'd made a move.

She wasn't the only female member of our gym, but she was the only one who incited locker-room porn stories. *Fuck.* I swear men were worse than women when it came to gossip.

"Back off, bub." Ellis shoved me away and upped the ramp on the treadmill. "I'm playin' it cool."

"Stay cool for too long, another one of these meatheads are gonna make their play."

"Nah, just look at her. That beauty's only got eyes for me." He lowered his voice. "She's looking right now, isn't she?"

She was, but I told him, "No. She's talking to Roarke." I threw a chin nod in the direction of the free weights.

Ellis whipped his head around so fast he tripped over his feet and damned near fell off the machine.

Laughing, I walked away and left him to his humiliation.

Numbskull. His dream woman had dropped out of the sky and into his lap, and he wanted to play games. I'd only shared two short conversations with the doe-eyed bombshell, but she was perfect for Ellis in every way.

I grew up on the same block with Ellis Chambers and Martin Roarke. Ellis was the big teddy bear with a bleeding heart. Martin, the smooth talker, had a temper as red as the hair on his head. Me? I was the scrawny kid who stuttered and wore glasses to correct my lazy eye for most of first grade. Unfortunately, kids didn't forget, and though I was right as rain by second grade, I'd been labeled "freak," and that stigma stuck through most of my elementary years. Teased. Bullied. Any time I was separated from my two best friends, the vultures attacked.

When I came home with my first black eye, Dad signed me up for boxing. Best fucking day of my life.

I finished my workout with half an hour on the treadmill, then headed upstairs to my office where I showered and then hit the books.

My mind was not focused on business but on a sweet little dish with killer legs and fuck-me eyes. The woman who'd slammed into me on the street like she'd been running for cover, then kissed me like her life depended on that one desperate, glorious lip-lock.

What was with that beauty? Our paths seemed destined to cross. Was it a sign? Was I supposed to help her in some way? Her boyfriend had been a hot-headed brute. Maybe he was abusive. Maybe I was supposed to teach her to fight. I was a firm believer in fate. Without a doubt, there was a reason she'd been brought into my periphery. After all, CFC was more than just a fight club. When construction was complete, the gym would front my new project, a safe haven for victims of domestic violence.

The thought made me twitchy. What if I couldn't help her? What if I offered and she blew me off? How could I approach her without coming off as a loon? That was, if I ever bumped into her again.

Shit. Maybe I was making a mountain out of a molehill.

I made my way to the rain-spattered window, made a mental note to call the cleaners, then watched the slow trickle of bodies maneuvering our street below, bobbing in and out of the bakery, loitering outside the antique shop.

A head of blond hair caught my eye, and I laughed. Ellis was headed toward the parking garage around the corner, a raven-haired angel by his side.

"Good for you, buddy. Good for you."

If ever a man was meant to settle down and raise a brood of rug rats, it was Ellis. The guy had a heart bigger than Texas and the patience of a saint.

Yours truly? I'd always wanted a family of my own, when the time was right. However, I believed a man should build his empire before settling down. Have a solid foundation to offer his wife, then grow his legacy from there, like my father before me, and his father before him. True, I came from wealth, but that wealth came from honest, hardworking men who lived their lives with honor, dignity, and integrity.

"God, family, work," my grandfather used to say. "Live your life in that order, you'll be unstoppable."

I didn't attend church every Sunday like Granddad had. Hell, I only talked to God on special occasions, but I'd been raised with strong morals, surrounded by a family that loved fiercely and lived modestly. Givers, through and through—to church and charity.

Which reminded me I needed to call St. Johns. Check their needs for the month.

My gut twisted. Seemed wrong to think about church when I couldn't stop thinking about the taste of that woman's lips. Or the press of her breasts against my chest. Or the burn her fingers left behind after gripping my neck. Or the way she looked at me.

Fuck. The way she looked at me, like I was familiar, like I was everything.

I rubbed the ache in my temples, sat at my desk, and forced unchaste thoughts from my mind. Then I picked up the phone and dialed the only woman who belonged in my head.

I slipped out the back entrance of the gym. Dirty clouds frowned down at me, mirroring my current mood. Heading toward the parking garage, I joined the rush hour dance, weaving and bobbing between hurried participants of the nine-to-five frenzy. That was the thing I loved most about the Belltown neighborhood—people walked everywhere. Sure, that had a lot to do with the lack of parking space, but everything a person needed was just around one corner or another.

I ditched my coffee mug and was about to pull my buzzing cell out of my pocket when a blur of green caught my eye mere seconds before barreling into my side, knocking me off balance. Something hard landed on my foot.

"Shit. Shit. Shit," came a frantic voice. "I'm so sorry." A wild mane of dirty-blond hair whizzed by. "So sorry!"

I looked down to find a nude heel. "Wait! You dropped your shoe."

L.O.V.E.

The woman stopped, her pink Adidas skidding on the sidewalk. The sexiest "Fuck!" I'd ever heard belted from her lips.

She turned, and her curious gaze settled on my face. Pink cheeks turned crimson. "Oh, crap."

God damn. There she was again. Swear to Christ, the woman was everywhere. "You."

"Yep. Me." She laughed, adjusted her black glasses, and whispered, "The kissing bandit."

What a beautiful sound, that nervous laugh.

I cleared my throat. Bent to retrieve the stiletto from the ground. "What's the hurry?"

"Late for work." She snatched the heel from my finger and tucked it into the bag slung over her shoulder.

She took me in, eyes, nose, mouth, and I knew, deep down, we'd met before, somewhere, somehow. She studied me with recognition, curiosity, and something else I couldn't quite grasp, but I wanted more of whatever strange connection we shared and, *good God*, those magnetic gray eyes. Fucking magic.

Plump, pink lips parted. She sucked in a breath. "Listen. Um, I'm really—"

"Tell me your name," I blurted, interrupting before she could run away. I needed to know, even though I had no right to ask.

"Nats! There you are," came a desperate voice followed by a large man wearing a black wool jacket and an angry face. Dark jeans covered log-sized legs, and with those thick-soled Timberlands, he could flatten her with one ill-intentioned step.

The woman sidled closer to my side, mumbled, "Fuck my life."

Her hair smelled like rain, and I refrained from ducking lower to smell her neck.

I recognized the guy from our scuffle in the coffee shop a month ago. If he recognized my mug, he didn't show it. He did, however, size me up, his chest inflating, fists clenched. Blue eyes darkened and then aimed at the girl by my side. "Babe. Please. We need to talk."

"Nothing to talk about."

"Plenty to talk about. Unless you've moved on already." The asswipe nodded in my direction, then ran a hand through his long hair.

Clearly, the guy upset her. He was twice her size, and she trembled next to me. I thought she was afraid and was about to step in when she moved between us and jammed a finger into his massive chest.

Without a lick of fear in her tone, she commanded, "Stop following me. Stop calling me. Stop everything that has anything to do with me. We are done." She finished with a hard slap to his chest, then marched away, her hips swinging something fierce under her long plaid coat.

I watched, stupefied, then chuckled when she shot me a glance over her shoulder.

The giant, overinflated douche rolled his eyes at me, mumbled, "Little lover's spat, that's all." His brows pinched, he asked, "Do I know you?"

"Can't say we've ever met," I lied. He'd never pressed charges for the beat down. Maybe because I'd paid for the damages to the coffee shop. Or maybe, judging by what little I knew of his personality, the guy wouldn't press charges because he'd be forced to publicly admit defeat. Or maybe, he was just that dense. Either way, I wasn't proud of my fib, but I had a meeting in less than twenty minutes and couldn't afford a scuffle of any sort.

"How do you know Nats?" he asked, chest puffing again.

He stepped closer. I held my ground. He had me by an inch and maybe fifty pounds and clearly enjoyed asserting his size. Nothing I hated worse than a fucking bully.

"Don't know her," was all I offered, and before he could respond, I walked away.

Wasn't easy. With every fiber of my being, I wanted to tear the man apart for making that lady tremble. And how fucked was that? I didn't know either of them. They were none of my concern, and I had no business letting that woman into my head.

But, goddamn, the way she looked at me.

Ellis met me at the corner coffee stand, ridiculous grin on his face, two mugs of coffee in his hands. "Can we skip poker tonight?"

I relieved him of one cup and brought the lid to my nose, absorbing the rich, nutty aroma. "What's up? You got a hot date?" I asked, knowing damn well he did.

"Lacey's making me dinner tonight."

We headed north toward the gym, the wet cement slick and growing darker as the annoying mist gave way to heavy drops of rain. "Getting serious with this lady?" I asked, ducking deeper into my coat collar.

Ellis hit me with a big, dumb grin, then lifted his latte to his lips, taking a slow sip for dramatic pause. "Fuck, man. She's the one."

"You sure, tiger? It's only been a month."

"What can I say? When you know, you know."

I couldn't bridle my smile. I loved Ellis like a brother, and he obviously adored the shit out of Lacey. The two of them had been joined at the hip since their first date.

I'd never met a couple more suited.

And speak of the devil—the hot, curvy firecracker came bouncing around the corner, smile bright, dressed in workout gear and a waterproof jacket, her dark hair covered in a huge hood. "Oh, hi guys!"

Ellis scooped her up with one arm and lifted her for a kiss, her toes inches off the ground. Sweetest fucking couple.

Suddenly I was bitter, having woken alone in my king-size bed *again*. I shook off the negative vibe and continued walking.

"Did Ellis ask you about this weekend?" Lacey said, taking two strides for every one of ours to keep up.

"What's up this weekend?"

She laid a hand on my arm to slow me down. "We're hoping to make a love connection. My best friend and Martin."

I snorted, spewing coffee. "Double date?"

"We were thinking more of a triple date."

I studied Lacey's pleading gaze, then shifted my attention to Ellis's puppy dog eyes. *Jesus. Fuck.* They were killing me.

"You sure you want to risk that, bud?" I asked, hating the bitter taste of those words. "Martin isn't exactly the dating type."

He tucked Lacey under his massive arm and argued, "He hasn't found the right lady yet, that's all."

Oh, Martin had found plenty of ladies. Trouble was, he could never recognize the beauty standing right in front of him, always looking for the next best thing, always wanting more.

We reached the door, and I shoved the key into the lock, wiggled the damn thing, then gave the door a hard yank. When the rush of sweat and leather and musty old building hit my nostrils, all tension left my body. I was home.

"I'm gonna head up to the office." I shrugged out of my jacket and gave it a shake, then gave Lacey a peck on the cheek. "You two enjoy your workout."

Small fingers gripped my elbow. "So you'll join us on Saturday? Please?"

"Of course." I nodded at Ellis. "Text me the deets."

"Yay!" Lacey squealed, then bounced away toward the locker rooms, yelling over her shoulder. "We're gonna have so much fun. I promise!"

I raised a brow, and Ellis only chuckled. "Don't worry. I won't let Martin fuck with this one."

Nobody controlled Martin. Since middle school, Ellis and I had become masters of damage control for our best friend. But that's what best friends did. Had each other's backs. Always. Even when your buddy had a knack for getting himself in trouble. Even when that kind of trouble could get your ass hauled to juvie, which by some miracle, we'd all managed to avoid. Stealing, drugs, gambling, fighting. Martin had played with fire and nearly burned us all more times than I cared to count.

"Whatever you say, man." I turned and jogged up the stairs. Fun? Probably not. But at least I'd get a few hours with my best friends and my fiancée in the same room.

4

Natalie

L ife had a funny way of throwing mean back at you. For example, the previous day, Holden sent me flowers, albeit after he stalked me to work, then sent me twenty-five text messages. He wasn't taking the breakup very well and had exhausted my good graces, so I forced the bouquet of roses through the shredder at work, then had them hand couriered back to the gym where I knew he would be. Mean, right?

I'm not proud of my actions. However, a full moon hung in the sky, so I blame my bout of insanity on that fact.

Back to mean...

"Your dress is gorgeous." Lacey finished tipping our Uber driver, then shoved her phone into her Tori Burch clutch. "Hugs your chest just right, shows the perfect amount of cleavage."

"Thanks." I held my coat open and twirled outside the swanky restaurant, then fell into Lacey's embrace, holding her for a fat minute and mustering the courage to go inside.

L.O.V.E.

My best friend smelled like cotton candy. Under her long jacket, she wore a simple black sweater dress that hugged her voluptuous curves. Red lipstick accentuated her full lips. Her cheeks boasted a pink blush no cosmetic could mimic. Love looked so beautiful on my Lacey.

"Ready?" she asked.

"Ready." Ready to get the evening over with.

Last thing I wanted was to dive back into the dating pool, but Lacey was so happy. So in love, lust, and all those fun things, and her guy was just the sweetest. His friends had to be awesome. Besides, Lacey would never set me up with a man unless she deemed him worthy. Her standards were far stricter than mine.

We swayed through the entrance of Bar Del Bruno, the hottest new Italian restaurant in Seattle. High ceilings. Amber lights dangling from the dark wood beams. Candles at every table. A grand piano sat nestled in a dark corner, a young man wearing a suit and a slicked-back undercut setting the mood for love, his long fingers dancing over the ivories.

"Bye-bye dating funk," she whispered in my ear, giving my fingers a squeeze.

No sense fibbing. I acted the runway model, working my heels, swinging my hips like a pro. The greatest accessory to any outfit was confidence. I layered myself in that shit, no matter how thin the veils, my dating-game face firmly in place.

I spied Ellis first, his six-foot-three stature hard to miss, and my racing pulse kicked up another thousand RPMs. Next to him sat a handsome man. Dark red hair, tan, square jaw. Fit. Tall. His focus was aimed at the woman who sat across the table from him, her back to me, and he laughed at something she said.

Ellis's smile was electrifying. "There's my girl," he announced, focused on Lacey while he pushed to stand.

The woman turned in her seat, her face coming into view. Platinum blond hair, high cheekbones, heart-shaped lips painted red. The perfect, straight nose was new. Not the inky black serpentine stare, though. I knew that glare all too well. Victoria Ford. My childhood tormentor.

See? Mean for mean.

My heart, lungs, muscles, and wits seized in one epic clunk, an old motor sputtering a final protest before rendering its host immobile. I tripped over my feet, but Lacey grabbed my arm, holding me upright, squeezing hard, conveying her own shock.

Without causing a scene, she whispered, "I had no idea. I'm so sorry."

There was no time to run or gather my scattered defenses. Lacey disappeared between Ellis's massive arms.

A warm hand surrounded mine. "You must me Natalie." His voice was silk, his gaze approving.

"Hi. Hey." I forced my attention from his paisley tie to his honey-colored eyes. Dear Lord, he was pretty. Clean shaven. Thick hair trimmed short. "Martin?"

His lips parted in an approving grin. "Nice to meet you."

Ellis cleared his throat. "Ladies, this is Victoria—"

"Ford." Lacey interrupted. "We know."

Ever the faithful friend, Lacey leaned closer and rested her hand on my shoulder, giving me a squeeze. "Hi, Martin. You look great. Love that tie." She cleared her throat and darted widened eyes toward Martin.

I realized I was still moving his arm up and down and dropped his hand.

Ellis waited for Lacey to sit before making himself comfortable, then gestured toward Victoria and asked, "How do you ladies know each other?"

Awkward.

Clueless to my discomfort, Martin pulled out the chair next to him, helped me out of my coat, and waited for me to sit, which I did, grateful to be a few feet farther from Victoria.

Much to my surprise, Victoria was the first to speak. "I tortured poor Nats all through high school."

Her gaze covered me like a flee-infested blanket, offering temporary warmth but the promise of misery.

Lacey's eyes narrowed, aimed in Victoria's direction, before she turned to Ellis. "I'm more interested to know how you and Victoria know each other."

Ellis offered Lacey a heartwarming smile. My chest deflated, envious of the adoration lighting his face. "She's Cole's fiancée."

Victoria hovered her hand over the table, wiggling her fingers, showcasing a moderate-sized diamond.

"Beautiful," I managed to squeak. "Congratulations." Either the poor guy was clueless to her depravity, or maybe she'd snared a masochist. My heart bled for the future Mr. Victoria Ford.

Holding back my ire made my stomach ache, so I excused myself to the ladies room rather than unleash a lifetime of stored retorts at the beaming bride-to-be.

Lacey shot me an apologetic grin.

On rubbery legs, I made my way through the tables, my confidence flaking away, layer by layer. The hallway leading to the restrooms seemed to expand with every step. When I rounded the corner, I stopped dead, feet cemented, heart racing.

In my path stood a man. Not just any man. Him. The guy.

Wearing dark gray slacks, a dark blue dress shirt rolled at the sleeves, tie loose, he leaned against the wall. His coat was draped over his left arm. He held his phone in his right hand. No ring, thank God. Head down. Attention on his cell.

Beautiful. Painfully handsome.

My pulse spiked, the roar between my ears so loud I feared the entire city would feel the tremors. The ladies' room was just out of reach, so close, yet a million miles away. If I moved, would he see me? Would he recognize me?

Of course, he would. I was the crazy woman who had kissed him on the street. Who'd barreled into him on the sidewalk. Who had unleashed her insane ex-boyfriend on him *twice*.

Why couldn't I move?

I was on a date, for crying out loud.

Forcing one foot in front of the other, careful not to click my heels, I pressed my palm on the door and braved one more glance. Thank the good Lord, he still stared at the phone. He raised a hand, raking his fingers through his hair and, dear sweet gods of holy, heavenly, lustful bliss, my entire body flushed with heat and prickly tingles.

I paused, only for a breath, but a moment long enough for the man to lift his eyes to mine. All at once, my lungs ceased to expand, my world spun at a nauseating pace, and I wanted so, so much not to be on a date.

On a raspy exhale he said, "You."

My knees buckled at the thick, raw, sensual tone.

I couldn't stop my grin. Mesmerized, lost in those eyes, I leaned against the doorjamb and whispered, "You."

He pushed off the wall, stood straight, and shoved his cell into his pocket, shoulders rolling forward like he bore

L.O.V.E.

the weight of the world, indecision flickering behind his heady gaze.

A tortured man if ever I'd seen one.

I wanted to jump into his arms. Talk to him. Touch, breathe, know him. Kiss that face. Make him laugh. Watch him cry. Bring him to his knees.

What was wrong with me? I was on a date.

Mean for mean.

But God, the way he looked at me.

A laugh carried down the hall, making me jump, tearing me from my fantasy, reverie, whatever the hell had me spellbound.

Before doing something foolish, I ducked into the ladies' room.

I made my way back to the table, determined not to let Victoria or that sexy stranger ruin my evening with the very handsome redhead. Eyes on the prize.

My cheeks heated at the way Martin's face lit up when I approached. He stood. Pulled out my chair. Waited for me to sit, then pulled his own seat closer. He smelled good, expensive cologne applied in a modest dose.

"Nats, you okay?" Lacey whispered in my ear. "You're red as a beet."

"Yeah. Yeah, just hot." I reached for my water glass and took a dainty sip when I really wanted to chug.

The weight of Victoria's stare bore through me, a dull knife sinking straight into my temporal lobe.

Martin cleared his throat. "We ordered a bottle of Barolo. Lacey said it was your favorite."

To which I replied, "We might need two bottles. Lacey and I can empty one in five minutes."

Everyone laughed. Martin had a nice laugh.

"Where's Cole?" Lacey asked.

"He got stuck with a client," Victoria answered, drawing her finger up and down the stem of her wine glass. "Should be here any minute. Said we can start without him."

The next twenty minutes passed with polite conversation. I learned that Ellis had considered being a medical doctor but instead became a pharmacist because he wasn't too keen on blood and gore. Martin was a pilot for a global distribution company. Victoria had spent the past three years on the East Coast, where she met her fiancé at a fundraiser for at-risk youth. He was a business owner and real estate developer who had recently returned to Seattle to be near his family and to open a gym as well as a women's shelter in honor of his late sister. He sounded like a good man. Victoria sounded head over heels in love.

"So the three of you grew up together?" Lacey asked, gesturing between Ellis, Martin, and the empty chair next to Victoria.

"Yeah." Martin nodded. "Grew up on the island."

"The island?" I asked, knowing damn well what he meant, despite the multiple islands surrounding the area.

"Mercer Island," Ellis stated.

"So you were a group of rich, entitled kids." Lacey winked at me. Neither of us had ever wanted for anything, but growing up, there'd always been a clear divide between the middle class and the upper class. More notably, the upper-upper class, those who grew up on the Eastside, which included "the island," a chunk of land that sat smack-dab in the middle of Lake Washington between Seattle and Bellevue.

Victoria snorted at the jab, then covered her mouth, trying to hide her laugh, throwing me off guard. The woman

I'd labeled "monster" almost seemed human. Maybe even likable.

She'd always been pretty. One of the prettiest girls in school. She was no longer simply pleasing to look at. Victoria was downright gorgeous, and dare I say, glowing?

Ugh.

"We were not spoiled rich kids, if that's what you think." Ellis gave Lacey's neck a squeeze.

"Yes, we were," Martin threw in, shooting me a wink.

"Okay, fine. We were," Ellis conceded.

I studied Lacey studying Ellis. She was a goner. And she, too, glowed. I wondered if a man would ever make me glow. Then I thought about the man in the hallway. I'd gone nuclear in his presence.

Then, as if I'd conjured him with my lustful musings, he came around the corner, tall and confident, and walking with a lithe grace that was both feral and beautiful all at once.

As he strode straight toward me, I imagined him to be Richard Gere in his Navy duds, and he was coming to scoop me up and carry me off, and we would live happily ever after in his bed for the rest of eternity.

Only, he hadn't noticed me. He wasn't giving me *the look*. Although his expression was warm and endearing, that gaze was not focused on me. Nope. Those thick-lashed beauties were aimed at Victoria.

Of course.

Mean for mean.

He strode to her side, placed a hand at her back, and bent low, his gaze flickering to me, then back to her before dropping a slow, chaste kiss to her lips.

"Cole," Martin said, pushing to stand. "You made it."

Cole. My dream man had a name.

The men exchanged a quick embrace.

Martin placed his hand on my shoulder, like he had the right, his fingers grazing the skin beneath my collar. "Cole. This is Natalie, my beautiful date for the evening."

Cole stood taller. Met my eyes with little-to-no interest, then offered his hand. "Pleasure."

Then Ellis chimed, "Funny thing, bud. Apparently, Natalie, Lacey, and Victoria went to school together."

"That so?" he asked his bride-to-be while settling into the empty chair and claiming her hand on top of the table.

Martin's fingers dusted my collarbone, lingering past the point of comfortable, souring the wine in my stomach.

Envy had no place in that room, and I hated myself for wanting to jump across the table and stab Victoria with my fork.

Victoria was the reason he hadn't kissed me back that day. Victoria was the reason he shared a table with me. Victoria was the reason I wanted to slink away into a dark corner and cry for a thousand years.

I'd be damned before I ever let her know she'd shaken me again. My body trembled with the vile poison filling my soul. Swallowing the bitter taste on my tongue, I turned my attention to my date where it belonged.

As far as I was concerned, Cole and Victoria no longer existed.

My office door opened with an ominous, slow creak.

"Sorry to interrupt." Gabriella, my coworker, apologized from behind a bouquet of flowers that seemed to float off the ground, so large I could barely see her black heels, tan legs, and wobbly ankles beneath. The scene would've been funny if not so creepy.

"What the actual fuck?" said Morgan, my favorite, and might I add, gorgeous and feisty client, her head tilting at an odd angle. She owned a chain of "bikini" coffee stands and had recently decided to expand into other business ventures.

The imposing display started to topple. Morgan and I shot forward, arms out, hands grasping, trying to find purchase, something solid to steady the tumbling flow of sunflowers, mums, gold poms, and orange roses.

We only made the situation worse, startling poor Gabriella. She screamed. I cussed. Morgan laughed. The bouquet fell to the floor, a morbid, though sweet smelling, pile of pick-up sticks.

Dropping to a squat, I rubbed my aching temples. "What am I going to do about him?" I studied the hodgepodge selection.

"File a restraining order." Gabriella pulled a rose out of the pile and brought the petals to her nose.

Morgan grabbed my elbow and helped me stand, giving me a motherly glare. "Ditto. Do it now. Don't wait another second. He needs to stop."

"Yeah." I nodded like a maniac, gnawing my thumbnail. "Didn't want to, but he's leaving me no choice."

Digging for my phone, I heard, "Nats! Baby! Fuck. Let go of me. Goddammit!"

Glass shattered. Grunts, smacks, and profanities followed.

My face heated. Head pounded. I peeked my head out the door, but Timothy, our astute head of security, ordered me to stay in my office. Like a cliché movie scene come to life, four—yes, four—men dragged Holden out the front entrance.

"Nats! I love you. Give me another chance. Please," echoed through the building and most likely down the block in every direction.

"Oh, honey." Gabriella pulled me into a tight embrace that I savored for a good thirty seconds before letting go to clean up the mess on my floor.

I could no longer tame the shake in my hands. Besides giving me gray hairs thirty years too early, that psycho was going to get me fired.

"You sure you don't need a few days off? I've got air miles I'll never use. Take a mini vacay. Get away from that nutjob for a while."

"What? And give up all this attention?" I joked, feeling not one lick of humor. "I can't. I have a date tomorrow."

"With that ginger hottie you told me about?" Morgan asked, gathering her coat and briefcase.

"Yes," I mumbled. I should have felt tingles at the thought of my date with Martin. Instead, I rubbed my temples.

Janet, my boss, came through the door, her suit impeccable, her smile sincere. "You okay?"

I nodded. "I'm sorry about the disruption."

"We'll meet with HR tomorrow. Talk about steps we can take to keep him from coming back. Take the rest of the afternoon off."

"I'm fine." I waved her off. "Besides, I've got two more meetings today." Holden was not going to ruin my day, or my numbers for the month.

Janet studied me before nodding. "Okay. If you're sure." With an approving smile, she headed down the hall.

I made quick work of the mess, swallowed a cocktail of pain relievers with lukewarm coffee, then collected my scattered nerves and landed two new clients for the bank, wooing them with numbers far more alluring than our competitors.

The pink-haired barista slid the Pumpkin Spice Latte across the counter with a pretty smile and a syrupy sweet, "Enjoy."

I shoved five bills into the tip jar because I liked her hair, and the world needed generous tippers.

I also felt extra spectacular because my last date with Martin had gone well. The man was pretty to look at. Polite. Respectful. We had shared great conversation over drinks at a fancy bar downtown, a romantic but chilly walk along the pier, a ride on The Seattle Great Wheel, where Martin held me close, then a hot kiss at my front door. And much to my surprise, he hadn't tried to get in my pants.

Also, I hadn't seen Holden since he'd been dragged away from the bank. Of course, I'd taken to sneaking out the back exit of my apartment building, and instead of walking the five blocks to work, took a new route, cutting through one smelly alley and extending my trek by two blocks, which was how I discovered the Mocha Maven.

I found a seat by the window, pulled out my cell, and dove in to my never-ending list of emails.

Sure, I was off the clock, but I liked knowing what to expect before I made it to the office.

My third email was from Janet, who wanted to see me the moment I arrived. "Aww fuck. This can't be good," I mumbled to myself. If Holden's shenanigans had gotten me fired, he was a dead man. I'd worked too damn hard for my spot on the corporate accounts team.

A deep chuckle came over my shoulder and I knew, like I'd heard that glorious sound a million times before,

Cole was standing at my rear. Tingles on my skin. Flutters in my belly. Erratic thunk, thunk, ker-thunk behind my breastbone. My body had never reacted that way to anyone.

Not one single soul. Ever.

Victoria was a lucky bitch.

Of course, knowing Victoria the way I knew Victoria, luck had nothing to do with her engagement to a man like Cole.

"Everything okay?" His voice washed over me like warm syrup, thick and coating every inch of me in sweet rapture.

"Hey, dude. How are ya?"

Dude? Oh, God. I sucked at faking apathetic.

Cole made himself comfortable in the seat across from mine. And, holy wow, did he fill that seat out well. Thick chest and wide shoulders. His mauve dress shirt complemented his complexion. An Armani model fresh off the page, an arm's reach away. *No. No. No.* I would not ogle.

Dreamy eyes locked on mine, and my tingles turned to full-blown lusty shivers. Yes. He was that beautiful.

His jaw tensed, but his gaze didn't falter, and *damn, damn, damn*, why did he have to look at me that way?

"What?" I asked, hypnotized.

"What, what?" He smirked.

"You're staring. Do I have something on my face?"

Cole blinked, crinkled a napkin, laughed, shook his head. "Sorry. Um." He scratched his eyebrow with his thumb. "There's just something about you."

Well. He wasn't one for bullshit. Respect.

"Sorry." He shook his head. "God. You must think I'm a creep."

No. He was the opposite of creep. If there were any creeping, it came from me. I closed my emails but opened my camera, waiting for the right moment. No denying, I wanted that man. To my bones, I ached with lust. And though it was wrong, and weird, I needed to capture the moment.

No bueno. Lacey's voice played in my head. I ignored her of course.

"Nothing creepy about you." I lifted my phone and took a shot, saying, "And believe me, I know creeps."

Eyes wide, he looked at my phone, then me, but much to his credit, didn't question. "About that." Again with the smirk and, oh my effin' jeez, those dimples.

"*That* being my crazy ex who attacked you for no reason?" I tried to make light of my predicament for fear of bursting into tears of shame.

One brow raised, he asked, "And chasing you down a busy street?"

"I was late for work." I slid my phone back into the pocket of my Fendi Tote, a graduation gift from my uncle that I broke out only in the fall and guarded with my life.

"You were running from a stalker," he practically growled, his fist tightening around that innocent napkin.

"Okay. Fine. I suppose I was."

He nodded, seemingly pleased with my honesty. "So, what are you doing in my coffee shop?"

"Oh. This is your place?"

"Not really. I own the building. They rent the space. But I do stop by once a day. Never seen you in here before." His lips were so pretty. And that chin cleft? I had no defense.

"Been taking the long way to work. Stumbled upon this little gem a couple days ago. Now, I'm hooked."

"Why?"

I lifted my warm cup off the table. "Because this is the best coffee I've ever had."

"No." He chuckled, killing me with that grin. "Why take the long way to work?"

"My ex has been a little overzealous with his apology." I slumped in my chair, the weight of the conversation exhausting. "And he wants me back."

"Can't say I blame him," he mumbled, then huffed.

My cheeks throbbed.

"Sorry. Not hitting on you. Promise." He raised his hands in surrender, then sat back, mimicking my pose. "What do you mean by overzealous?"

"There's too much to tell, honestly. Let's just say, I've taken to sneaking out the back door of my building."

Cole sat straighter, long fingers curling around his paper mug. "Are you in danger?"

"Oh, no. From that doof? Please. He would never hurt me."

"You sure about that? He tried to kill me because I looked at you. You ask me, that's a man to be wary of."

One thing I knew for certain about Holden was he'd never hurt a woman. Not physically. But one thing I suspected about Cole was he wouldn't fall for any bullshit. I wasn't in the mood to argue, so I conceded. "I know. You're right. Security had to drag him out of our building last week."

Cole's eyes narrowed. "He's escalating."

That icy glare was unexpected. As was the tick in his jaw. My jumbled brain didn't know how to process his reaction.

"Can we change the subject?"

He stared at me. Correction. He stared into my soul, like he could read my past, present, and future.

"It's a gorgeous morning. I don't want it tarnished with reminders of my latest bad mistake."

Cole blinked. His shoulders relaxed. He drank. Nodded. Studied something over my shoulder.

Good Lord, the man was beautiful. Suits, or workout wear, he commanded attention, confidence shifting the air around him.

"Okay. Subject changed." He tapped a slow rhythm along the seam of his cup, then shocked me by asking, "What's the deal between you and Victoria?"

He may as well have poured Drano down my throat. "You'll have to ask Victoria," I said with a nasty bite.

"I did."

I should've walked away then. Instead, I prodded. "What'd she say?"

"That she wasn't nice to you."

"Wasn't nice? That's her recollection?"

His gaze dropped to the dark table, then bounced back a little softer. "She told me about the grape juice incident."

Grape juice, spit, snot. God only knows what else was in that cup she'd poured over my head on our freshman year picture day.

My face had to be purple at that point, or charred black, because I was a furnace ready to blow. "Did she now?"

"Sounds pretty awful."

How dare he look sympathetic.

The weight of memories, the ghost of my tortured past, the vile, vile anger welled, bitter on my tongue, and I could no longer meet his eyes, afraid to reveal my scars.

I pushed to stand, my chair making a terrible screech. "It was nice to see you, Cole, but I need to get to work."

Cole stood, too, as if on reflex, and cleared his throat. "I hit a sore spot."

"Something like that." I didn't wait for a response or bother with niceties. I made for the door without a backward glance.

What a shame. I loved that coffee shop, and now I could never return.

Cole

"You taking her out again?" I shoved my gloves into the locker.

"Tonight." Martin dropped his ass on the bench and rubbed a towel over his head.

"So things are going well?" I asked, yanking a T-shirt down my damp torso and avoiding eye contact, afraid of revealing my ire.

"Yeah. I mean, you've seen her." He chuckled, blew a low whistle.

I wasn't amused. "Looks aren't everything."

"But you saw her, right?" Elbows to knees he stared at the floor. "Seriously, though. She's great. Smart. Funny. Low maintenance."

"Where are you taking her?" I stepped into my jeans.

"That new place in Bellevue everyone's raving about. Top of the Tower. Had to call in a favor to get reservations. Worth the sacrifice, though, for that view."

The words, "Don't go there," flew out of my mouth before considering the sentiment behind them. *Jesus. Fuck. Shit.* Why was the locker room so damn hot?

"Why the fuck not?"

Why? Who the hell knew? But I was digging a hole I'd never escape. I needed to backpedal, and fast. "She doesn't strike me as the gold digger, arm candy type."

"Explain." His phone buzzed.

"You take a woman to a place like Top of the Tower to impress your colleagues. See and be seen. Show her off."

"And?" He looked at his screen and shoved the cell into his duffel bag.

"Come on, Martin. You really want to expose her to the bullshit so soon?"

"No."

"Take her someplace quiet and quaint. Where you can sit close, get to know each other. No pressure."

"Yeah. Yeah. That makes sense." His leg bounced jackrabbit speed. "Fuck. You'd think I've never dated before."

Shit. The guy was nervous. Maybe he really did like Natalie.

"Wouldn't call what you do dating."

"True." The word came out more triumph than reality check, and that right there was what had me riled more than anything.

I leaned a shoulder against the locker, arms folded. "Don't fuck around with Natalie, for Ellis's sake. She's Lacey's best friend. You make Lacey unhappy, Ellis is unhappy, and then he'll make you and I fucking miserable. And that dude deserves some happy, yeah?" I clapped Martin's shoulder hard to make my point, but also to release some unbidden frustration.

Martin was one of my best friends. A brother. He was also an unapologetic player. Killed me to admit I didn't want him anywhere near my girl. Shit. Not *my* girl. *That* girl.

My girl was currently at lunch with the wedding planner.

That girl, Natalie, was none of my business, so why was she rattling around in my head? Why the urge to protect her?

"Sure. Makes sense." Martin scratched his chin. Dipped his head. Nodded. "I know the perfect place. She'll love it."

I didn't want her to love it. I wanted her to hate everything about the date. Even Martin. Because that pretty boy was a charmer, and women fell head over heels for him on the daily.

If Natalie fell for my best friend, I would see her all the time. We'd be forced to hang out. I would have to pretend she had zero effect on my engaged ass.

Victoria was everything I'd always wanted in a partner. Faithful. Giving. Smart. Did I mention faithful?

Fidelity was top of the list. *Thou shalt not commit adultery.* That commandment had been drilled into my conscience for as long as I could remember. My father. His father. My uncles. God fearing men, all of them.

Yet there I stood, angry at my best friend for dating a woman I had no right to give two shits about. I should've been happy for him.

His cell buzzed again. Giving me his back, he rifled through his bag, mumbled, "Fuck." Then over his shoulder, he said, "I gotta skip lunch today. Something came up at work."

"Sure. Sure. We'll catch up later."

He turned, threw me his signature smile, confident and cocky, but also one of his tells. He was hiding something. I hoped to hell he wasn't back to gambling.

"You sure this is a good idea?" Victoria asked, looking down at herself, then adjusting her black skirt.

"Why not?"

With a huff, she said, "I was really awful to her."

I helped her out of her coat, then turned her to face me. "How awful?"

Victoria looked to my left, then my chest, then my mouth. "I don't want to tell you."

I caught her chin before she could turn away. "Vic. How bad was it?"

"Bad, baby. I'm not proud of who I was back then. I was jealous and lonely and bored. She was beautiful, inside and out, and she had friends. Everybody loved Natalie. And well, you know what I went through with my uncle. Messed me up. My therapist said I fixated on Natalie."

That was the first I'd ever heard of a therapist. "Did you ever try to apologize?"

"No." She stood toe to toe, looking up at me with a pout.

"You feel like that's something you can do now?" I shrugged off my own coat, then handed both to the woman behind the counter.

"Maybe."

I dropped a kiss to her pert nose. "Martin's going to be around forever. If he's with Natalie, that means we'll be seeing Natalie. The two of you will have to work things out."

Anger flashed in her blue eyes before she composed herself, so quick I almost missed the expression. Then she fell against me, gripping my arms. "I'll try. But I don't think she'll ever be able to forgive me. I wouldn't forgive me."

"Let her see the amazing woman you are now. The woman I fell in love with."

"I don't deserve you," she whispered.

"There they are." Martin's voice came over my shoulder.

Every muscle in my body tightened. I wrapped an arm around Victoria before turning to greet our friends.

And fuck me, there she was, four feet away but under my skin, scorching my veins, wearing a clingy dress the color of sangria, her hair twisted on top of her head, her eyes made all the more enticing painted in shades of gray. No glasses, and though I had no right, I was mesmerized by the smokey hue of her irises.

Martin released Natalie's hand and pulled Victoria in for a cheek kiss, then gave me a hard clap on the shoulder before checking their coats.

Natalie offered a sweet smile and soft hello to me, then shot Victoria a nervous glance. "Hi, Victoria." She didn't wait for an answer before moving past and heading to the host station.

A tall man wearing a tailored suit stepped out of the shadows, his piercing gaze aimed at Natalie. He pulled her into an intimate embrace, his large dark hands resting against her pale skin. She leaned back to look into his face, her smile endearing, his dark eyes far too focused on Martin's date.

I yanked at the knot on my tie. Why the hell had I let Martin talk me into this get together?

Victoria whispered, "Shit. Not him," before pressing herself into my side.

They exchanged private words before Natalie turned, the man's arm still wrapped protectively around her waist.

"Guys." Natalie beamed. "This is my cousin Finn."

Cousin? Interesting.

Martin released a heated breath and then moved forward to shake Finn's hand.

Natalie made introductions. When it came Victoria's turn, Finn's chest puffed, eyes narrowed, his long arm cinched Natalie.

"Victoria Ford." He forced a smile. "Thought you moved to the East Coast."

The man had to be six-four. Wore it well. Dark skin. Dark eyes. Solid underneath his expensive duds. Shaved head that added to his intimidation factor.

"Hi, Finn." Victoria stuck to my side. "Moved home a bit ago. This your place?"

Finn nodded.

Natalie patted Finn's chest. "He reserved us a table close to the stage, but it'll be a tight squeeze. You guys okay with that?"

Nobody said a word, tension stifling the air.

A nervous laugh escaped her full, pink lips. "Trust me, drinks here are the bomb, and we won't find better entertainment. The tight quarters'll be worth it."

Martin moved again to Natalie's side. "Sounds perfect." Only when he grabbed her hand did Finn release Natalie.

We followed him through an already crowded lounge toward a small stage, its floor lit with dim red bulbs, a spotlight aimed at a worn wooden stool. Red velvet curtains hung in the background, black and gold damask wallpaper covered the walls on either side of the room that reminded me of on old theatre turned speakeasy.

An unseen artist stroked a haunting melody on a piano tucked in a dark corner, some old tune I recognized but couldn't place.

L.O.V.E.

Our table was round, made for two, but we settled in, Victoria to my right, Natalie to my left, Martin directly across from me, the stage at my back. My knee bumped Natalie's thigh but she didn't seem to notice, and I made no move to adjust, mostly for lack of room but partly because there was something enchanting about the connection.

Wrong. True. But like a magnet, I was drawn to her.

I needed a drink.

Finn disappeared. Two minutes later, a woman floated our way. She had a face like Zoe Kravitz and a body like Adele, and damn she was breathtaking. Her red gown shimmered under the dim lights and hugged every beautiful curve.

"Doll. You came," she said to Natalie, her voice smooth like a single malt whiskey.

"Finn told me you were back. I couldn't wait to see you." Natalie wrapped her arm around the woman's waist and gestured around our table. "Everyone, this is Finn's wife, Mona. She's our entertainment tonight."

"Pleasure to meet you all." Mona offered her hand to Martin first, then Victoria, then me.

"Cole Adams." I gripped her soft palm. "Pleasure."

"Cole?" Mona laughed, a seductive grit to her tone, then shot Natalie a wink.

"What's funny?" Martin asked.

"Natalie King. Cole Adams." She waited for us to connect the dots.

We didn't.

"You don't understand." Her hazel eyes lit up. "But you will." With that, she turned and sauntered back toward the stage.

Natalie sucked her lips between her teeth, fighting a smile. And damn, she glowed like a kid on Christmas morning.

64

"How is it you're related to them?" Martin asked, clearly confused by their different skin tones.

"My dad's brother, Joe, met his wife, Angelique, in Barbados. Fell in love, brought her back to the US when his contract ended over there. Anyway, they had twins. Finn and Felix, who I—I mean, we "—she gestured between Victoria and herself—"went to school with."

My fiancée's pale skin turned ghostly white.

Natalie continued. "Finn stayed in Seattle. Felix is in telecommunications and currently heads a project in Morocco. Finn met Mona five years ago. Fell in love. Bought this bar to showcase her talents."

"Aw, shit. That's Mona King." Martin scrubbed a hand over his face, then leaned closer to Natalie and kissed her neck. "You didn't tell me you knew her."

It didn't go unnoticed that Natalie had zero reaction to Martin's lips on her skin.

"When you mentioned you liked her music, I thought it'd be more fun to surprise you." A proud smile cracked her face.

When Martin stole a proper kiss, I turned away, a knot forming in my gut. I slid my fingers through Victoria's under the table. She trembled, and I pulled her hand to my thigh.

"You okay?" I asked, leaning close so no one else could hear.

"Never better," she forced through clenched teeth, meeting my eyes for a brief second before focusing again on my best friend and his new girlfriend, the woman I was getting damn tired of trying not to think about.

"Another round?" our waitress asked, her red hair pulled back, not a strand out of place, her makeup flawless, her dress straight out of an episode of *Boardwalk Empire*.

I gestured yes. I'd need at least six to survive the evening unscathed.

Conversation was polite. Martin did most of the talking. We avoided the subject of Victoria and Natalie's past, and I raved about Victoria's new ventures, hoping to show Natalie that my fiancée was no longer the same woman from high school.

At one point, Natalie looked at her phone, her face going ashen before she dropped the device into her handbag. I shot Martin a glance. He hadn't seemed to notice and rambled on about his last adventure in Vegas.

Natalie was fully engaged while Victoria seemed distant. She didn't lose her cool often, but when she did, she could go days without talking. That undercurrent of rage vibrated the air between us. I could do nothing to soothe her while we were in public, but I'd do everything in my power to ease her tension when we got home.

The lights dimmed, thank fuck. The piano went silent.

Natalie bounced in her seat, then clapped her hands. "She's about to start." She stood and turned her chair around to face the stage. Following her lead, I turned, too. Natalie's knee touched mine again, but she shifted and crossed her legs, breaking our sinful connection.

Double dates were bullshit.

Martin and Victoria were now at my back, but I looked over my shoulder to make sure Vic was okay. She smiled her killer smile and let me know not to worry and enjoy the show.

The whole crowd silenced as if holding a collective breath. Natalie brought her steepled hands to her lips.

A single blue spotlight hit the stage, and there she stood, Mona King, graceful and glorious at the mic.

Without moving her head, her eyes darted left, then right, a smirk. A deep breath. Then she belted the first line of, "I Put A Spell On You."

In the background, the piano came into play, enhancing the emotion, but not a single soul in that bar could tear their gaze from the queen on the stage, commanding and regal. Her voice weaved through skin and bone, then pierced the heart and caressed the soul.

Nina Simone, Ella Fitzgerald, Billie Holiday. Some I recognized. Most I didn't.

But under Mona King's spell, I fell in love. With life, with music, with crowded bars. I heard a sniff and tore my gaze from the stage. Tears rolled down Natalie's cheeks, but she smiled, silently singing along, every bit in love with the performance as I was.

A hand came over my shoulder, then soft breaths in my ear. "I'm heading to the ladies' room. Be right back." Victoria kissed my cheek.

"I'll go with you." I pushed to stand but she held me down.

"It's okay. Stay. Enjoy the music. I'll be two secs." She kissed me again.

When Mona started her rendition of "Someone To Watch Over Me," fingers dug into my thigh.

"My favorite song," Natalie said to the stage.

She looked down and jerked the offending hand away. "Oh, God. I'm sorry." She flashed an impish grin.

I mourned the loss of her fingers, the warmth, the physical connection. I blamed that bullshit on the music.

L.O.V.E.

Because I was not a cheater.

The song ended, leaving my emotions drained, but my soul sated.

Then Mona spoke into the mic, her voice sultry still. "Before I take a break, I have a special song for two lovebirds out there. Nat and Cole, this one's for you." She shot a wink our direction, though I was sure she couldn't see us.

"Oh, no." Natalie groaned. "She thinks were together." She laughed and shrugged, then settled back into her seat.

Mona crooned a familiar tune. "L-O-V-E" by Nat King Cole. I smiled, a flood of memories washing over me. My grandfather singing to my grandmother, swinging her around the room. Then I laughed, finally understanding. Natalie King. Cole Adams.

Mona sang. Natalie sang along. I was no longer mesmerized by the artist on stage but the woman sitting next to me. I fell in love. Again. With the song. With life. With crowded bars. With a woman I hardly knew.

My insides shifted. My gut twisted.

I reached behind and grabbed Victoria's drink, downing her half-empty glass in one shot.

Where the hell was my fiancée? And where was Martin? I stole his whiskey and downed that, too.

Natalie was clueless to my agitation. Good.

I stared long and hard at my best friend's girlfriend. Tried my damnedest to rile all the hatred and disgust I could muster.

Only, I couldn't find one thing I didn't like about the temptress, aside from the fact she was bewitching.

Mona finished. Promised she would return shortly.

The lights came on. Natalie wiped more tears. "God, she gets me every time." She gave me a playful nudge with her elbow.

Temptress.

I excused myself to the restroom. I stopped at the bar. Ordered a shot. Then made my way to the men's room.

Martin was nowhere to be seen. Maybe he'd gone outside for a smoke. He was notorious for falling into old habits after a drink or two. Be it nicotine, women, or bad decisions.

When I returned to our table, Vic was typing on her phone. Martin and Natalie sat close, having a private conversation. He rubbed her thigh. She seemed to like his attention. Good.

Natalie King was less attractive in my best friend's arms.

Six drinks. Three sets of sultry love songs.

One Uber ride home.

Victoria helped me to bed.

The last thing I remembered was tasting cigarettes on her lips and asking when she'd started smoking.

I woke to an empty bed again. In an empty house, the brick Georgian Colonial I'd bought for my bride-to-be in the Madrona neighborhood.

A note on the kitchen counter read: *Hangover cure in the fridge. See you tonight. XOXO, Vic.*

I wadded the scrap paper, made for the garbage, then sucked in a breath, flattened the crumpled note, and stuck it in the drawer where every note from Victoria landed.

She called it a junk drawer.

I called it sentimental safekeeping.

Whatever.

L.O.V.E.

Fuck the hangover cure. I dressed and went for a run, heavy metal blasting through my earbuds, the angry gray sky blanketing our neighborhood in a damp winter chill.

Breakfast. Shower. Shave.

I briefly considered checking on Martin, but then I'd have to hear about Natalie. Didn't want that siren on my mind because, fuck, she was like a tiny gnat with a mighty roar buzzing around my head, and that woman was not welcome in my head.

I dialed Ellis, hoping he'd be up for a spar. "Hey. Heard you had a great night. Sorry we couldn't make it."

"No worries. What're your plans today?"

"Heading to Bainbridge, hanging with my parents for the day. Wanna join us?"

"Nah. Got work to do. Thanks, bud. Have fun."

"See you Monday?"

"Yep."

I ended the call.

My phone rang. Victoria. Tension eased, and I settled into my couch. "Morning, beautiful."

"How are you feeling?"

I huffed. "Like shit. You should be in bed with me. Where'd you go?"

"I reminded you last night, don't you remember? Lauren's cousin, Cora, owns that bridal shop in Portland. I told you about her a couple weeks ago. Anyway, she said she'd open her store just for us today. Catered lunch. Drinks. We're making a day of it."

I rubbed the ache in my temples. "It's Christmas Eve tomorrow. You'll be home tonight?"

We'd yet to decorate, both too busy.

"Not sure. If we have too much to drink, we'll crash at Cora's, head home in the morning."

"Yeah. Okay." I looked around my empty living room, the home I'd bought for my fiancée. The home she'd decorated to impress the friends who rarely visited. The white paint. Velvet couch. Art by some artist whose name I couldn't pronounce hanging on the walls. Not much in the way of personality. Nothing inviting. Or maybe my hangover was worse than I thought. Maybe I was tired of living alone in the home built for a family.

"And Cole?" Her voice softened, a silky seduction.

"Yeah?"

"Mom and Dad just called. I'm gonna head to Hawaii with them next week. Spend some quality time before I get too busy with the wedding."

Too busy? I refrained from laughing. We rarely spent time together as it was.

I waited for an invitation that didn't come, then said, "I'll see if Martin's available to pilot the plane."

"He is. I asked him last night."

Of course, she did. While I was too drunk to pay attention. "I'll call ahead and make sure the condo is stocked."

"You're the best, sweetheart."

I wasn't. But I would be better because my future wife deserved the best version of me. "Be safe today. They're predicting snow."

"We will." She sighed. "Gotta go."

"Victoria?"

"Yeah, babe?"

"Love you."

"You, too. See you tomorrow."

The call ended. My phone made a disappointing sound as it crashed into the wall and landed on my shoe. I must've kicked them off last night, as one sat wonky against the wall, the other under the side table.

L.O.V.E.

I had a good relationship with my future in-laws, but Victoria was always hesitant about sharing them. Didn't make sense.

The last thing I wanted was to be stuck alone with my thoughts. Options limited, I fired up the flat screen and settled into a mind-numbing click, click, click.

When I passed a black and white clip, I paused. A familiar tune passed through the speakers. "The Christmas Song" by Nat King Cole. My heart raced. Head pounded. Thoughts of Natalie danced through my aching skull.

Two more bars into that wretched song, I hit the *Power Off* button and tossed the remote.

Shit.

God was testing me. Had to be.

I was not in love with Natalie. I couldn't even be in *like*. I didn't know the woman.

Her smile was a ruse.

Her laugh a curse.

Her skin a guise.

Her eyes a seduction.

A test.

And I was fucking failing.

I wouldn't fail. I was engaged. I was committed to Victoria.

PART TWO

Oh my God, You're Everywhere

Natalie

"Wow. You're everywhere, aren't you?"

I stopped cold. Shivered at the tone. Turned.

Cole sat at the corner table, black thermal hugging his strong arms, dark jeans encasing his thick thighs, well-worn boots on his feet. Half-finished plate in front of him. Dimples on full display.

For the love of God, I needed a distraction.

My heart skipped a beat when I forced my gaze to his plate and spied the strips of steak. "Crying Tiger. Good choice. One of my favorites."

Dropping his fork to his plate, he asked, "You know what this is?"

With a nod, I answered. "Have to order it special."

"You've been here before." He twirled a small metal object in his right hand between his thumb and forefinger.

When he caught me looking, he leaned back and tucked the trinket into the front pocket of his jeans.

L.O.V.E.

"Many, many times," I said, taking in the room. Sage green walls. Dark, refurbished wood. Amber mood lights. A hidden gem. My hidden gem.

"Must be fate." He smirked.

"Fate?"

With a shrug, he said, "Us bumping into each other."

"I don't believe in fate." Much to my mother's dismay.

"What do you believe in?"

"Hard work." His fiancée taught me that lesson, relentless in telling me I'd never graduate college, let alone find a man willing to take care of me. I'd proven her wrong. I'd taken care of myself.

Cole considered my answer, nodded to the chair across from him. "Join me."

A dinner alone with Cole would only lead to bad, bad things. "Oh, gosh. That's nice, but I was planning on curling up on my couch with a good movie." I lifted my arm in case he hadn't noticed the to-go bag dangling from my fingers.

"Natalie. Don't make a guy beg. I hate eating alone. Besides, it'd be a shame to hide in your apartment when you look so pretty."

I looked down at my denim jacket, thigh-length sweater, worn leggings, and Moto boots. I hadn't washed my hair all weekend, and forget about makeup.

"It's cold and dreary outside. I just want to take off my bra, curl up on the couch, and binge watch *Ray Donovan*." And pout, I left unsaid, feeling sorry for myself because Lacey had spent every waking moment with Ellis since the day after Christmas.

"Sounds fun." He gave me a once-over, not inappropriate by any means, more like he was trying to figure me out. "But here, you can eat with a quasi-handsome gentleman who happens to be good at conversation."

He made a good point. And he was far more attractive than Liev Schreiber, and that was saying a lot. "Okay. Yeah. Why not?" I made myself comfortable in the chair opposite Cole's and arranged my Styrofoam containers on the table, popping the lids and savoring the garlic aroma.

"And for the record, you're more than quasi-handsome," burst from my lips like a shaken can of soda exploding all over the room, leaving a sticky mess.

"Yeah?" he countered with double dimples, knocking me for a loop.

"Definitely." *Good Lord*! I couldn't stop myself, and I needed to stop.

He belonged to another. Victoria of all people. The scar on my forehead itched, a sobering reminder of the situation.

Rubbing the annoying tingle with the back of my hand, I asked, "Buy any new buildings today?"

A sly grin. "As a matter of fact, I did." His eyes sparkled, swirling with pride.

"You should be celebrating."

"I am." His gaze slid to the table.

He was lonely. Just like me. God, how I wanted to throw my arms around that solid neck and kiss some joy back into his sullen gaze. Instead, I asked, "This is celebrating?"

"Sure." He gestured to his food, then me. "Good food. Great company."

Our gazes locked for longer than appropriate, and I heated in places that should be immune to his charm.

Cole cleared his throat, breaking the spell. "I don't enjoy going out. I'd rather stay in, celebrate on the couch with a good movie, cold beer, my lady, clothing optional, of course." He shot me a wink.

I tried to dodge the damn thing, but he gave good flirt, and that wink, innocent or not, hit my chest dead center.

Won't lie. I liked that he flirted with me. I loved that Victoria's fiancé was paying attention to me, the girl she'd tormented, the girl she'd stolen friends and boyfriends from, the girl she'd tried to break.

Were I a lesser woman, I would've played our mutual attraction to the bitter end, taken a bat to Victoria's chance at a happily ever after.

But I wasn't that person.

I would not continue the cycle.

I would deflect the flirt.

"Martin talks about your exciting adventures all over the world, all the fancy parties, swank hotels, and whatnot."

Cole's grin faded. The mention of his best friend, whom I happened to be dating, deflated our nice little bubble.

Leaning closer, he confessed, "Honestly? The guys love that shit, so I go along for the ride."

"And you front the bill."

He quirked his head, thrown by my blatant observation. "Martin tell you that?"

"No. Figured that one out all on my own."

"They're not using me if that's what you think."

"I don't." I didn't believe his friends were using him, anyway. Victoria? Entirely different story.

"Good. It's not like that between us. We grew up together. Been through hell and back together. I have more money than I can spend in two lifetimes. If they want to blow off steam once in a while, I'm happy to oblige."

"Yeah. I could tell that about you."

"How?"

"You're swimming in dough, yet you're sitting in this hole in the wall while your fiancée is on her way to Maui with your best friend via your private jet."

"That's his jet, not mine."

"No, it isn't. It's yours. Martin told me you like to say it's his since he's the only person you let pilot the damn thing."

"Okay, fine. Busted."

"You don't need to talk him up, ya know. I like him already."

Cole hit me with a hard, unfocused glare. "He's a good guy." He blinked. Nodded. Poked at his rice. "Needs to find a good woman."

Sinful, I know, but I didn't want Victoria or Martin soiling my conversation with Cole, so I changed the subject matter to more mundane topics. He wasn't only gorgeous to the eye, he was beautiful on the inside, too, and fun to talk with. I learned about his favorite charities. There were seven that he supported. His music depended on his mood. Lime green was his favorite color. We both hated cats, but while Cole loved big dogs, I was partial to smaller breeds. He moved back to Seattle to raise his family close to his parents, whom he seemed to love and respect deeply.

Cole didn't look at his cell once throughout dinner. My phone buzzed relentlessly. Unknown caller. If I answered, a certain jilted lover would be on the other end.

"You sure you don't need to get that?" Cole asked, collecting our garbage from the table.

"I absolutely do not want to answer those calls."

He stood taller, searing me with the heat of his glare. "Your ex still bothering you?"

I melted into a puddle on the worn linoleum, exhausted by the turn my life had taken since the whole coffee shop incident. "He's relentless."

Cole stared long and hard, a thousand questions dancing in his eyes, his fingers tightening around the plate he held. "File a restraining order?"

"No," fell like a lead weight from my lips, landing between us with a dull thunk, and I stared at the floor, feeling the fool.

"C'mon." He stood and made his way to the trash bin. "I'll walk you to your car."

"Oh, that's not necessary. I live just around the corner."

"Then I'll walk you home." His hand landed on the small of my back, urging me toward the exit, leaving no room for argument.

Cold, damp air blasted through my too thin jacket. My shivers, though, had nothing to do with the temperature and, shamefully, everything to do with the man holding the door open.

Cole walked me home. We stood outside my building and talked for another half hour, speaking nothing of consequence, sharing friendly banter.

It wasn't until I entered my apartment that I realized I'd used the front entrance to my building for the first time in ages. And I hadn't looked over my shoulder all night.

"Thanks for dinner, Nats. That was amazing." Martin tossed the dishtowel in the sink, hooked an arm around my waist, yanked me flush against his hard body, and doused me with kisses, starting at my cheek, traveling down to my neck, then to my collar bone.

"You're welcome," came out breathy and hopeful.

He hovered over my breasts and lifted his eyes to mine, brows quirked in a silent plea for permission.

I lifted my chin, allowing him access.

Warm hands slid under the hem of my blouse, then traveled upward, his thumbs blazing a trail over the lace covering my tight buds.

I ached with need. But it wasn't Martin's touch I craved.

He moved one hand to the button of my jeans.

God, how long had it been since a man had made me orgasm?

Martin had yet to get me into bed. We'd started many intense make-out sessions that always ended before the fireworks began. His phone would ring, calls from work. He didn't have condoms. I had my period. New Year's Eve had been a dud—he drank too much and passed out on his couch the second we got back from a ridiculously lavish party Ellis had invited us to attend.

Funny thing? I was always relieved.

Still. We had fun, though I never got the feeling I was a priority. His cell rang all hours of the day, and he was often called away at the drop of a hat.

Maybe that's what I liked about Martin. He wasn't clingy. And Lord knows, I'd had my fill of clingy men.

But I was a woman with needs, and as he worked my jeans open, then down my hips, I shivered with anticipation, because I was finally, finally going to get some much needed relief.

Martin was attractive for sure. And if he made love like he kissed, I was in for a treat.

He helped me disrobe, then hoisted me onto his counter, the gray quartz cold on my backside.

His khakis had made it to his ankles when his phone buzzed.

Face flushed, he huffed, "Jesus. Fuck. I'm sorry. Gotta take this," then dropped a kiss on my nose, righted his pants, and left me naked in his kitchen.

Bits and pieces of his conversation drifted my way and went something like, "Yeah. No. No. Not busy. Tonight?

Fuck yeah. Does he know? Sure. Sure. I know. I know. No. No. No. Come on. What do you think?" He huffed. "You know that can't happen. Okay, I'll be there. Bye. No. Bye."

Martin found me in the same position he'd left me. He scrubbed a hand through his thick hair. "So sorry. Have an emergency flight to Georgia."

"Tonight?"

He stepped between my legs, pulling me against his arousal. "Be back day after tomorrow. We'll go somewhere special."

"Sure." I shoved him away before he could claim my mouth, then dropped to my feet.

"I'm sorry, Nats. It's my job. I'll make it up to you."

"No worries. Really." On with my jeans.

"You're mad."

Duh. "I'll be fine." Hook the bra. Shirt next. "This works out great, actually. I've got a super busy weekend planned, and now I don't have to worry about juggling my time." I shoved my feet into my Uggs, snagged my handbag off the coffee table, and made my way to the door.

Martin stopped me, palm to the wood, towering above me, worried eyes meeting mine. "What kind of plans?"

"Girl stuff."

A strong hand curled around my neck, thumb caressing. "I'm sorry, baby."

He didn't get to call me baby. *Baby* was a term of endearment reserved for lovers. Soft and slow, I gripped his wrist and pulled his arm away from me. "No need to be sorry. It's your job. I understand." I gave his shoulder a quick rub. "Fly safe."

Martin leaned in for a kiss. I slid to the left, slipped through the door, and threw over my shoulder, "Good night. See ya' around."

I loved Barolo. Two bottles resided in my wine rack at all times, for special occasions such as finding myself alone on a Friday evening after almost getting ravished by a handsome redhead with a killer body but sent on my merry way. Whatever.

I had wine. I had a *Ray Donovan* marathon. I had my comfy couch.

Two episodes and one and a half glasses of wine behind me, my phone buzzed under my left butt cheek. Took some finagling, but I managed to untangle myself from my throw blanket and find my cell.

"Hello?"

"I hear you'll be a swinging single tomorrow evening."

Every nerve in my body tingled, his rich voice like a verbal massage, hitting all my erogenous zones.

"He told you?"

"Cried like a baby. Said he had to go out of town and you were upset."

"I'm not." Irritated would better describe my mood.

A heated pause. "Does it bother you, Martin going out of town all the time?"

"No," I answered, not entirely dishonest. "I really do enjoy my alone time."

"So why did he call me, worried he'd ruined things with you?"

I couldn't wrap my head around the fact that Cole had called me. Cole the uber-rich guy. Cole the most beautiful man alive. Cole the fiancé of my nemesis. Cole, who was under my skin and grating my nerves. "None of my comings and goings with Martin are any of your business." I should have ended there, but Barolo. "Especially the lack of coming, due to that workaholic taking a fucking phone call in the middle of getting busy on his kitchen counter."

Long, uncomfortable silence passed. Enough time for Ray Donavan to put a bullet through a priest's head.

Cole blew a hard breath through the speaker. "He left you hanging?"

"He left me hanging."

"The fuck's wrong with that guy?" Two more heavy breaths. "On behalf of my douchebag best friend, and men everywhere, I apologize."

"Not necessary." I pointed the remote at my flat screen and pushed *Pause*. "Cole."

"Yeah?"

My phone buzzed in my hand, alerting me to incoming texts. I ignored them. "How did you get my number?"

"Martin."

Shamefully, I wasn't upset that Cole had my digits. "Why are you calling me?"

He huffed a nervous laugh. "He wanted me to check on you."

What kind of man does that shit? If Martin was worried, he should've made the call. "Okay. So we're back in junior high?"

A deep, chocolatey, gooey chuckle reached my ears. "You're right. Immature. Again, I apologize."

"You're forgiven," slipped my lips, and I sank deeper into my cushions.

"Uh. Wanna meet for dinner tomorrow? Victoria's heading to Portland for a bridal shower. Ellis and Lacey are MIA."

I hadn't spoken to Lacey in days. I was lonely, and maybe that was why talking to Cole seemed like a necessity. But savoring the sound of his voice was wrong on too many levels. "I don't think that's a good idea."

"Why?"

"I think you know why." I swallowed another long pull of my wine.

"Are you drunk, Natalie?"

"Maybe a little." Why did he care? "Barolo never lets me down," I whispered, saddened by the truth of that statement. "I'll never love a man more than I love Barolo."

"Listen. I'll be at Wall Street Thai tomorrow at six, having my usual. Join me or don't. Just thought I'd offer, seeing as we're both without our significant others for the weekend."

"Significant." I laughed. "That's funny." Martin was of no importance to me. Not really. Pathetic, I know.

"What's funny?" His voice echoed like he was in a large empty room.

"Never mind."

He grunted, then released a long exhale, the sound of metal clinking in the background.

"Where are you?"

"Gym."

I glanced at the clock. Ten thirty-six PM. I remembered him boxing with Ellis, his grace. His power. I sighed.

"You okay?"

No, I was not. "I will be, soon as Ray ditches the priest's body."

"What?" His breaths quickened and a thump, thump, thump, thump reached my ears.

I emptied my glass. Swallowed. Lay back down, stretching my legs across the sofa. "It's sad how we root for people to die, isn't it?"

"The hell you talking about?" His breaths came measured in sync with the background noise. Thump, thump, whack. Thump, thump, whack.

85

"It's wrong for us to take pleasure in their deaths, yet we do."

"Who died?" Whack, whack, whack.

"Take Ray Donovan for example. The priest abused him. Raped countless children, including Ray's brother. And while that old fucker sits there on the couch, bleeding, we're silently hoping, please Ray, please, just end that bastard. Don't take him to the hospital. Don't forgive his sins. Just end him. And *bam*! Bullet to the head. And I'm happy. Happy that a man was murdered. Does that make me a bad person?"

"No." Huff, thump. Huff, whack. Huff, thump, thump.

The sound was a lullaby, a calming caress. I let my guard down, closed my eyes, and whispered, "I used to wish someone would kill Victoria."

"Natalie," he whispered, low and gruff. A warning, perhaps.

"Sorry. Oh, God. I'm sorry."

"How bad was it?"

"I've had too much to drink. I should go."

A mumbled "fuck" reached my ears. "Why won't either of you talk about what happened?"

"She's your fiancée. I won't." I wanted to. "I can't." I had no right. He wasn't mine. "Goodnight, Cole."

I powered down my cell. Drank through two more episodes. Woke the next morning with a killer headache, a sour stomach, and Cole on my mind.

"Wasn't expecting to see you here." Gone were the dimples. Even wearing a scowl, the man was devastating. He wore a light blue sweater, worn jeans, and black sneakers. His messy hair only added charm.

The flutter in my chest was wholly inappropriate, and the very reason I had waited for him to finish eating before walking through the door and to his table.

"I only came to apologize for last night. In person. Not over the phone."

"You have no reason to apologize." He cleared his throat and dropped his wadded napkin on the empty plate, then tilted his strong square jaw to meet me eye to eye.

My glasses slid down my nose, an irritating distraction. I pinched the rim, sliding them back into place. "I said some things."

"You were intoxicated."

Damn wine. "That's not an excuse."

"Natalie." He sighed, pushed to stand, and then pulled out a chair. "Sit with me."

"No." I moved back a step. "I need to get home."

My phone buzzed in my hand, breaking the tension, and I glanced down at the screen.

I see you.

Fucking whore.

Pulse kicking, I looked out the window across the street. A glance left, then right. No sign of Holden or his Tundra.

Over the past couple weeks, the texts had changed from pleading to ugly. I blocked every caller, yet new messages kept coming. I would have to change my number, but I feared even that wouldn't stop his efforts.

Cole whispered, "What?"

"What, what?" I asked, not sure where to aim my attention, gaze bouncing from the phone to Cole to the phone to Cole.

"You're white as a ghost." He stepped around the table, standing close enough I could smell his laundry soap. "Is it him? He still bothering you?"

I hadn't the energy to lie. "Yes." I showed him my screen.

"Natalie," he said, voice dark and gritty. "We have to do something."

The word *we* floated between us, a slip I didn't dare acknowledge.

Cole cleared his throat. "The guy is unhinged. You need to be careful."

"I know." I shoved the cell into my handbag.

"What are you doing to protect yourself?"

"Security won't let him into our building at work. He can't get into my apartment building. I haven't seen him in days." I stared at the table, my words falling weak.

"We offer self-defense courses at the gym. Why don't you come in? Take a class. See how you like it." He gripped my elbow and gave it a squeeze. "Hell. Bring Lacey. You two can get the friends and family discount."

"Yeah. Maybe," I mumbled, moving just enough to break contact. Even though the gesture was innocent, his touch ignited an unholy flame under my skin. "Might be a good idea."

"Good." He nodded, seemingly satisfied. "Good," he repeated, then tugged his wallet out of his back pocket and dropped a handful of bills on the table. "Did you walk or drive?"

"I walked."

"Okay, then." Again his fingers wrapped around my arm. "I'll walk you home."

"That's not necessary. It's—"

"I'm walking you home," he interrupted, scooting me toward the door, leaving no room for argument.

Cole kept the conversation light, though I noticed he was on alert, keeping an eye on our surroundings, staying close, too close, our arms brushing, shoulders bumping.

We reached my building and I turned to thank my hero for the day but, dear Lord, the man smelled delicious and looked downright edible. I hadn't eaten all afternoon, and I couldn't manage one single word for fear of drooling all over his feet.

Shoving his hands in his front pockets, he asked, "Should I walk you up?"

Walk me up. See me in. Tear off my clothes. Take me against my front door.

"No. That's not necessary." The words traveled up my throat like oatmeal through a straw.

Cole stared for a long hard spell, then his brows furrowed.

He leaned closer. I hadn't the strength to back away, to stop what I sensed was coming, because I wanted the freight train that was Cole Adams to come at me full throttle, pulverize me, leave me dead but wholly satisfied.

Indecision pained his face, wrinkles bunching between his brows, a snarl forming on his lips. Closer still, he came, and my heart punched through my chest to steal the man that should be mine. The man that was not and never would be mine.

His hand landed on my neck. My fingers rose to his chest. Push or pull? Life or death? God, I wanted those lips. That body. That brain. Those dimples.

"Don't move," he said, his lips sinfully close to mine, moist from his tongue.

Move? His touch rendered me immobile. His heat, his scent, his quickening pulse beneath my fingertips, spellbinding. Heavy breaths hit my face.

The intimacy was wrong.

I was wrong.

Because he was right.

Right for me.

Right now.

Right for eternity.

I raised my chin to accept his mouth, a sigh escaping, or maybe that was the last of my conscience.

"Aren't you a little devil," he rasped, jerking away. "Got you." He straightened, held his hand up.

On the tip of his finger, a tiny brown beetle shimmied back and forth, then spread his wings and buzzed away.

"Oh." My chest deflated. My stomach sank. A blowtorch scorched my cheeks.

"He was caught in your hair." He assessed my eyes, then my cheeks, then my mouth. "You okay?"

No. I was fucked in so many ways. All of them caused by the man that stood too damn close. Who smiled too damn bright.

He looked down at my hand, the offending appendage that still rested on his chest.

Our eyes locked, and a groan rose in his chest. I slunk back a step, my arm falling to my side.

"Natalie." He swallowed. Looked over my shoulder. "I...um..."

"Nats?" A familiar, angry voice drew my attention to the man approaching on the sidewalk.

Holden wore a scowl, his features sharper than the last time I'd seen him. He wore black running pants, a black jacket zipped to his neck, and a black beanie, his hair now reaching almost to his shoulders.

Cole stepped in front of me, a vibrating wall of testosterone, an impenetrable shield between me and any threat.

"Baby," Holden pleaded, though I couldn't see him, only Cole's back. "I'm not here to cause trouble. Just want to talk."

"She's got nothing to say to you." Cole's voice vibrated the surrounding air.

"I think that's her decision," Holden countered, eerily calm.

"Natalie," Cole said over his shoulder, "your call."

Obviously, I was not in the right frame of mind to make any judgement call. "I just want to go to bed." I turned, keyed the number pad, and pushed the door open the moment it buzzed. As I escaped behind the glass, I threw over my shoulder, "Holden. You bother me again, you're going to jail." An empty threat since I hadn't filed a restraining order. But I would. First thing in the morning.

It wasn't until I'd reached the elevator that I realized Cole had followed me inside. It wasn't until we reached my door that he said, "You thought I was going to kiss you."

I died a thousand deaths right then and there.

"Yes." I stared at the keys in my hand, then swallowed my shame and forced my gaze upward.

"I love Victoria," he said, though I could swear, he winced, his gaze sliding to something over my shoulder before hitting me hard.

"I know." All the men did. And none of them survived unscathed.

"We're getting married soon."

God. Was he trying to torture me? "I know that, too."

"I hate cheaters." Such conviction in his voice.

"Me, too," I threw back with all honesty. Every boyfriend I'd had in high school had cheated on me with… guess who? Victoria.

Raking a hand through his hair, he murmured, "But you were going to let me kiss you."

"Because I'm a terrible person."

He didn't try to convince me otherwise, instead announcing, "I should go."

"I think that's a good idea."

With a nod, he took a step back. "Okay." Then he stopped and asked, "You haven't told Martin about your ex, have you?"

"No."

"Why?"

"It's my problem. I don't want him to worry. Please don't say anything."

"Saying nothing gets women killed," he said, glaring straight through me before dropping his head.

There was a story there, hiding behind his gruff tone and frustration. A story that was none of my business.

Hands to hips, he gnawed his bottom lip, then assured me, "I won't say anything. As long as you promise to show up for those self-defense classes."

"It's a deal."

He turned to leave. Stopped. Faced me again. "I'm sorry if I gave you the wrong impression."

I had no words because my heart was leaking, shame and guilt flooding my chest.

"Are we okay, you and me? We'll be seeing a lot of each other with Lacey and Ellis."

I nodded yes, though inside I screamed *no, no, no.*

"Good." His dimples appeared. "Friends."

Then he was gone.

Cole

"You talked to her?" Dark circles framed Martin's eyes.

Last time he'd looked so worn out, Ellis and I had been dragging him out of a brothel in Nevada.

"You asked me to check up on your girl, so I did."

"And?"

"And you're good, bud." The fib left a sour taste in my mouth and a gnarly ache in my gut. But, fuck, Martin sucked at relationships, and if one little white lie could help steer him the right direction, then my integrity could weather a hit.

Martin tracked a leggy brunette on her way to the weight room, a predatory gleam in his eyes, and my guilt for lying evaporated. I refrained from smacking him but, damn, how I wanted to shake some sense into the bastard.

"Hey, guys," came a heavenly voice over my shoulder, her timing spot on.

Martin snapped his head toward the sound, face blazing. "There's my girl." He pulled Natalie into an awkward embrace, giving me a good view of her backside.

She wore baggy sweats, the drawstring pulled tight but hanging low on her hips, highlighting a round, firm ass, and a slim waist. A black tank top clung to her fit back and arms, her skin pale and delicate, too clean and pretty for the likes of my friend.

Martin went in for a kiss. Got nothing but cheek. Interesting.

"Be right back." She gave him a friendly pat on the back. As she passed, she shot me a quick glance and raised a hand in greeting. "Hey, Cole."

Her dismissive tone stung.

Every emotion rolling through my body was wrong. A betrayal. *Fuck.* I needed to ghost. With a clap to Martin's shoulder, I retreated to my office, where I wouldn't be tempted to watch the self-defense class or the woman I'd persuaded to attend said class.

As if God himself were trying to right my wrong, Victoria glided through the door.

"Hey, baby," she sing-songed, swaying my way, all long legs, bare midriff, and ample bosoms on display.

She landed in my arms, stiff but pushing all her soft, sweet curves against my rigid planes, staking her claim, a sobering reminder of where my head belonged. "Take me to lunch after my workout?"

"It's a date," I whisper-growled in her ear, pulling her tighter. "Wasn't expecting to see you until dinner. You hate working out here."

"I do." Her nose scrunched, protesting the musty smell of my yet-to-be-remodeled workspace. "But I was in the neighborhood and wanted to see my man."

Victoria hated that my office was the loft above a dirty "fight" gym, rather than sharing space with my father, who had a million-dollar view from atop his ivory tower.

"Everything okay?" She tipped her head back, inspecting my face.

"Yeah. Just missed you. Why aren't you at work?"

With a shrug, she said, "Wasn't feeling it," and wiggled free of my embrace. "No big deal."

"You've skipped work three times this month."

"I've got my sugar daddy to take care of me," she teased, throwing in a wink. "Besides, soon as you knock me up, I'm going to resign. We've already talked about this, Cole. I want to raise my children, not hire someone for the job. Have you changed your mind? Because that's a deal breaker. If you're going to be one of those husbands that says he wants his wife at home, then complains to his friends that he's the sole breadwinner in the family, we need to rethink our relationship. Because that's just bullshit, and you know how important family is to me."

"Jesus, Vic. I'm worried about you getting fired. How the hell did we go from you shirking your responsibilities to me being a bastard?"

"Oh, God, Cole. Sorry. I'm such a mess with all the wedding preparations." Her pink-tinted lips dotted my cheek. "I need to hit the treadmill so I can fit into my dress. See you at lunch."

"Vic, wait." *Christ.* I couldn't wait for the wedding to be over. The moment I'd proposed and put that ring on her finger, she'd hit the ground running, leaving me dumbfounded, choking on her dust.

My cell rang.

"Love you, babe. See you soon." With a pat to my chest, she sauntered away to work out at a gym she hated.

L.O.V.E.

Deep down, I knew lunch wasn't her motive for showing up; otherwise, we'd have met at a Victoria-approved restaurant. Something was up. Had I not been distracted by a call from my father, I would've locked her in my office and made her talk. Instead, I answered my cell and followed her back downstairs.

"Hey, Dad."

"How's my boy?"

"Doing great."

"And that lady of yours?"

"Perfect. How's the knee?"

"Therapist said I'm back to working order."

"Good to hear. You gonna come by, go a round?"

"Ha!" He barked a belly laugh. "Learned my lesson the last time. I'll leave the fighting to you young punks." When I was a kid, Dad loved getting in the ring with me. He wasn't trained, but that never stopped my old man. Hands on, my dad, even if he suffered an ill-timed hit or two. Wasn't until years later, he told me it made his heart soar to see the way my confidence grew with those gloves on.

"And the gym? How're things coming along?"

"Renovations on the apartments upstairs are due to start next month."

"That's perfect, Son. Can't wait to hear all about it. Lunch next week?"

"See you then. Love ya, Dad."

"Love you too, Cole."

I stood on the last step, scanning the space. Victoria was MIA, but Martin and Ellis stood in the entrance to one of the training rooms, each leaning against a doorjamb, arms crossed, lovesick smiles on their faces.

I came behind the two lugs, about to make my presence known, when I caught sight of the scene. Lacey lay on her

96

back, the instructor crouched over her, giving instructions. All the other students watched with rapt attention. All but one.

Natalie stood, arms crossed, the heel of one bare foot perched on the other, her gaze narrowed, not on the floor, but at Victoria, who stood at the opposite corner of the room, cheeks red, chest rising and falling as if she'd sprinted a mile. Victoria wasn't watching the class either, but had her ire aimed at Martin and Ellis, looking ready to blow. *What the fuck?*

I stepped between my brothers. Victoria's eyes widened. She smiled, raised a hand, then disappeared around the corner.

"Jesus. Look at you lovesick bastards." I gripped their shoulders. "Give the ladies some privacy."

Ellis shrugged me off, his puppy dog eyes heartwarming.

Martin, on the other hand, leaned closer, voice low, almost genuine. "Why's she taking a self-defense class?"

"She's your girlfriend. Ask her," was all I offered. Wasn't my business. Victoria, however, was my business. "Either one of you say something to piss off Vic?"

Martin grunted a, "No."

Ellis mumbled, "Haven't talked to her in days, why?"

"Nothing. Never mind."

I checked my clock for the fifth time, then curled my hand around the beer glass, giving it a swirl, the dancing foam a flimsy distraction from my swelling aggravation. Wasn't like Victoria to be late.

"Seriously?" A voice floated over my shoulder. "I see you everywhere. My coffee shop, my favorite restaurant, my bar."

"My gym," I added, trying not to smile.

Ouch. Her laugh pinched my chest.

I turned to face Natalie, my breath catching. She wore a black dress, tight around her chest, but falling loose to just above her knees, and black heels that— Fuck, I was staring again.

"Like it's fate or something," I joked, though humor eluded me.

"Why're you pouting into your beer alone?" Ellis clapped my back, then claimed the empty stool next to mine, and I wondered what the hell was happening.

"Hi, Cole." Lacey came around Natalie, dropped a kiss on my cheek. "I thought you weren't able to join us tonight," she said, sliding between Ellis's knees.

"I wasn't. I mean, *we* weren't. Vic wanted a night alone. Said she read about this place. Wanted to meet here."

Of all the bars in all of King County, she'd picked the very same one Natalie was at. Just my fucking luck.

"Imagine that," Natalie mumbled, then shimmied onto the barstool next to Ellis, effectively putting a mountain between us. Good play. I was in no mood to banter with the temptress.

"Where's Martin?" came out gruff.

"On his way," Ellis said, gesturing to the bartender.

I turned back to my beer, catching sight of Natalie through the mirror behind the bar. The blue lighting in the dark space amplified the silver shimmer in her eyes. My chest beat something fierce. The room blurred, then snapped back into focus, making my head spin, desire and guilt a nauseating cocktail.

Minutes passed, slow and soggy, drenched with stolen glances and forced restraint. Drinks were bought.

Conversation shared. We moved from the bar to a table. I switched to hard liquor.

I called Victoria. She didn't answer.

Martin arrived twenty minutes after we'd been seated. We said our hellos. He embraced Natalie, moved in for a kiss, but she gave him her cheek. Her rejection made me happy, and a fucking bastard.

Victoria arrived ten minutes later. Relief washed through me, and I stood to greet her. She sauntered my way, her killer curves and hungry smile all for me.

When she caught sight of the table, she faltered in her red heels, but righted herself before anyone who didn't know her tells could notice. Shoulders back, chin high, she greeted everyone, hugging my brothers but only acknowledging the other ladies. I waited for her to sit, settled into my chair, and kissed her neck, then whispered, "You're gorgeous, you know that?"

Her shoulders relaxed. I kissed her again. Inhaled. "New perfume?"

"What?"

"You smell different."

Hands trembling, she cupped my jaw, pulling us face to face, mouth to mouth. She laughed. "Martin's cologne. He hugged me. Now I'll reek of him all night."

"Ellis and I have told him a million times to tone it down. The guy doesn't get it."

When we kissed, my stomach settled. "I want you to myself. Let's get our own table."

"No. That would be rude. We'll have a few drinks, then you can take me home. I bought something special for you."

"Yeah?" I leaned in for another nibble of those lips I rarely tasted.

"Mmhmm." She put a finger to my mouth. "But you'll have to get me naked to find it."

Jesus, how long had it been since I'd sunk between those creamy thighs? "I've had enough to drink. Let's go now."

Natalie laughed at something Lacey said, and my heart slammed against my rib cage. Victoria lifted my whiskey to her lips and finished it in one swallow. "Let's stay a little longer."

We stayed too long. Enjoyed too many drinks. Natalie and Victoria didn't speak, but Lacey made an effort to include Victoria in the conversation. I loved her for trying.

I made eye contact with Natalie only twice by accident.

Lacey excused herself to the ladies' room. Martin followed suit. Lacey returned. Victoria excused herself. I stared at my drink, studied the handblown glass light fixtures on the ceiling, calculated the blonde to brunette ratio in the room, anything to keep from staring at that damn temptress sitting across the table.

Lacey and Natalie, clearly inebriated and having a blast, told funny stories of growing up together.

Ellis shared the story about when he was four and used his dad's razor to give the dog a haircut. Natalie laughed so hard she cried.

I wanted to lick her tears. I wanted to make her cry. I needed to leave and never look at her again.

I ordered another drink.

Ellis and Lacey kissed. Natalie stared at me, cheeks flushed, lips stretched in a cute smirk. She rolled her eyes, made a funny face, then snapped a picture of the couple with her cell. Before tucking her phone away, she aimed the camera my way and said, "Say cheese."

I laughed. The knots in my gut loosened.

We could be friends. I could do that. For Ellis.

I checked my phone. Victoria had been gone for ten minutes.

Martin returned, shirt rumpled, reeking of smoke.

"You see Vic back there?"

"Yeah. She's on the balcony." He pointed over his shoulder. "Said she needed some fresh air."

I joined my fiancée outside, the night sky refreshing. When our lips met, I tasted whiskey and smoke. "I thought you quit."

"Sorry. I'm trying, Cole. It's just hard, watching those cunt—" She shook her head. Swallowed. "They hate me. And I'm trying. For your sake, I'm trying."

"You're brave, baby. I appreciate your efforts, but if it's hurting you, we can go."

"I don't deserve you." She stared through the glass doors, our table visible at the end of the long hallway. Martin's arm hung loose over Natalie's shoulder.

Victoria mumbled, "Hands off..." but her words were carried away by the warm breeze.

"What did you say?" I asked.

"Nothing," she snapped, cheeks blazing, eyes narrowed. "Can we go?"

"Yeah. Let me hit the head. I'll call for a car."

"I can drive," she said, words clipped.

"You've had more to drink than I have."

She opened her mouth to argue, but I pinched her lips and shook my head. "We've both had too much to drink."

"Yeah. You're right."

"Meet you at the table?"

"Meet me outside." She walked away, her gait only a tad shakier than mine.

L.O.V.E.

Two men stood at the bathroom sink. Suits and shiny hair. They shot me simultaneous nods and continued their conversation.

"You hear those two going at it in here?"

"Fuck, yeah. That bitch was hot."

"Pretty sure she came twice."

"In five minutes."

"Wager a Benjamin on which one of us can get a lady in here first?"

"Deal."

They shook hands. Washed. Left.

I laughed. I'd fucked in a bathroom stall once in college. Wasn't easy. We were both drunk and horny. I came. She didn't. Never saw her again.

Victoria would shudder at the thought of sex in a public setting. My cock ached. I needed to get my fiancée good and naked.

She passed out on the drive home. I carried her to bed. When I tried to help her undress, she slapped my hands away. I set a glass of water and pain relievers on her nightstand.

In the shower, I stroked my raging hard on, imagining a blond beauty wrapped around me, back pinned against a bathroom stall, riding my cock and screaming her release. Only it wasn't Victoria's cries I heard. It was Natalie's. And it was Natalie I saw when I came all over my hand.

I cranked the hot water and washed away the shame. God, I was such an asshole.

I crawled into bed, head pounding, gut churning, and curled my arms around my fiancée.

She reeked of whiskey and smoke. I held her tighter, guilt settling like a set of kettlebells in my chest.

I vowed to never jack off to another woman.

Natalie and I could not be friends. I could never see her again.

"Oh, my God. You're everywhere," came the voice I tried to disdain yet heard every time my eyes closed. "Is any street corner safe?" she teased.

I shifted my attention from the construction crew across the street. There she stood, a lone daisy in a concrete wasteland, bright eyes, brighter smile. Tan plaid coat over faded jeans and a white T-shirt. Glasses with a pale pink frame that matched her jacket and her lips. Hair piled on top of her head in a just-rolled-out-of-bed way. "Hey, Natalie."

Cars weaved through the busy intersection behind her. Above the mostly gray buildings, the clouds hung thick and dark, promising a downpour. Stormy like those silver, beguiling eyes of hers. She belonged on a billboard or the cover of a magazine. A city girl, if ever I'd seen one.

"You stalking me? Do I have to file a restraining order against you, too?" She laughed.

I wanted to hit something, but instead felt for the little gold trinket in my pocket and rubbed its smooth edges. "Your ex still harassing you?"

"I haven't seen him in a coupla weeks."

"Good." My chest deflated. "How are the classes?" I'd avoided the gym during class hours to avoid bumping into Natalie, putting the whole out of sight, out of mind theory to work.

"Great! Thank you for suggesting them." She adjusted her purse strap higher on her shoulder, her smile bulldozing my rectitude.

"Good," I repeated, apparently struck dumb by her beauty.

Lifting her head, she squinted. "I joined your gym." Her nose crinkled, as if waiting for me to protest.

"I heard."

Since then, I'd taken to using the back entrance to my office and getting my workouts in before sunrise to avoid bumping into her. It was then I realized how fucked my life had become. A man of honor should be able to resist temptation. Shouldn't have to rearrange his life because a woman who wasn't his fiancée stole his thoughts, conscious and otherwise.

"Something wrong?"

"No." I wanted to hate her. I wanted to hurt her for making me weak. "Nothing. Why?"

"You seem distracted."

I pretended to be interested in a passing BMW. "Meeting my dad for lunch."

"Oh." She shoved her hands into the front pocket of her jeans. "That a bad thing?"

"No. Why?"

A shrug. "Like I said, you seem distracted."

She had no right to care. She had no fucking right to be concerned for my emotional wellness. I was such a bastard for liking that she'd asked. I had to end the poison between us.

"Natalie. Look, here's the thing. You and Victoria share a past. I don't know what happened. But there's tension whenever the two of you are in a room together. She's going to be my wife. I have to have her back. Be in her corner. Understand?"

My gut tightened when she stumbled back a step.

Gaze dropped to the ground, she mumbled, "Sure. Sure, I get it. Being friendly with me feels like you're betraying her."

"Yes."

She scratched her forehead. Angry eyes lifted to meet mine. "So when we bump into each other, like we seemed cursed to do, should I pretend like I don't know you?"

Cursed was a little harsh. "That's not what I'm saying."

"Really?" Her right brow lifted.

Aw, shit. The woman was pissed.

"So what should I do exactly? Pretend I don't see you and keep on walking? Or maybe I should forget the years of torture, the four years of therapy, and next time we're all in a room together give Victoria a big ol' bearhug, thank her for the scars I wear, inside and out. Let her off the hook. Is that what I should do, so that life can be more comfortable for you?"

"She's trying."

Stepping closer, she pounded a pointed finger into her chest. "I'm trying, too, for Lacey."

"You wanted to know why I'm distracted. I answered." God, I was an ass.

"I'm the reason you're distracted? Me?" Hands to hips, she stepped closer, raising her chin in challenge. "We agreed to be friends. I'm being friendly."

"Maybe I can't—"

"Cole." Dad cut me off, his large arm coming around my shoulder.

I hadn't noticed his approach. I stepped away from the fiery woman. She stood her ground.

"Who's the lovely lady?" my father asked.

"Dad, this is Natalie King. Martin's girlfriend."

"King?" Dad offered his hand. "Any relation to Joe King?"

Natalie gave him a firm shake and a genuine smile. "That's my uncle. You know him?"

"He's the only man I trust with my finances."

"Wow. Small world." She tucked a loose strand of hair behind her ear. "Well, nice to meet you."

"You, too." Dad shot me a glance, then asked, "Why don't you join us for lunch?"

"Oh. Thank you, really, but I have an appointment." She pointed across the street.

"Pleasure to meet you, Natalie," Dad said, clueless to the tension.

"You, too." Natalie offered Dad a small wave, shot daggers my way, mumbled, "Cole," and punched the button for the crossing signal.

I glued my gaze to my father so as not to watch her walk away, so as not to give away my unfaithful thoughts. I only relaxed when, through my periphery, I noted she'd made it across the street and inside the building opposite from where we stood.

"Shame what happened to that girl."

"What do you mean?"

"If I remember right, she was tormented in high school. There was a big scandal involving her and her cousins, Joe's kids."

"Didn't know that."

"She's a fighter, though. Didn't quit or move away. Earned a full ride at UW. Shall we head inside? I'm famished."

We were seated at our usual table beside the window. Only after we'd ordered did I dare a look across the street. The name on the building Natalie had entered read *Joyspring Wellness Center*.

Dad laughed, snapping me back to attention.

"What's funny?" I asked.

"Natalie King." He held my gaze, head bobbing, waiting for me to get the joke.

I didn't. "And?"

"Cole." He lifted his hands to the sky, like the answer was obvious. "Nat King Cole."

"Jeez, Dad. Really?"

"You know, your grandparents were huge Nat King Cole fans. Dad had all his albums. He used to dance your grandma around the kitchen, singing all those oldies to her."

The weight on my chest lightened. "He used to sing to me and Cadence, too. All the damn time."

Dad laughed, highlighting his wrinkles. "He was the only one could get you to sleep sometimes. You'd cry until you were purple-faced. Your gramps would come over, take you out of your mama's arms, shut himself in the bedroom with you, and start crooning. You'd be out cold in no time." His eyes shimmered. "God, I miss him."

"Me, too, Dad. Me, too."

I stood outside the bank, feeling every bit the jackass, but determined to right my wrong.

At five thirty-five, a scrawny security guard escorted Natalie though the door. Her smile fell from her face when she saw me, that disappointment a sledgehammer to my chest.

She turned to her friend and said, "See you tomorrow, Tim," then came my way.

Though we stood mere feet apart, miles of wrong separated us. Her red-rimmed glasses matched her floral blouse and red wool coat. God damn, the woman must have stock in an eyewear company.

"What are you doing here?" she asked, staring at my chest.

Black slacks covered her legs, thank God. Made focusing on the task at hand easier. "I'm sorry about yesterday."

"Okay." She moved past and headed toward the intersection. "Apology accepted."

I followed a pace behind. "I was rude and insensitive."

"No," she said over her shoulder, her steps hurried. "Just honest. I like that about you."

I reached for her, then reconsidered. That should've been the end of our convo. I apologized; she forgave. But my conscience wasn't eased, so I asked, "Can I walk you home?"

"Sure. On one condition." She reached the street corner and pounded the crosswalk button.

I stood at her left, an arm's length away, giving her space. Or giving me space. I wasn't sure. "What would that be?"

"No flirting."

"Fine."

"No smiling either," she said, staring across the street.

"Seriously. Why?"

"You have dimples." Her lips curled. "Dimples make me stupid."

"See. I feel like that was a flirt."

The signal changed and Natalie stepped off the curb. "No. Not a flirt. A fact."

"Okay. Christ. Can we start over?"

"Sure."

"Listen. I was talking with my Dad yesterday. He mentioned an incident in high school—"

She threw up a hand, cutting me off. "That's very personal."

"I need to know, friend to friend, was Victoria involved?"

"Cole. You'll have to ask your fiancée. Will she tell you the truth? I don't know, but that's between you and her. It's not my business."

"You're going to therapy because of her."

A huff. "Yes."

"Would it help you to know that Victoria's been in therapy as well?"

"Help me? No. Surprise me? Yes." She did a little hop to avoid a crack in the sidewalk.

"How horrible was she exactly?"

"Oh, my God." Bringing her hands to her cheeks, she shook her head. "Can we not with this conversation? Please?"

I smiled, hoping to break the tension.

Lips pursed, she shook a pointed finger at my face. "I said no smiling."

"I can't help it. You're kind of funny when you're mad."

"Don't make me angry, Cole Adams. You won't like me when I'm angry."

"Okay, Bruce Banner. This is me backing off."

Natalie stopped in front of a hipster boutique, shoulders slumped, handbag dangling from delicate fingers. Worried eyes met mine, a trace of sadness leaking through. "What do you really want, Cole?"

"Truth?"

"Yes." She nodded, her gaze floating over my shoulder, then settling back on me. "Let's just get it out in the open so we can move on."

I moved closer to block her from the biting winter wind and shoved my hands in my pockets because, fuck me,

I ached to touch what wasn't mine. "We're attracted to each other, no sense denying it."

"I won't deny it."

"But it's more than physical. There's something about you I can't shake. I feel like fate brought us together for some reason. And that's why I tried to be friends."

"I feel a 'but' coming on." Chin tucked into her coat, she stared at my chest.

"I abhor cheaters."

"So do I. What's your point?"

I would burn in hell for saying so, but heaven help me, I needed to purge. Natalie deserved the truth. "I'm cheating on Victoria every time I close my eyes and see you instead of her. I'm cheating every time I wake up in the morning and wonder what you're doing before I realize her side of the bed is empty."

"Stop." Liquid eyes met mine.

"I'm committing adultery every time I remember the taste of your lips or get fucking hard thinking about that kiss."

"That's not fair, Cole," she whispered, shaking her head. "I didn't know you were with anyone when I kissed you."

"I'm being unfaithful every time I get jealous listening to Martin talk about you. How he loves falling asleep at your side, waking up with you. When he complains about being exhausted because the two of you were at it all night."

"Stop, Cole." Brows pinched, she stepped back, bumping into the shop window.

"You're all I see, Natalie. Every time I close my fucking eyes. I need you to know I'm not just being an asshole when I shut you out. It's just that... Fuck, this isn't coming out right."

"Oh, you're on a roll. Don't stop now."

Christ. I needed her to understand.

"I can't like you and I can't ignore you, so I'm trying to hate you, Natalie King. Because hating you is still a feeling, and I'd rather have that than nothing."

Natalie stared long and hard. Her tears were like acid, a slow IV drip straight into my chest. What a fucking disaster.

"Say something."

With a nod, her eyes met mine. Then she swung, her designer bag hitting my shoulder. With her free hand, she struck my chest. Again with the bag, the strike aimed at my face. I dodged but didn't counter. I deserved her wrath.

The little seductress exploded, her cheeks flaming, her finger poking at my sternum. "Fuck you. Fuck you and your dimples. Fuck you and your name. Fuck you for looking at me the way you do. For being everywhere all the fucking time. And fuck you for being in love with the devil." She raised her chin, challenging. "Yes, I said it. Your fiancée is Satan's spawn, and she's going to drag you to the pits of hell. Have fun on that ride, by the way."

Two angry strides announced her farewell until she stopped and turned. "I don't know what line of bullshit Martin is feeding you, but that lying bastard has never stepped foot inside my apartment. We've never spent the night together. Hell, since we're dropping confessions, Martin and I have never had sex. Which means, he's probably getting his rocks off with someone other than me."

Jesus. Fuck. What have I done?

She took another step back, another agonizing six inches between us. "Thank you for walking me home. Thanks for showing me what kind of man you are. Thank you for giving me a reason to dump your philandering friend."

L.O.V.E.

A warm breeze blew hair across her face, a mask. A shield. "Yeah. This is good. No more reason for us to hang out. Your conscience can be clear. This is me, bowing out gracefully." She bent at the waist spreading her arms, mocking, then stood straight, an ice-cold fucking statue. "But know this, Cole Adams. We bump into each other again? I'll be throwing all my hate right back at you."

8

Natalie

"**Y**ou dumped him?" Lacey whisper-yelled, her eyes going wide.

"Yes."

"I don't understand." She leaned her hip against the counter, crossed her arms, and scowled. "Last week we were considering a couples trip to Aruba. You seemed happy."

"There just wasn't any spark." I stuck my head in the fridge, pretending to search for something.

"What happened? Did he hurt you?" she asked my back, her breath blowing my hair.

The truth would upset Lacey, which in turn would upset Ellis, who no doubt would have a talk with Martin. And who knew where that would lead? They were best friends. I wouldn't be the cause of a rift between those men.

I grabbed a bottle of ginger beer and turned to face my friend. "Lacey, I wanted to like him. I really did. I gave it a good shot. But like I said, there wasn't any spark. Wasn't fair to waste his time."

"Waste whose time?" Mom came around the corner, folded dishtowels in hand.

"Martin." Lacey pulled a drawer open, then snatched the towels from my mom and started her ritual of arranging them two across and four high.

Hands to hips, Mom prodded, "Who's Martin?"

Lacey gasped, clutching her chest. "You didn't tell Linda about Martin? Oh, Nat Brat. You really don't like him."

"I tried." I moved from the fridge to across the room, a nice buffer but still stifling considering the topic.

"Well, good for you, Nugget." Mom pulled a dryer sheet off her pant leg. "You've put yourself back out there. That's great. Mike Harkness said his son is moving back to town. He's—"

"No!" Lacey and I shouted in unison.

Mike Harkness Junior was handsome and likable as long as he kept his lips zipped and shoes on his feet. They guy was smarter than sin, but cited oddball facts nonstop and had an unfortunate and seemingly incurable case of smelly feet.

"Okay. Okay." Mom, the perpetual matchmaker, surrendered with a laugh. "So who's Martin?"

Lacey's brows pinched. "Ellis's best friend."

"Is that going to be awkward when you all get together?" Dropping her arms to her sides, she hit me with a worried glare.

"No." I shook by head too hard and too fast. "Our split was amicable." Hell, Martin had barely blinked an eye when we met for coffee and I gave him the, *it's not you, it's me* spiel.

Hunched over his phone before he stood from the table, he'd left me sitting with two full coffees and a half-hearted, "See ya around, kid."

I could handle a run-in with Martin. He meant nothing to me.

But Cole? Mister *I can't like you, and I can't ignore you, so I'm trying to hate you. Blah, blah, blah.* Well, he'd already decimated me with his cruel, yet beautiful, confession. Another encounter with that man, I'd be ground to dust, my honest intentions the mortar, my sinful desires the pestle.

Cole liked me. And that sucked. Because I liked him, too. Too much. Only, I couldn't like him. How foolish to think I would've been okay being part of their group, watching from the wings, while the one person I hated in the world lived her happily ever after with the man I had an agonizing crush on.

So I took myself out of the picture. Easy-peasy. Problem solved.

"You girls staying for dinner?" Mom asked.

"No," I grunted, throwing all my muscle into popping the lid on my drink. "Just here to pick up the suitcase."

To which she replied over her shoulder, "Dad set it in the hall for you."

I turned to my best friend. My happy, giddy, so-in-love sister. "So, where is he taking you?"

"It's a surprise."

"I love surprises," Mom said from the refrigerator.

Bottle to my lips I asked, "How do you know what to pack?" I chugged, then winced, the ginger burning my throat.

"He gave me a list." Lacey's cheeks blazed, meaning juicy gossip was in my future.

Mom's head popped up. She whipped around to face us, cauliflower in one hand, a bottle of IPA in the other.

L.O.V.E.

"Come on, before Mom goes Katie Couric on you." Hooking Lacey's elbow, I made for the front door. "Bye, Mom. See you Sunday. Love you!"

"Bye, Mama King," Lacey yelled, her sandals scuffing along the hall. "Thanks for letting me borrow your suitcase!"

"Bye, girls."

Safely inside the car, I begged. "What's on the list? What's on the list?"

"Nothing," she said with a shrug and an evil grin. One thing I hated about my best friend? Although she wore her heart on her sleeve, she was a master at feeding you juicy details only a nibble at a time, making you drool for more.

"Lacey. Come on." I squeezed her wrist. "You can tell me. You know I keep a secret better than anyone."

"That's why I love you. But seriously. The list was blank. Well, except for the picture he drew at the bottom." She pulled a folded piece of paper out of her handbag, carefully straightened the page, then handed it over. The header read: *What to pack for our trip.*

Below was a numbered list, one through five. Each number read *NOTHING.*

At the bottom of the page, he'd hand drawn a beach chair, a beach ball, a pair of flip-flops, and an umbrella, indicating she only need dress for warm weather.

"Oh, my God." I slapped a hand to my chest. "He's taking you to a private beach. The two of you are going to be naked all day and all night, boinking on the beach."

"Boinking on the beach?"

"You better stock up on sunscreen."

"Oh, Natalie." She dropped her head back on the seat. "I didn't know it was possible to fall for someone so hard and so fast."

"Love looks good on you, Lacey Lulu."

"You're really not sad about Martin?"

"Not even a little bit." Truth.

"I'm sorry we didn't make a love connection."

I'd made a connection all right, just with the wrong man. But that was a burden I'd carry to my grave. "C'mon. Let's go home and get you packed."

God was testing me. He had to be. After my last run-in with Cole, I'd un-joined his gym to avoid any uncomfortable altercations. I'd managed one week without a glimpse of his smolder. I had even started driving to work rather than walking to avoid bumping into him on the street.

Yet, there I stood, peonies in hand, face-to-chest with the man I was supposed to hate, and I couldn't rile one ounce of indignation.

Even when I asked, "What are you doing here?" with as much vinegar as I could muster, my voice sounded light and airy because every cell in my body sang for joy in his presence.

Wrong on too many levels.

With a shrug and a huff, he answered, "Buying flowers."

"In *my* flower shop?"

"Technically"—he gestured around the space with a sweep of his arm—"it's mine."

I was done. "Give me a freakin' break. You own this building, too?"

"No." He unleashed a deadly dimple. "Not yet. Should be mine by the end of next week, though."

"Seriously." I poked his cheek, knowing full well I had no right to touch. "Put that thing away."

The skin between his brows bunched. His dimple faded. "Since you're here, and I'm here, can we talk?"

Another test.

"There's nothing for us to talk about." I stepped left to move around him.

Cole blocked my escape. "You ended things with Martin."

"It was for the best."

"Why?"

I pinned him with a challenging glare. "You really need to ask?"

"No." He looked over my shoulder. Scratched the side of his head. Dropped his gaze to my bouquet. "Listen, I'm sorry."

"For what?"

"You left him because of me, because of what I said."

Dear Lord, the room was hot. "I didn't leave him, Cole. To be honest, we were never really together."

"How do you mean?" He shifted the long wrapped box from his left hand to his right.

"He was never really with me, even when he was. His attention was always elsewhere."

"Fucking prick." With a huff, he shook his head. "Don't get me wrong, I love the guy. I'd die for him, but he's oblivious when it comes to relationships."

"Well. That's not my problem anymore."

Cole stared long and hard, not his usual melt me into the tile stare, but more a probe."I like your glasses." His voice was gruff, hesitant almost. "How many pair do you own exactly?" There was no judgement or mocking in his question, only curiosity.

Some women loved shoes. I loved eyewear. "I like to match my outfits," was all I offered. I would not, could not, acknowledge the wholly inappropriate butterflies in my belly.

I would not fail the test.

I reminded him there was no reason for us to be talking, or friendly, or in close proximity for any reason by bringing that one reason to the forefront of our conversation. "Are those flowers for Victoria?"

Cole lifted the box in his hand. Swallowed. Nodded. "She's been under the weather." Shoulders tensing, he shifted, putting distance between us. "Who are you buying flowers for?"

"My mom loves peonies," I lied. It was me. I loved peonies. Every year on my birthday, Lacey bought them for me. Only this year, she was naked on a beach somewhere with the man of her dreams. So instead of pouting over my scrambled eggs, I walked to the floral shop, *my* floral shop, and bought my own damn flowers.

"Nats," came an unwelcome voice over my shoulder, shooting prickly bites up and down my spine.

I whipped around, my back slamming into Cole's front. Rock hard, warm, and not budging.

Holden stood five feet away. Eyes red-rimmed. Cheeks crimson. Veins popping in his neck. "This your boyfriend?"

"That's none of your damn business." Knowing that answer wouldn't suffice, I closed my eyes. Inhaled. Released a slow breath. "He's not my boyfriend." Calm, cool, collected, I asked, "What are you doing here, Holden?"

Holden's face cooled five shades, regret flashing in his blue eyes. "I love you, Nats. Did our time together mean nothing to you?"

There was no right or wrong answer. So I stayed silent.

He ran a hand through his unwashed hair, glare bobbing between me and Cole. "Can we talk? Alone. Five minutes."

I shook my head. "Talking won't make a difference."

At his sides, his fists balled, veins mapping a violent trail up his arms. "You can't give me five fucking minutes to apologize?"

At my back, Cole's chest tightened. His hand came to my neck, fingers curling into a loose grip.

I shrugged him off. Everything about his presence and my reaction added fuel to my fire. I stepped away from Cole, closer to Holden, my heart beating a daunting rhythm. "You don't get it. You don't have reason to apologize. You are who you are. The very first time I was uncomfortable with your behavior, I should've walked away. But I didn't because I was blinded by your beauty and so damn desperate to be wanted. So that's on me."

"We had something good, baby." His pecks rippled under his Gold's Gym T-shirt.

"No, we didn't."

Holden winced but quickly recovered, shoving his hands into his loose sweatpants. I couldn't remember ever seeing him out of sorts like this. His public persona was everything.

Pleading eyes met mine. "I would do anything for you."

"What's my favorite color?"

"Blue. You always wear that blue shirt."

"No. I wore that because you liked that it showed off my tits." I stabbed at my chest, poking too hard.

"What's my favorite food?"

"Pizza," he mumbled, unsure. "From Lennon's."

"No." I huffed. "What's my favorite song?"

"'Someone to Watch Over Me,'" Cole whispered to my back.

Oh, my effin' Lord. Emotion pricked my eyes. I blinked the threatening tears into oblivion and took another step away from Cole, the man I could never have, and one step closer to Holden, the man who never had me.

"Do I like to dance? Do I sing in the shower? What perfume do I wear? What do I do at my fucking job?"

Silence.

"You can't love me," I shouted, throwing my head back in frustration. "You don't *know* me."

"Nats."

"And I hate being called Nats. It's Natalie." I turned to leave, then faced him again. "You need to find someone who you can't help but learn those things about. Someone who'll learn those things about you without you ever telling them."

Hands to hips, Holden dropped his head. Huffed. Laughed. Stared at the floor. Chin down, he raised his eyes to meet mine. "Fuck. Fuck! I really fucked up with you, didn't I?"

"We weren't meant to be. That's all."

"I don't agree." He nodded. Rubbed his chin. "But I hear you."

That was too easy. Something wasn't right, but I continued. "Please, Holden. Can you stop with the stalker shit?"

"What are you talking about?"

"The phone calls. The posts on my social media."

"I don't know what you're talking about."

"The calls, the texts, all hours of the day from different numbers. The threats."

Holden reached for me then dropped his arm. "I stopped after they dragged me out of the bank. I haven't called you since."

"God! I'm so done with men."

"Natalie, I'm telling you the truth. I called your number three times since that day. Yes, I met you outside your apartment, hoping you'd talk. I was on my way to the gym when I saw you come in here. That's it. I swear."

His sincerity no longer mattered. "I gotta go."

Strong fingers wrapped around my arm from behind. "Let me walk you."

"No!" I snapped, jerking free of Cole's grip and shoving past. "Just no."

I hurried my pace, refraining from looking over my shoulder or scanning my surroundings when I reached my car. Un-fucking-believable. Bullshit, Holden hadn't been calling me. My phone buzzed. I didn't bother to look. And Cole? Seriously? How dare he know my favorite song?

I was officially done with men. With dating. With going to the gym. Or the flower shop. Or my favorite restaurant. Or anywhere in public.

Maybe a transfer out of state was in order. Yeah, that was a good idea.

My phone buzzed again. And again. All the way to my parent's house in Ballard. I only dared to look after I parked in their driveway.

Lacey. Thirty-two texts. Ten *Happy Birthday* wishes. One picture. Her hand. A giant, shiny, glittering diamond ring.

I squealed. I cried. I didn't call her back until after dinner.

"Not another word from him?" Lacey asked, hand shoved behind the left side of her black halter, adjusting her boob.

I swirled my straw in a slow circle before taking a sip of my vodka cranberry. "Radio silence."

"That's great!" Seemingly satisfied with the way her babies were hanging, she slapped her hands on the table.

In the opposite corner of The Rusty Ram, a rowdy group of twenty-somethings engaged in a shouting match. Security swarmed the corner, dragging one man outside.

"*No bueno.*" Eyes narrowed and aimed at the commotion, she pursed her bright red lips and asked, "You ever feel like we're getting too old for this place?"

Hand to my heart, I shouted, "Never!" then added, "but I think I'd be just as happy sharing mozzarella sticks at Applebee's."

"God, I know."

Lacey and I finished our drinks and maneuvered to the center of the crowd. Sweaty bodies bounced in unison, the heavy base a mind-numbing escape from the burden of the daily nine to five.

I watched my best friend, my heart full to the brim with love and joy. Every few minutes, she checked her hand as if afraid to lose her ring, or perhaps to remind herself that Ellis was real. She was on the brink of an epic adventure.

I swallowed the thick lump of bittersweet sentiment balled in my throat, realization crashing my buzz. Our girls' nights were over. Our movie marathon, binge-eating sleepovers would soon be a thing of the past. My Lacey Lulu was no longer a *she* but a *we*. A *we* that did not include me, but instead, a man who was worthy of my best friend.

I fought to keep the emotion at bay, but a tear escaped and then another. Lacy stopped bouncing. There had never been such a wide divide between us.

Another fight broke out near the exit. Lacey ignored the disturbance. "We're gonna be okay, Nat Brat. I promise." Brushing a tear off my cheek, she smiled.

"I know. I'm just so damn happy for you."

A *pop, pop, pop* rose above the music, loud enough to cause pain. Bodies blurred. *Pop. Pop.* Something wet hit my face. Something hard knocked me sideways. Lacey fell. I was shoved and pushed and carried away in a frenzied stampede of panic and mayhem.

I scrambled through a sea of skin and sweat, fighting a violent current to get back to my friend. Despite my efforts, I landed outside, Lacey nowhere to be seen. I scanned every face, every head of dark hair.

Soon the street was flooded in blue and red lights. Muffled voices surrounded me, none of them recognizable. The entrance was blocked.

Someone in a blue uniform made me sit against the wall.

I tried Lacey's number. No answer. I sent a text. Waited. No response.

In a panic, I texted Ellis. I begged the woman in blue for help. She ordered me not to move.

My ear rang, pain clouding my senses. I closed my eyes and prayed.

"Natalie."

That voice. Gritty and anguished. Muted.

"Natalie. Jesus. Fuck. Somebody help her."

I blinked my eyes open. My angel. My soulmate. My sinful temptation crouched in front of me. I'd managed two weeks without seeing Cole Adams.

"What are you doing here?" My words came out muffled.

"We were close when you texted."

"We?"

"Ellis and I." He reached up to touch my face, then dropped his hand. "Why isn't somebody helping you?"

"Me? I'm fine. My ear just hurts."

Again, he lifted his hand as if to soothe me, then changed his mind, gaze bouncing from my head to my

124

chest, my cheek, my ear. His brows pinched tight. "What happened?"

"I think there were gunshots. I don't know. We were dancing, then everyone started to run out. I lost Lacey." My chest constricted. "Oh, my God! Where's Lacey? She fell. Then I couldn't get back to her."

"Shh. Calm down. Try not to move."

"We have to find her." I tried to stand.

"Ellis is looking for her right now." Cole clamped his hands on my thighs, holding me in place. "Natalie, don't move." He looked over his shoulder, yelled, "What the fuck's taking so long. Get someone over here now!"

"Why does everyone keep telling me not to move? I'm fine. My ear just hurts."

Cole's eyes were liquid and angry. "You're not fine."

I dropped my head in frustration. A dark, wet, sticky blob landed on my hand. Violent trembles rocked my body. Another drip from my head.

Cole finally touched me, his finger tapping under my chin. "Natalie, look at me, not your hand."

His face blurred. "No. No, no, no."

"Look at me, Natalie."

"No no no no no no."

"Hey. I'm here. I got you. Just stay still until they get someone over here to clean you up."

"That's blood. That's someone's blood." It wasn't mine. I'd know if I'd been shot. I lifted my hand for inspection. "Oh shit, is that bone?"

Cole caught my chin again, holding my head steady, his hand trembling. "Natalie, just look at me, okay?"

"It's in my hair." On instinct, I reached up to inspect the damage.

"Natalie." He grabbed my wrists and held them in place. "Please. Trust me. Don't move." He yelled over his shoulder. "Get someone over here now!"

"It's not my blood," I mumbled, unsure which of us needed the assurance most. I couldn't look at Cole. I refused to look at my hand. I stared at his chest, rising and falling in short rapid bursts and tried my best to ignore the gore in my hair, or think about who the blood and bone had belonged to. Or how close I'd come to being shot.

My stomach lurched.

"Natalie." Cole's voice calmed. "I see Lacey. Ellis is with her. She's on a gurney. It looks like they're inspecting her leg. She seems fine."

"Thank you, Jesus," I said on a loud exhale.

Cole seemed to share my sentiment and fell on his ass next to me, releasing a long shaky breath, his hands now as bloody as mine.

The world spun. I barfed my drinks all over Cole's lap.

"Say again?" I asked, my hearing still fuzzy.

I stood over Lacey's bed, her hand in mine, her ankle in a wrap and properly elevated on a stack of pillows.

"I'm pregnant," she whispered into my good ear, blinking at me through her one working eye.

"I don't..." Pregnant? "I can't..." Bittersweet elation filled my chest. "You're gonna be a mom?"

Lips sucked between her teeth, she nodded.

"I'm gonna be an auntie?"

Lacey squeezed my fingers. "Best auntie ever."

"Lacey." Tears welled. "Lacey, this is crazy."

"I know, right? Proposed to, caught in a gang shooting,

nearly trampled to death, and impregnated all in the same month."

"How did Ellis handle the news?"

"He wants to get married as soon as possible. Maybe a Vegas wedding next month. Or as soon as we can coordinate everyone's schedules."

"This is really happening, isn't it?"

"Yes."

It was too soon. "He's a very lucky man."

"Nat Brat, you have to be there. You just have to. I can't imagine doing this without you. If you can't get time off, we'll wait, but—"

I climbed into her bed and wrapped her in a full body hug. "I'll be there. I'll be there. Of course, I'll be there. I wouldn't miss it for the world."

"Miss what?" came Cole's gruff voice, sending my heart racing.

I raised my head off Lacey's chest to find Cole, Martin, and a sheepish looking Victoria standing just inside the doorway, each holding a bouquet of flowers for my crippled, bruised, and newly knocked-up friend.

"Do they know?" I whispered, hiding our faces behind my hair.

Ellis barreled through the crowd, taking up half of Lacey's room, then piled on top of me hugging us both. "I'm gonna be a daddy." He kissed my cheek, then hers. "And we're heading to Vegas so I can make an honest woman of my lady."

Martin's face lit up, and he made a move to tackle his friend. For as large as he was, Ellis moved like a gazelle, springing to action, hugging his friend away from Lacey's injuries.

Victoria stared at the floor.

Cole stared at his buddies, blinking his eyes. I could swear he was fighting tears but, damn, his dimples were tuned to megawatt. His feet shifted on the hardwood before he came our way, then bent to drop the sweetest kiss on Lacey's forehead. "Congratulations, beautiful. You're going to be a great mom."

He was so close I could taste his breath—coffee and caramel. So tender with her, I swooned. So dreamy, I sighed.

Oh, shit.

I bolted to the sitting position. Cole's gaze sliced right through me, quick and razor sharp, on his way to join in the man hugs with his buddies. As much as I wanted to stay with Lacey and cry, hug, and celebrate, I could not share that stifling space with Martin, Cole, and especially Victoria.

"I'm gonna head out." I lifted Lacey's shirt and dropped a kiss on her belly. "Bye, baby. Can't wait to meet you."

Her long fingers raked through my hair. "We'll talk tomorrow?"

"Of course." I kissed her nose.

"Bye, Nat Brat."

"Bye, Lulu."

"Hey, Victoria." I offered a pathetic wave as I passed.

I couldn't hear if she responded, my traitorous heartbeat deafening, the need to flee hurrying my pace.

I made it to the hallway and halfway to the elevator when a hand wrapped around my arm. "Hey, Nats, can we talk?"

My chest deflated, a slow leak. "It's Natalie," I reminded him. "And I have to get home."

"Listen." Martin dipped his head, wrinkles deepening between his brows. "You don't have to leave on account of me."

I shrugged free of his grip. "I'm not."

His sigh was more irritation than relief. "We can be friends, you know."

"Sure." I took in his freckled face, his full lips. Felt nothing. "We can be friends."

"We're gonna celebrate." He nodded toward Lacey's door. "Why don't you join us?"

"You guys have fun. I have to do laundry." Ten paces from the elevator. Nine. Eight.

A heavy hand landed on my shoulder. "Nats. No need to be a bitch. This is about Ellis and Lacey, not you. So we didn't work out. No big deal. We have to get over it for our friends."

Bitch? Bitch? I turned so fast I teetered and instinctively grabbed Martin for balance.

Chest to chest, we locked gazes, mine heated, his hungry.

"Fuck, you're beautiful." Snapping his arms around my shoulders, he dipped for a go at my mouth.

When my palm met his cheek, he jerked back, then shoved me away, hard enough that I slammed into the wall and bounced right back to where I'd started.

"You fucking cunt," he growled. "You don't know what you're giving up."

Then and there, I lost my shit. I slapped him again. He thought I was done. I landed two good strikes before he wrestled my hands behind my back and had me pinned to his chest.

"Stop hitting me."

"Stop being an ass."

Whiskey-laden breaths hit my face. "Tell me the truth. Why'd you break up with me?"

"I'm not attracted to you. Simple as that."

L.O.V.E.

I had wanted to be. The man was definitely pretty to look at. Great body, not that I'd ever seen all of it. Sweet job. Fun to talk with when he wasn't being a dick.

"We can give it another go." He leaned closer. "I'll be more present this time."

"No, Martin. Now let me go." I wiggled.

His grip tightened. "Not until you tell me the truth."

"You want the truth? Fine. I'm in love with another man." And that was true. So pathetic and painfully true. "I'm in love with a man I can never have. Happy now? Can you let me go?"

He didn't. He walked me backward to the wall, then rested his forehead on mine, breaths labored. "We're not so different, you and me."

"How's that?"

"I'm in love with a woman I can never have. Really fucking sucks."

He wasn't talking about me. That I knew. There was someone else. Had he cheated on me with the woman he loved, or had he cheated on her?

"We can help each other out." His lips brushed my cheek. His hips curled, grinding against me. "Help each other forget these...other people.

"No." I shrugged in vain, his hold too strong. "Let me go. You're hurting my arms."

"Not until you give me a goodbye kiss."

"Let her go, Martin." Cole's face appeared inches from mine, murderous glare aimed at his best friend.

Martin didn't back down, not right away. His tongue dragged along his bottom lip. He sneered. Looked at me. Looked at Cole. Then released my arms, throwing his own up in surrender as he backed away.

His cheek shone crimson where I'd hit him. He took a breath, then another. "I'm sorry, Natalie. I got carried away. I'm sorry."

He ducked his head and turned back toward Lacey's door, where Victoria stood shooting me a lethal glare.

"You okay?" Cole whispered, gruff and shaky.

I looked over his shoulder. Martin and Victoria were gone. "I'm fine."

He stared long and hard, unconvinced but seemingly unsure how to proceed.

"I'm fine. Really." Still pressed against the wall, I slunk away from the brooding man. Jesus. What was wrong with me?

I stood straight and announced, "I have to go do laundry," then pressed the call button for the elevator.

Behind me, Cole huffed. "Natalie."

I stared at the panel on the wall. "What?"

"Who's the man you're in love with?"

My shredded heart flapped in the breeze like tattered rags caught on a power line. He'd heard my conversation with Martin.

I opened my mouth to no avail. Thankfully, I didn't have to lie because Cole cleared his throat and snapped, "Never mind. None of my fucking business."

The elevator dinged.

Behind me, retreating footsteps.

On the ride up to my floor, I vowed to never again share space with Cole Adams. After the wedding, anyway.

9

Cole

Lacey's dress was simple, playful almost with its plunging, heart-shaped top and a short, ridiculously puffy skirt. But what did that matter when she stood next to Ellis in his white tuxedo, and they both stood before Elvis, who wore a red Hawaiian shirt and drawled about love and honor, and 'til death do you part? The whole setup was ridiculous, and perfect.

Martin even fit in, standing next to Ellis, donning pressed khaki shorts and his Avanti palm tree button-up.

Natalie, however, put everyone in the small chapel to shame, including the bride. Her face was flawless, shades of pink dusting her cheeks. Her lashes, darker than normal, framed a haunting set of eyes that shimmered with emotion. Her glasses were tinted yellow with thin gold frames that matched her shoes. Her rosy lips quivered, three times that I'd counted, before her smile, that damn beautiful smile, took charge.

Her hair was pinned back on both sides, the rest coiled in soft, touchable curves that fell down her bare back. The strapless, pale yellow dress hugged breasts that teased of spilling over the silky fabric. The skirt hung to just above her knees in a loose drape that would be easy to lift were she bent over a chair, or a desk, or...*fuck*. What the fuck was I doing?

I squeezed Victoria's hand.

She leaned closer, rested her head on my shoulder, and whispered, "God, Cole. I can't wait for our wedding day."

Fuck, my unfaithful heart. "Maybe we should elope, too. You know, while we're here. Skip all the fanfare and just be man and wife."

"That's not even a little bit funny, Cole. All the time I've put into making our wedding perfect."

I was painfully aware of all the time stolen from us. I missed my Vic. Missed being a couple. I was jealous of my own fucking upcoming nuptials. However, my best friend's wedding wasn't the time or place to vomit my concerns. "I'm sorry."

Victoria shifted, crossed her tan legs, pulled her cell out of her clutch and thumbed through the multiple texts spanning her screen.

I forced my eyes forward and focused on the back of Ellis's head, ignoring Vic's rude behavior and avoiding another glance at the temptress standing next to Lacey.

"Hey." An elbow dug into my ribs. "The girls just landed. How long is this going to take? They want to meet us at the club."

Biting back profanities, I waited three breaths, then whispered, "You invited your friends? Seriously?"

Ellis and Lacey laughed. Elvis must've made a joke.

Angry eyes caught mine. "I'm sorry, baby. I get nervous and agitated around those two." She pointed toward Natalie. "You have to understand how hard this is. They hate me. You get that, right?"

I didn't answer. She wouldn't have heard me anyway, her attentions back on her screen. Maybe I'd been wrong inviting her to Vegas.

Lacey and Ellis said their I do's. They kissed. They danced while Elvis sang about wise men and falling in love. We cheered. We followed them to their limo, said our farewells, then watched while the newlyweds were swept away to the penthouse suite I'd gifted them for the weekend.

Natalie stood off to the side and wiped a tear from her cheek, watching passing cars.

Victoria yawned.

Martin clapped my shoulder. "Where are we kicking off the celebration?"

"Mind taking me back to our suite, babe?" Victoria laced her fingers through mine. "The girls are meeting me there. We'll hit the shops for a bit, give you some guy time, then meet you later."

I gave her fingers a squeeze. "Sure."

"Perfect." Martin rubbed his hands together, giving Natalie his back, a wild look in his eyes that promised trouble. "That leaves you and me and a whole lotta options."

Yeah. I knew what that meant. Drinks. Gambling. Girls. I'd rather follow Victoria and her friends around than spend the evening babysitting Martin. Then again, if I didn't keep a close eye on my playboy best friend, he might disappear for days, and we would not have our pilot come Sunday afternoon.

"Sounds like a plan." I checked my watch. "Ellis made dinner reservations at eight. Should we meet at our suite, say seven thirty?"

Our black town car pulled to a stop in front of us. "Natalie, we'll give you a ride to your hotel."

"Oh, no." She looked at everyone but me. "That's fine. I've got an Uber coming. He'll be here in five."

"You can cancel." She'd refused to stay in the same hotel as the rest of us, the rooms I'd bought.

"Really, it's fine."

Martin shoved past and ducked into the car.

"You have a free ride right here."

"Don't push, Cole. If she doesn't want to come with us, it's fine." Victoria tugged on my arm. "She's a big girl."

Call it instinct, or manners, but I hated leaving her alone on the street. Still, I had no right forcing the subject. "We'll see you for dinner?"

"See you tonight," she said to her shoes, gnawing on her bottom lip.

I held the door while Martin and Victoria settled into their seats, then gave Natalie one more glance before folding into the buttery leather.

As we drove away, I refused to look back. Instead, I watched my fiancée, who wore a scowl while she watched Martin, who wrenched his neck to watch Natalie as we pulled into traffic.

Natalie wore a different dress to dinner. Pink straps tied around her neck created a plunging neckline and glorious cleavage, not that I was looking. Her cheeks glowed from too much sun, and she wore little, if any, makeup. Her hair was pulled into a complicated twist on top of her head. Her tone legs were on full display, and her stiff, bare shoulders were the only sign of her discomfort.

L.O.V.E.

I slammed my drink and gestured to the waitress for another.

Natalie's smile faded when I stood to greet her. "Where is everyone?"

I stepped around the table and pulled out a chair a safe distance from mine. She fell, more than sat, into the cushion.

I settled back into my seat. "Victoria decided to hit the clubs early with her girlfriends. Martin is passed out in my room. Ellis hasn't returned my texts. It's safe to assume we won't hear from the newlyweds tonight."

"Oh." She stared at the empty shot glass in front of me. "I bet their neighbors are hearing plenty, though." She laughed at her joke, then met my gaze. "Get it?"

I was speechless, confused, angered by my weakness around Natalie King. Disgusted by my inability to think straight.

"You know, 'cause they're ... " She made a circle with her index finger and thumb on one hand, and pistoned her other index finger through the hole, making a funny face.

What a dork. What a gorgeous, delightful, perfect dork.

I laughed. She laughed. Her shoulders relaxed.

I'd never wanted to kiss someone so bad in my life. "What'll you have to drink?" I asked as the waitress came our way with my Johnnie Walker.

"Oh. I probably shouldn't."

"We're celebrating."

She snorted. "You know what? You're right." She lifted her chin, shifted in her seat, then said to the waitress, "I'll have what he's having."

The waitress nodded. "Are you ready to order?"

"Give us a few minutes," I responded.

"Of course." She dipped her chin and backed away.

Natalie lifted her menu, hiding that gorgeous glow, giving me time to pull my fucking shit together, steel my spine against her unconscious attack on my morality, shoot a quick prayer to the Man Upstairs to strengthen my resolve.

She lowered the menu only enough to peek over the top. "I don't know what any of this is."

Although no longer hungry, I used my own menu as a barrier and pretended to consider my dining options, but caught myself studying Natalie instead.

Her dress blended perfectly with the pink, cream, and gold tones of the room. When she smiled, laughed, blinked, breathed, or just existed, I wanted nothing more than to claim her, make her mine, throw her on top of the table and show my appreciation for everything that she was.

I wanted to punish her for showing me everything that I wasn't.

She was not safe in our private dining room. Neither was I.

"You know what?" I stood, pulled out my money clip. "What do you say we get out of here? Go someplace more—"

"I'd kill for a cheeseburger right about now." Her menu hit the table with a smack, and she was on her feet. She finished my drink in one long swallow. "Come on. I know the perfect place."

Fuck. I was so fucked. A gentleman would've taken her arm and escorted her through the busy restaurant. I shoved my hands into my pockets and wrapped my fingers around Cadence's cross.

"I'll try Lacey and Ellis again. See if they want to meet us."

"Let's go by your room, get Martin off his drunk ass," she suggested, fiddling with the tie around her neck.

I dropped enough cash on the table to cover our failed dinner. When I looked up, our gazes locked, hers tormented, dropping to my mouth and then to the floor. "You should try Victoria again, too. She might be hungry by now."

Good play, bringing my fiancée into the conversation. Smart woman, dropping that bucket of ice water over my faltering integrity.

I followed her toward the exit, and only by accident noticed the sway of her ass in that dress, only briefly appreciated the shape of her legs, only for one moment considered placing my hand on the small of her back.

While we waited for the car, keeping a safe distance between us, I asked, "They have drinks where you're taking me?"

Martin must've caught his second wind. He was MIA. Victoria refused the invite, but made me promise to meet her and her girlfriends later.

Ellis and Lacey had worked up an appetite, thank fuck, and joined us on our trek to In-N-Out Burger, which did not, unfortunately, serve drinks. Lucky for me, I'd made sure the car was stocked with a wide variety of libations.

I was currently on my fourth? Fifth? Aw fuck, what did it matter? Ellis and I enjoyed a killer bottle of bourbon with a bag of burgers between us while we sat on the trunk of the town car. Lacey and Natalie sat on a blanket they'd spread in the grass and shared fries while they whispered and laughed, staring at the view.

Jeremy, our driver, had taken us to a "top-secret" location, a closed park that boasted the best view of the city skyline. That man had earned himself one killer tip because he had been right—the view was unreal.

The burgers were the bomb. The company was perfect. And I enjoyed a mind-numbing buzz. I only accidentally ogled Natalie twice.

Alcohol was to blame. Not the dress. Not her laugh or her smile.

We finished our meal. We joined Victoria and her girls at the club. I drank. I watched Victoria dance, joining her twice. I only accidentally, from the corner of my eye, caught a drunk asshole grinding against Natalie. I might have smiled when she pushed him away.

Victoria was surrounded by her friends, and she was happy. She laughed more than I'd seen her laugh in months.

Martin finally showed. He joined the girls on the dance floor. He danced too close to Natalie.

She allowed him to touch her for one song, then joined Ellis, Lacey, and me at the table, sweaty, breathless, and... playing with her breast? She dug around behind the fabric covering her left boob, then pulled out her cell and read the screen.

Her smile faded. "Seriously?" she mumbled, searching the room, eyes wide, panicked.

Before considering ramifications, I snatched the cell from her hand and read the screen.

I see you

Slut

Ugly whore

U should b working the streets, not the clubs

I should kill u now, save the planet

Turning my back to Ellis and his bride, shielding Natalie, I asked, "Who sent this?"

"I don't know." She gnawed her lip. "Don't say anything to Lacey, please? It'll ruin her night." She reclaimed her phone. Tucked it back into the hidden compartment in her dress. "I haven't gotten one of these since I ended things with Martin."

"You think Holden followed you to Vegas?"

She looked over my shoulder, then made a quick assessment of our surroundings and said, "I need to go."

"Jeremy will drive you," I ordered, leaving no room for argument.

She replied, "Thank you. I appreciate the offer."

Natalie made an excuse to her best friend and said her goodbyes. I walked her to the car and waited while Jeremy merged into traffic and disappeared. Then, I dialed a longtime acquaintance who happened to head a personal security crew in town and made sure someone had an eye on Natalie for the rest of her time in Vegas.

Then, I called my buddy back home, Detective Waters.

When I returned to my friends, Martin came my way with a wicked grin on his face and lipstick smeared on his chin.

"Can't keep it in your pants for a minute, can you?"

"Not surrounded by all this eager beauty." He clapped my shoulder. "Where's Nats?"

"Called it a night."

His grin faltered but only for a blink. I let the details rest. He'd been stupid enough to let Natalie slip through his fingers. Her concerns were none of his business.

My only concern should have been my bride-to-be. "Anyone seen Victoria?"

Ellis pointed toward the back. "She headed for the restroom. Said she needed a touch-up."

I ordered another drink. Victoria came back, fresh as a fucking daisy, tits on display, silver shiny dress covering only the required parts, legs begging to be parted in a pair of silver, glittery, fuck-me heels.

Her lips met mine, her breath a hefty dose of minty menthol. Her tits pressed against my chest.

"You having fun?" I growled in her ear, dragging my fingers up the length of her bare thigh.

"A blast." She curled into me. "Where's Natalie?"

I dared explore higher, breaching the hem of her dress. "She left." I pulled her earlobe between my lips. "Think it's time for us to go, too." I stretched my fingers, dusting the curve of her ass. Fuck, it'd been so long since I'd touched her. I couldn't remember the last time we'd made love.

She curled her face into mine, but she shifted her hips, pulling away from my touch. "Baby, I want you so bad right now, but I started my goddamn period."

"You know I don't care about that shit."

Cupping her jaw, I pulled her in for a kiss. Her entire body stiffened.

"Vic," came Martin's voice over my shoulder, "one of your girls is getting sick in the bathroom. She's asking for you."

Victoria cussed into my mouth. Pulled away. She brushed soft fingers through my hair and promised, "Let me go take care of this. Be back in a sec."

Victoria didn't return. Forty minutes later, she sent a text to tell me she'd taken her friends back to their hotel and would call for the car when she was ready.

Martin disappeared into the sea of women.

I ordered more drinks.

Jeremy drove Lacey, Ellis, and I back to our hotel.

I opened another bottle of Jack and waited. Alone.

10

Natalie

"Natalie." *Bang. Bang. Bang.* "Natalie, open up!"

I stood at the door, eye to the peephole, and debated whether or not to proceed.

The man outside was clearly inebriated. He swayed where he stood, his eyes unfocused, his hair rumpled. He had no business being at my hotel room. I should've called security.

Bang. Bang. Bang.

A man yelled from a few doors down. "Shut the fuck up!"

Oh, jeez. I couldn't leave him out there to get arrested, or possibly beaten to a bloody pulp.

I opened the door and stood aside, anticipating the effects of alcohol mixed with gravity.

Much to my surprise, Cole didn't fall.

Holding a bottle of Four Roses in one hand, he stumbled but caught himself on the wall. Paused. Gained his bearings. Turned his head to find me. "Natalie. Natalie

King. Nat King." He dropped his arms and swayed, then smiled and punched at this chest. "And Cole. Nat King Cole. Get it?" He laughed a hard belly laugh.

Tears streaming down his face, clutching his gut, he slid to the floor.

I closed the door, dug pain relievers out of my suitcase, snagged a water bottle out of the mini fridge, tossed the lid, then joined him on the carpet. We sat opposite each other, but a safe distance apart.

"What's going on, Cole?"

"Do you think I'm stupid?" he asked, eyes trying to focus but missing their target.

"Of course not. Why?" I offered him the bottle of water.

He swatted my hand away. "I love her, you know?"

"I know." I didn't know because, honestly, I knew nothing about their relationship. On purpose. Because it was none of my business.

"I'm a good catch, yeah?" He bent his legs, planted his elbows onto his knees, scrubbed a hand through his hair. "My parents raised me right. Taught me the value of hard work, integrity, how to treat the ladies in my life right. Respect."

"They sound like great parents."

"They are. They really are." He laughed again, then his features fell dark. "They've never liked Victoria."

They were great judges of character obviously.

"She asked me out first. Did you know that?"

I shook my head no.

He nodded yes. "Pursued me for weeks. I had taken a friend of hers out once or twice, and I really liked the girl, but she just stopped calling. Ghosted me. Then Victoria was there. Just everywhere. I didn't want to date a friend of a girl I'd been with, so I politely declined Victoria's advances.

But, damn, she was relentless." He dangled his arms over his knees. "I figured, if she was going to all that trouble for one date, I had to give it a shot."

"Sounds like a great love story, Cole," I said to appease, the words so sour on my tongue I wanted to vomit.

Head dropped between his arms, he murmured, "She hasn't fucked me in months."

"What?"

"Not since... Shit." He looked to the ceiling. Laughed. Dropped his gaze, missing my eyes, and landing on my mouth. "Not since the night you met Martin."

I tried to do the math in my head, wariness making it difficult. How many months ago had that been?

How could she be with Cole and not want him every hour of every day? He was gorgeous, virile, sweet, and so goddamned sexy.

Months? She hadn't touched him in months?

"Is she sick or something?" I blurted in a mild state of shock.

He huffed. "No. Always busy, or tired, or distracted, or out of town."

"You're a saint, Cole Adams. I don't know many men who would put up with not getting laid for months at a time."

"I'm no saint." He twisted the top off his half empty bottle, took a swig, then scratched his forehead with his thumb. "If I were a saint, I wouldn't have you on my mind every time I jack off." He then pointed at me as if accusing. "I wouldn't be here, hoping to get lost in you. Wishing you would hate my fiancée so much that you'd let me fuck you, use me, use my body, just to get back at her. Sometimes I wish you were a heartless bitch who didn't care about morals or being faithful so I could do all the dirty things I want to do to you."

My throat shriveled. Tongue stuck to the roof of my mouth. God, it would be so easy. So easy to take what I wanted from Cole. Only, I wanted everything. All of him. That included his happiness, his success, in life and in marriage. A union that regretfully did not include me.

I snatched the bourbon out of his hand and suffered two swallows, the warm liquid heating me from throat to gut.

Cole watched, his tongue sweeping between his lips. I set the bottle out of his reach. He rocked forward, landing on hands and knees, jaw tight, eyes tortured yet determined, our noses threatening to touch.

He breathed. I breathed.

"You ever think about us, how we met, how great we'd be together?"

"No," I lied.

"I don't believe you," he snarled, staring at my lips.

Oh, sweet Jesus, he wanted to kiss me. My soul begged for that connection. But I had to be the strong one. Cole was currently incapable.

"I would leave her. If you asked me, I would leave my fiancée. That's how fucked I am over you."

"You're drunk, Cole." My pulse raced, body hummed.

"I am." He leaned closer, our mouths dangerously close to colliding. "I'm so fucking wasted. So tired of fighting this pull between us."

I hated Victoria with everything I had in me.

"You love her," I reminded him.

"Is there anything more powerful than love?" he asked, his whiskey breath warming my skin. "Because that's what I suffer. Every fucking day. It physically hurts, not being able to touch you." He pounded his chest. "How can I feel this way? How? When I don't even know you, not really."

145

My skin tightened, shrinking, tingling.

The word *destiny* came to mind, then escaped my lips, breathy and exhausted.

Our hearts belonged side by side. I had no doubt. Or maybe the alcohol was kicking in. Or sleep depravity.

I was not a cheater. Cole was not a cheater. He was drunk. I was love drunk but still had my wits. And yes, my morals, too, despite hating them at the moment.

I placed a hand on Cole's chest, pushed him far enough away that I could stand, then walked to the other end of my small room, severing our heated tie, or maybe stretching it, because I believed that tie to be unbreakable. Stretched and weakened, but never broken.

My body ached for Cole Adams.

Cole retrieved his bottle, lifted the alcohol to his lips, and slumped against the wall.

I called Lacey.

When Ellis and Jeremy showed up at my door thirty minutes later, Cole was out cold.

Ellis didn't pry, only asked, "Are you okay?"

"Yes," I assured him. "He'll be hurting. Not sure how much he drank before he got here."

Ellis stared at the floor, sucked in a breath, then confessed, "This is my fault. Tomorrow is the anniversary of his sister's accident. We should've had the wedding on a different weekend."

Speechless, I watched as Ellis and Jeremy hoisted Cole off the floor, and without question or judgement, carried him toward the elevator.

I locked the door and turned. Something sharp dug into my foot. "Jesus! Fuck!" I yelled, hobbling, "Ow, ow, ow." I flipped the light switch and found a gold crucifix on the floor, dainty and too beautiful not to be hanging from a chain. One of the men must've dropped it. I curled my fist around the warm metal, then tucked the pendant into a pocket in my handbag.

I dozed poolside, a glass of orange juice and bottled water on standby. Two children squealed and splashed in the shallow end, their mother enjoying a book under the shade of an umbrella.

I dared the Vegas sun to scorch the Seattle pale clean out of me, enjoying one last dose of vitamin D before heading to the airport.

My phone buzzed.

"Lacey Lulu."

"Nat Brat."

"How's Mrs. Chambers this morning?"

"Oh, my Lord. Say that again. I love being called Mrs. Chambers."

"Mrs. Lacey Lu Chambers." I sighed. "How was your wedding night?"

"Perfection. Are you joining us for breakfast? Everyone's here."

I hated letting my girl down, but I could not face Cole Adams. Not without self-combusting. "I'm sorry. I changed my flight. Heading home today."

Lacey whispered, "Hold on one sec." A chair scratched. Muffled voices. Lacey excused herself. Heavy breaths. "Okay, I'm alone. Are you leaving because of what happened last night?"

"No." Yes.

"You wanna talk about it?"

"No." Never. With anyone. Ever. Because admitting my feelings for an engaged man would make me a horrible person, though not as horrible as actually having those feelings. For allowing them to take root, let alone grow into a deadly jungle.

After a long, pregnant pause, she asked, "How did he end up at your hotel?"

Good question. I hadn't told anyone which hotel I'd booked. "I don't know, Lacey. He showed up. He was drunk. He babbled about Victoria. He passed out."

"He looks like shit today."

A red and white beachball bounced my way, and I kicked it back toward the pool. "I'm surprised he's out of bed, honestly."

"I wonder if there's trouble in paradise? Victoria showed up in a separate car. She had a giant freaking hickey—"

"None of my business," I blurted. Because I knew things already that I didn't want to know. I didn't want to hope that there was trouble, that Victoria might suffer a broken heart. I wouldn't be that person.

"Are you sure I can't change your mind? We had a whole day planned, all of us."

"I'm sorry, Lacey. Please don't be mad."

With a huff, she freed me. "I know you have your reasons. And I know you well enough not to push. Let me know when you're home safe?"

"I will." I paused, fighting tears, hating that I was letting my best friend down. I wanted to ask her about Cole's sister, but again, none of my business. "Enjoy your first day of being Mrs. Chambers."

Lacey laughed her genuine laugh, not her courtesy laugh. She would be fine without me. She had Ellis now. She would be better than fine for the rest of her life.

"Love ya," I whispered, biting back tears.

"You, too."

I enjoyed the sun for another half hour. Took a quick dip in the pool. Showered. Packed. Checked out. Waited outside for my shuttle to the airport.

My phone chimed.

Fucking cunt

I see you

Ugly cow

Hope ur plane crashes

My skin prickled. I didn't look around. I no longer gave a shit.

"We need to talk," came a weary voice over my shoulder.

"No," I said, tucking my cell into my handbag, keeping my back to the man who seemed determined to ruin me.

"I'm sorry about last night."

"I'm sorry I let you in." I stared at the hotel sign across the parking lot.

Cole huffed, his breath blowing my hair, making me shiver.

"I was shitfaced. But I knew what I was doing, what I was saying. And I shouldn't have dumped that bullshit on you. I was so fucking selfish, hoping you'd be the one to cross that last line, to give me permission to—"

"Stop." I whipped around and clamped a hand over his mouth. "Just stop. We are not going there. Do you hear me? This is over. No more. We are never to be in the same space again, got me?"

He couldn't answer, my hand sealed tight over his lips. He studied me, my entire face, his eyes liquifying. He blinked. Nodded. Took a step back.

My arm dropped to my side, and a hefty weight lifted from my shoulders. I would have to be the one to go. I would have to step away from my best friend so she could be happy with her new life. I would be the one to distance myself so Cole could move forward with his commitment to Victoria, torment free, temptation free.

"Walk away. I don't want apologies. I don't want to see you ever again. We are nothing." I turned my back and exhaled, settling into my new reality.

"Thank you, Natalie." His breath blew over my shoulder, making me shiver despite the desert heat. "Thank you for being stronger than me."

The first tear fell when I spied the shuttle down the street. The next fell when his footsteps retreated. I straightened my spine, sucked up the emotion, and tamped that shit down tight, low in my gut, where it would be sure to fester and poison me later. But that was fine, because I was not going to lose my shit in public over a man I had no right falling for in the first place.

I poured water out of my bottle into the soil of my neglected peace lily, its leaves sad and droopy, much like that stupid organ in my chest.

"How are you feeling?" I forced a smile, though Lacey couldn't see me through the phone.

"Oh, aside from not being able to eat and dry heaving at everything I smell, I'm doing great."

"Are you all moved out?"

"Yes."

My heart sank. I'd miss having Lacey in the same building. Sure, she was only moving to the other side of town, but that eight miles seemed a continent.

"Martin, Ellis, and Cole did all the work. I sat with my feet up."

"Like the queen you are." I meant every word.

My boss appeared in my doorway, her eyes dancing with mirth. "Have a minute?"

"I'll call you tonight, Lacey."

"Of course. Bye, Nat Brat."

I shoved my cell into my desk drawer. "Hi, Janet. Did you get the lead I sent over?"

Janet nodded. "That's a big fish. Be great to land that client." She came through the door, followed by a tall man wearing a gray suit and a boyish grin. "Natalie, this is Mr. Griffin."

Mr. Griffin offered a warm, firm handshake, his blue eyes sizzling.

"Nice to meet you." I gestured for them to sit and waited before settling into my chair. "What can I help you with, Mr. Griffin?"

The man studied me for a moment, still wearing that grin. He leaned forward, resting elbows to knees, his jacket pulling tight around broad shoulders and solid arms. "Please, call me Caleb."

The room darkened, shrinking, narrowing to the small space surrounding me and *Caleb*. Suddenly, everything was off balance, tilted, wonky but thrilling, too, like a ride on a rusty carnival coaster.

Caleb. Caleb. Caleb.

Your soulmate, Mom's voice rang in my ears.

"Of course. What can I help you with Mr. Grif—I mean, Caleb?" God, the name I'd heard all my life tingled my tongue. The man was a looker, thank the Heavens. He wore his golden hair in a pompadour, smooth and slicked back, had a meticulously trimmed beard, and if I had to guess, I'd place him mid-thirties.

Janet leaned back, crossed her legs, and folded her hands on her lap, giving Caleb full run of the conversation.

"I'll cut right to the chase. There's an opening in our Whisper Springs branch. Several high-profile clients. The team is small, but we'd like you to join the Corporate Accounts division."

Caleb's lips moved, but the words ceased to register, the heady weight of his gaze throwing me off balance.

Blah, blah, blah...client approval rating.

Caleb.

Blah, blah, blah...yearly increase in margins.

Caleb.

Blah, blah, blah...substantial growth.

Caleb.

"Regardless, you are our number one choice, and I understand it's a big move, so take some time to consider the offer."

Had he made an offer? "Thank you."

He rose to stand, and Janet followed suit, shooting me a wink before making her exit.

Caleb waited for me to see him out. Halfway through the door, he turned, pulled my hand between his in a gentle shake and said, "I hope you'll join the team in Idaho. We need that spectacular brain of yours."

I only nodded, mesmerized by the spark in his eyes but mostly by his name. Caleb. Could he be? No, no, no. Ridiculous.

Mom's story was absurd. But there he stood, Caleb, my possible soulmate, offering a free right turn at the exact time I needed a change of course.

A quick glance at his hand, and there was no ring on his finger. "I'll give your offer serious consideration."

His smile widened and, holy shit, what a fabulous set of pearly whites. "I hope so. I look forward to getting to know you better."

"Nice to meet you, Mr. Griffin."

"Likewise, Miss King."

I watched him saunter down the hall, and when I should've been thrilled, nausea hit and my lungs constricted. What if he was *the* Caleb?

He was attractive, no doubt, but where were the butterflies? The zing of electricity when he shook my hand? The clouds didn't part, no birds sang, my knees were steady.

I needed to clear my head.

I grabbed my handbag and told Janet I was taking my lunch, then headed outside before she could wrangle me into a conversation.

I rounded the corner, unsure where I was headed, but craving the fresh air. There was no place more beautiful than Seattle in the spring. When the gloomy gray cleared and the sun shone, the city came alive, a kaleidoscope of bright, happy color, the buildings, the people, the energy. I lifted my face to the brilliant blue sky. My heel caught on the uneven sidewalk. White hot pain shot up my left leg. My right knee landed with a crack on the cement, but my palms took the brunt of the fall, my Coach shoulder bag landing between my hands.

Time froze while I accessed the damage, the searing points of pain. My ankle, my knee, my hands. My head?

Wait.

Drops of blood pitter-pattered over the leather. I looked to my right and, yep, there was blood and even a chunk of hair on the raised planter where my skull had connected on the way down.

Not since the infamous scissor incident in high school had I seen that much of my own gore. Funny. Last time, I'd been able to stay conscious.

"Thanks again, Mom," I mumbled through the fog of painkillers flowing into my veins.

"You thirsty?" She lifted the plastic cup to my lips before I could answer. "The doctor wants to keep you overnight. Keep an eye on that head."

"Okay." I squeezed her fingers. "Thanks for coming."

"Of course, baby." Mom leaned close, studied my face. "Are you in pain?"

"Not too bad." The room blurred. I found her eyes and focused. Mom had beautiful eyes. "Thanks for coming."

"You've said that already, honey."

A deep, sleepy voice came from behind the green curtain, his speech sloppy, like his mouth was packed with cotton. "Yeah. Twenty-one times to be exact."

Mom rolled her eyes, and I stifled my laugh.

A nurse came by with her machine on wheels, bypassing my bed and heading to the man behind the cloth barrier.

"Well," Mom said, dusting a finger over my cheek, her smile sad, "now you have matching scars."

"That, I do. Lucky me."

She kissed my nose. "Makes you look kinda badass."

"I am, don't you know?"

She laughed, then tucked the blankets tighter around my legs. Worry wrinkles and all, Mom was still the most beautiful person I knew. "Thanks for being here, Mom."

"Twenty-two," shouted the groggy man.

That time, I did laugh, then cried out in pain. Damn, I hurt everywhere.

"I'm gonna run to your place, grab you some clean clothes. They should have a room ready by the time I get back."

"Mmmkay," was all I could manage.

Mom waved and disappeared.

"Ow, Jesus. Fuck," the man hissed.

To which the nurse replied, "One more."

Another hiss.

"There. Done. Not so bad, huh?" A machine beeped, then buzzed. "The doctor will be in shortly."

"How long?" the man grumbled.

"Well, let's see," the nurse replied, no constraint in her tone, "when he's done assessing the damage you inflicted on those five men, setting that broken arm, resetting that dislocated shoulder. Patching up five split lips, one broken jaw, two broken noses, seven—"

"I get it, I get it."

Footsteps came my way, the wheels of the machine squeaking. Before the nurse rounded the curtain, she stopped, and over her shoulder, asked, "I heard you were defending a lady's honor. That true?"

"What the fuck ever," the mystery man grumbled.

She only chuckled, offering me a wink as she passed. "I'll be right back, sweetheart."

Damn, emergency room drama put any telenovela to shame.

I wanted to question the man, but he seemed grumpy, and I wasn't in the mood for conversation.

"Where is he?" someone bellowed from down the hall. "Where the fuck is he?"

Shuffling feet and heavy footsteps ensued.

"Sir. Sir. Excuse me."

The curtain next to me billowed. My neighbor muttered, "Fuck."

I relaxed into my pillow to enjoy the show.

"What the fuck is your problem?" the intruder yelled.

"The fuck's your problem? You had her and you couldn't keep your dick in your pants long enough to realize the best woman you're ever gonna meet was right there, right fucking there for the taking."

"How the hell is that any of your concern?"

"Where the fuck did you get that video?"

"Doesn't matter. I got it."

"And felt the need to show it to everyone in the goddamn bar? Why? Because she dumped your sorry ass? You bitter fucking prick."

"Again, why the fuck do you care?"

"You know what this will do to Ellis and Lacey."

The weight of a two-ton puzzle crashed over me, pieces clicking into place, crushing my body.

Ellis and Lacey. Video?

My drug stupor lifted. "What video?" I yelled over the angry voices.

"The fuck?" one of the men grumbled.

"What goddamn video are you talking about?"

The curtain rustled. Martin came around the corner, his face a bloody, swollen mess. "Nats?" His lower lip was two sizes larger than normal. "What the hell happened to you?"

"Natalie?" the other man said. "Are you fucking kidding me?"

More rustling. Martin was shoved aside. A bloody and not as bruised as Martin, but still damaged Cole, stepped into my field of vision, blocking everything out of sight.

"What the hell?" His fingers were on my face, too delicate for a man his size, too tender for a man who wasn't mine. "Who did this to you?"

Heart racing, my breaths came jagged. "What video?" I asked again, terrified of the answer.

Cole only stared at me, jaw tight, gaze hard.

His chest rose and fell four times before I shouted again, "What video?"

Nothing.

"Martin?" I tried to peek around Cole. "Martin! What video?"

Martin stood at the end of my bed. Bloodshot eyes, three-day stubble. He pulled his cell from his back pocket.

"Don't fucking do it, man," Cole warned.

"Yes," I argued, pushing Cole away from me. "Show me."

I knew. In my gut, I sensed what was coming.

Martin thumbed his screen, his tongue darting out to lick the cut on his lip. He handed me the phone.

And there it played in glorious HD. *The* video. The culmination of my years of suffering under the sadistic hand of Victoria Ford.

The image of me, a naked white girl, smashed between two large, dark, muscular bodies—my twin cousins—seemingly entwined in passion.

"Hey," Martin smirked. "If I'd known you were into that kinky shit—"

Cole's fist hit Martin's face, laying him down for the count.

I couldn't find it in me to care about Martin.

I needed so desperately for Cole not to jump to conclusions. "It's not what you think."

"Doesn't matter what I think. This is bullshit. The fucking video should not be passed around."

"That was high school," I muttered.

"What that is, is none of my business. I did some fucked-up shit back in the day."

"You don't understand..." God, how could I tell him?

"It's not my business." He stepped back. Shook his head. His laugh came cruel. "I thought you were a little too close with your cousin when we met a few months back."

Sword through my chest.

He couldn't look me in the eye. His obvious disgust hurt deeper than any physical wound.

When he turned to walk away, I spilled my guts, because fuck Victoria. He'd fall victim eventually. "That was right before graduation. I bought myself a new bikini. Lacey, Finn, Felix, and I were minding our business, found our own little corner of the beach. I got up to use the restroom. My ex was there, waiting for me, said he wanted to talk. Wanted me back." I sucked in a shaky breath. "You see, he dumped me for Victoria two weeks earlier, just like all the other guys I dated. We talked. I said there was no chance of us getting back together. I headed back to the beach. Next thing I know, someone is laughing behind me. I hear a snip, snip, and my top falls off. I'm trying to cover my chest, more snips, and there goes my bottoms, too. I turn to find Victoria holding a pair of scissors and her phone, she and three of her friends recording the whole incident.

"There was nowhere for me to go, so I ran toward my towel, but I tripped. My cousins ran to the rescue and threw themselves over me to cover my naked ass."

I shivered, fighting a wave of nausea. "I'd had it with the bullying. With her hatred toward me. Lost my shit. I fought my cousins and tried to get up. I didn't care if I was naked. I was going to kick her scrawny little ass. I got one punch in, but then she stabbed me in the head with her scissors, screaming at me like I was the crazy one. What you see in that video is me fighting, trying to get free of my cousins, while they're holding me down. Victoria cut the video, made it look kinky. Shared it with everyone in school."

My breaths came strained. Violent tremors shook my hands.

Martin rose from the floor, bloodier than before.

Cole stood over me. A statue. Unreadable.

Footfalls came our way. A soft voice blurted, "Martin, I came as soon as—" Victoria skidded to a halt, eyes wide, bouncing from Martin to Cole to me, then back to Cole, who stared right through my aching skull.

"Cole, sweetie, what happened?" She stepped behind her lover, placed a hand on his arm.

Martin growled and disappeared.

"What's going on?" Though her tone was measured, her glare was feral, and I had no doubt, were there not witnesses, she would stab me again, a fatal blow.

Cole snapped a hand to the back of Victoria's neck, said, "That's a good question, Vic. Why don't you tell me what the fuck is going on," while he ushered her away from my bed and disappeared.

Dad had the best arms. Solid and strong. Readily available for hugs. Perfect for hauling his drunk daughter home from his best friend's bar.

Damn alcohol. Stupid pain meds.

"All right, where's your key?" he grumbled, holding me snug against his side and shuffling through my handbag. "There we are." He unlocked my door, scooted me forward.

I flopped onto my couch, the room tilting, my stomach churning, my sorrows thoroughly drowned.

Lip quivering, I avoided his glare, staring instead at his brown loafers. "I'm sorry, Dad."

L.O.V.E.

"You're lucky Hank was on shift tonight." He made his way to the kitchen, filled a glass of water, then stood at my side. "What's going on with you?"

I snagged the glass and guzzled, then wiped my lips with the back of my arm. "I just wanted to stop by Harry's. Say hello to everyone."

"Bullshit." With a huff, Dad shrugged off his jacket. "You never go to a bar alone. Not even to Harry's." He dropped next to me, making the cushions bounce. "What the hell were you thinking?"

I blew a raspberry through numb lips. "I don't have Lacey anymore."

"Of course, you do."

"No, Dad. You don't understand." I grabbed his arm to make sure he paid attention. "I can't see Lacey anymore."

"That's ridiculous. Of course—"

"She's married now," I sobbed, releasing my pain, my heart too soft and bruised to carry all the sadness.

He unsuccessfully fought a smile. "That doesn't change anything."

"You don't get it." Hands to the sky, I schooled my father. "She has Ellis. And where Lacey goes, Ellis goes. Where Ellis goes, Cole goes."

Dad nodded. Rubbed his chin. "Who's Cole?"

I licked salty moisture off my lip. "The man I'm in love with." *God, that word.* Love. Four simple letters. One ridiculous wallop.

I tested it's weight on my tongue. "Looooove. L.O.V. E."

Dad's chest bounced with what was sure to be restrained laughter. "You're in love with a man, and I haven't met him?"

"I'm so ashamed." Again with the tears.

"Talk to me."

Face buried in my hands, I confessed. "I don't know how or when it happened for sure. He's Ellis's best friend. He looks at me like I'm his reason for existing. And he's everywhere. Just everywhere. I've tried to avoid him. But somehow, he's always there."

"Okay." My father shifted, his reliable arm weighting my shoulder. "So what's the problem?"

"He's engaged."

"Well, that's not good."

"To Victoria Ford." I fell against him then, burying my face in his chest.

His body stiffened, arm tightened. "That's the most fucked-up twist of fate I've ever heard."

"See?" I looked up, searching for comfort in his weathered face. "See why I needed a drink?" Or three.

"Natalie." He curled both arms around me and rested his chin on my head. "I'm sorry that you're hurting, but you're smarter than this. You know better than to get drunk over a guy. You've put years of hard work into getting over the shit Victoria put you through."

"I know, Dad."

He gave me a shake. "And the girl I raised would never pine over a married man."

I raised a pointed finger. "With the exception of Kit Harrington."

Dad chuckled. "Okay. Yeah, I'll give you that one."

I snuggled closer to my dad, my rock, savoring the healing comfort of his heartbeat. "I've tried to get him out of my head. I know it's wrong. Why is this so hard?"

With a long sigh, my father slumped. "Maybe this is fate telling you to take that job in Whisper Springs."

Dad's words cut deep. Had to kill him to speak that single, heavy sentence, because I was his only child, and family was everything to my dad. But he'd always had my back, and he'd always known best.

I must've passed out in my father's embrace. I woke sometime later, covered in a wool blanket with a pillow under my head. Dad sat in the kitchen, eating a sandwich. A soccer game played on mute on my flat screen.

"How ya' feeling, kiddo?" he asked, not taking his eyes off the television.

"Okay."

"I flushed your pain pills."

"Oh." I rubbed the haze from my eyes.

"You don't need that shit. Acetaminophen and ibuprofen from here on out."

"Sure." I tried to sit up, but the effort made my head throb.

Bathed in flickering light from the television, Dad's shadow bounced against the far wall like a guardian angel watching over my home. I dug my phone out of my back pocket and captured the moment because my father, truly, was a gift from God. Patient. Wise. Stern when he needed to be. Tender when my heart ached. My rock. My safe place. My hero.

"Your milk is expired." He popped the last bite into his mouth.

"Okay. Thanks."

The screen went black. Dad rinsed his plate, then came my way with another full glass of water. "I know you'll do the right thing, Nugget. You've got your mom's brains, her grace, too. I don't doubt for a second you love this man, otherwise, you wouldn't say it. So I know you're suffering, and you can talk to me about anything, anytime. You know that, right?"

I nodded. He set the glass on the coffee table.

"I'm gonna get out of your hair, but you need to make a promise."

"What?"

"No more going to bars alone, even Harry's."

"I promise."

He snagged his jacket. Kissed my forehead. "Love you, Nugget."

"Love you, Dad."

"I'll check on you in the morning."

"'Kay, Daddy."

The lights went out. So did I.

PART THREE

Very Extraordinary

Natalie

The text on my screen read: *Open your door*.

Same message as the last three.

I stood my ground at the counter, filling my goblet. Wine first. Uncomfortable altercation second.

Four desperate knocks hit the front door.

Two deep breaths, one slow sip, and I made my way toward the unwelcome visitor. Hand to the knob, I closed my eyes and prayed for strength and wisdom.

Sinful beauty greeted me. A test. A trap. My forbidden fruit disguised in jeans and a baseball cap.

"For the love of God, what are you doing here?"

Cole white-knuckled my door jamb. "We need to talk."

"We really don't." Because talking reminded me of everything I wanted and couldn't have.

The muscles in his arms bunched. Gnawing on his bottom lip, he stared through me as if weighing his options.

Options were not on the table.

"Who in the hell buzzed you in?" I hoped the heat from my cheeks would fuel the glare I fired his direction.

"Some sweet old lady with a feisty corgi."

Mrs. Mariani. "Traitor," I mumbled, though I couldn't be angry at the woman. No doubt he'd wielded his magic smile, charmed her into compliance.

Uninvited, he stepped over the threshold. I backed away, his beauty too cruel, his presence an affliction.

For one whole month, I had managed to avoid Cole Adams and his cheek porn. I'd beaten my addiction to those damn dimples.

Five seconds in his presence, and I was jonesing again. "Get out of my house."

"I can't do that." He closed the door. Turned the lock.

Golden eyes met mine, and I was transfixed. Victim to the wonderment that was Cole Adams.

"The wedding is off." His lips moved.

The words registered but my thoughts faltered, several beats behind.

"Hmm," was all I managed to say. I headed for the kitchen, stealing a moment to collect my wits, which Cole had splattered all over the entryway.

"Did you hear me?" He followed, personal space be damned. "Victoria and I are over."

"So what?" I turned and threw my hands in the air, exasperated. "People break up every day. People kiss and make up every day. It's none of my business, so why are you here?"

Expression pained, he lifted a finger and traced a delicate line below the scar on my forehead. "You know why."

"I know nothing, Jon Snow," came breathy and unbidden.

Pop. Pop. Dimples. Wielded like weapons, knocking me dizzy. Cole caught my waist and with little effort, lifted me to the counter, pressing his forehead to mine. "You're killing me, you beautiful dork."

Oh, sweet Jesus, the proximity. Unbearable. Unbelievable.

"Tell me you know why I'm here." His lips teased mine, soft, unsure, and definitely unreciprocated. "Tell me you've wanted this since that day in the coffee shop." He towered over me, tall and confident and, damn, he smelled so good, his cologne soft and citrusy. His breath, minty and sweet.

"Tell me I'm not alone," he pleaded, capturing my chin and killing me slowly with his hopeful gaze.

"This is wrong," I argued.

"Why?" he asked, strained, raspy. "We're both single now. Why is it wrong?"

Because we'd been wrong for too long. "You only just left her."

"Four weeks ago." He pulled a strand of my hair through his fingers, studied my face, my scar. "Right after the hospital incident."

Lacey hadn't mentioned the breakup. Then again, I'd forbidden any talk of Victoria.

"Tell me what happened."

"Doesn't matter." He stepped away, face flushed. "We're over."

"It does matter, Cole." Nobody survived Victoria untarnished. If he'd ended things because of me, Hell would rain down in one form or another. "What happened?"

He leaned against the counter opposite me. Arms crossed. Stance set wide. So sure in his conviction. "Truth is, things had been off with us for months. And then that video." He scratched the back of his head. "I found out some things." His eyes seemed to lose focus, something weighing heavy.

"What things?"

"Don't get mad," he said to the floor.

My skin prickled. "Tell me."

"I have a buddy in the SPD. A detective." He cleared his throat. Nodded. Hit me with a hard stare. "I called him after you received that text in Vegas. Those messages you've been getting? They were—"

"From Victoria," I blurted, heat flooding my face, shivers dancing up and down my arms. *Oh, God.* He'd been watching out for me.

"You knew?"

"I suspected." She'd played the same game in high school, using multiple numbers via burner apps to harass me.

The air thickened. Cole's eyes darkened. I expected anger, but instead, he nodded in understanding. "When I questioned her actions, she didn't deny a thing, but she didn't defend herself. She screamed and cried, made like I was the bad guy, threw her ring in my face and stormed out."

"She left *you*?"

Cole tore the cap off his head, roughed a hand through his hair. Chin down, he whispered, "I'd been emotionally unfaithful."

Painful knocks invaded my chest.

His tortured gaze ripped my chest wide open.

"And because I struggled with that sin, I would've forgiven her. But she didn't give me the chance." With a flick of his wrist, his hat landed at the end of my counter. "And when that door slammed behind her, my first thought was...I'm free."

He stepped between my thighs, lifted my glasses off my face and set them down next to my fruit bowl. My eyes burned with unshed tears.

"I'm free to be with the woman who's invaded my thoughts." He licked his lips, stared at my mouth. "The woman whose kiss haunts my dreams." Warm, trembling hands cupped my face. "I'm free to explore this extraordinary woman who makes me laugh, makes me want, makes me fucking crazy."

Cole went for the kill. Lips, tongue, teeth, moans— God, the noises he made. Auditory porn.

He sucked any fight clean out of me.

Skin to skin, breath to breath, his soul for mine in a frantic exchange. I was lost to the euphoria, the silent confessions.

My doubts withered, turned to dust, floated away on the soft waves of his hums.

My legs opened, inviting him closer. Heat and denim filled the empty, aching space. My shirt disappeared. His lips traveled lower. Mine remained parted, drawing precious oxygen while he tasted and ravished my neck, my collarbone, then moved lower still to my breasts in a manic exploration.

Cole sucked and nibbled and licked, giving my breasts equal attention, driving me mad. And his touch? Sunshine to a morning glory. A desert rain. A baby's first breath. I was reborn under the heat of those fingers.

He pinched a tight bud between his thumb and forefinger, giving a gentle rub and twist, causing a flood of heat between my legs. He let go, then pulled the skin between his teeth, and sucked in slow, languid pulls, a rhythmic pulse that carried down my spine, pooled in my belly, and swelled.

L.O.V.E.

He sucked. Relentless. Determined. My hips moved, commanded by that pull, seeking more. Desperate for the friction, I cinched my legs around his thighs, writhing against the hard bulge behind his denim, silently cursing the barrier between us.

Cole slid one arm around my back, never breaking the seal of his lips on my breast, continuing his slow, deliberate pulls, then rolled his hips, helping me bump and grind against his steel-hard heat. Mindless and molten and delirious with need, I begged for more, my head falling back. He held my weight, sucking, my breast a thousand pounds of lust, and the room became unbearably hot. I lost sense of everything but our bodies and the power of that pull, his mouth commanding me to... "Oh, God, Cole. Oh, God. I'm coming. Fuck. Fuck."

My eyes slammed shut, my toes curled, and I came, a full body tremor, gasping for breath, strange noises coming from my lips. I hugged his head, holding the man hostage to my chest.

And when the ecstasy melted to utter devastating exhaustion, Cole rested his head between my boobs but held me steady, the broad expanse of his back rising and falling, and when I gathered my faculties, I raked my fingers through his hair and forced him to look up.

"What the hell was that?" Death by nipple-gasm, I suspected. Because, I swear, I had caught a glimpse of the pearly gates before crashing back to earth.

Eyes wild with lust, he begged, "I need you."

Three simple words.

I held all the power, but God, I was powerless because there was nothing I could deny the man. "Take me to my room, Cole."

He carried me with impossible grace and breathtaking strength. My back hit the mattress. I shimmied out of my pajama bottoms, my skin tight and tingly, my insides liquid heat.

With sure hands, Cole worked the button of his jeans, those muscles in his arms bulging and flexing. Before dropping his denim to the floor, he pulled a stack of condoms from the pocket and tossed them on the bed. A stack. Not one, but two, three...*oh shit*, five.

Face flushed, lips parted, gaze weighted, Cole stripped naked, revealing years of conditioning, his body thick and defined. Dark hair covered his chest and blazed a trail over ripped abs down to his heavy erection. Oh, my Lord. Perfection.

Cole prowled over me, admiring every inch of flesh as he passed, eyes alight with appreciation, and I'd never felt more cherished. I grabbed a foil packet, ripped that baby open, and did the honors, my fingers trembling, not from nerves but anticipation.

Wet lips met mine, and his cock nudged my opening.

I'd waited my entire life for that one singular connection. Slow and steady would not do. I curled my legs around his waist, dug my heels into his ass, and pushed him inside me, and oh, shit...the stretch. The burn. The delicious fullness.

Something akin to a moan escaped my lips. Cole growled in my ear. Then, he started to move, and oh, sweet mother of mercy, the man was fluid and precise. As if we'd danced that dance a thousand times before, my body rolled into his thrusts, our hips finding a frantic rhythm.

He slid one hand behind my head, gripping my hair, tilting my head to accept his mouth. But before he plunged, he whispered, "I knew you'd be perfect."

Cole fucked my mouth with his tongue before pulling back and mumbling, "I knew you were meant to be mine."

L.O.V.E.

My heart soared to the moon. My body melted under Cole's attention, his command, his thrusts, grunts, and kisses. God, the man kissed me into oblivion. He staked his claim, smothering me in orgasms and promises.

We used the last condom on Saturday morning before breakfast. We ate. We laughed. We planned dates. We walked to the corner store and bought more Trojans.

I couldn't get enough of those dimples. That smile could inspire a thousand paintings, a million love songs.

My heart, my body, my soul was so full of Cole Adams. By Saturday evening, we crashed on my couch, bodies tangled, and fell asleep watching *Ray Donavan*.

Somewhere around midnight, Cole carried me back to bed. We lay in the dark, face to face, his hand on my hip, his erection tickling my thigh.

"I'm a goner," he whispered, our breaths mingling. "I'm not letting you go." He rolled me to my back, kissed me dizzy, and as he slid into me, whispered. "You're my one."

My heart soared so high I lost my breath. I'd known from the beginning he was my one. To hear him say the words changed me on a molecular level.

Cole made love to me one last time, kissing the tears from my cheeks, and when we fell, tangled, into slumber, I knew my life would never be the same.

I woke, a heavy weight in my gut, an angry warning in my chest.

"I don't understand. How could this happen?" Cole's gruff voice came from my kitchen.

I stretched my sore limbs, headed naked to the bathroom and, unable to tame my rattling nerves, hurried through my morning routine.

Ten minutes later, I found Cole on my couch, elbows to knees, head resting in his hands.

Dear Lord, he was beautiful, wearing nothing but boxers, his muscles taught, hair a rumpled mess.

"Good morning," came out raspy and breathy. I stepped close and roughed my fingers through his gorgeous mane.

He didn't look up but gripped my hips and nuzzled my belly, releasing a long sigh.

My heart dropped to my toes. "Hey. What is it?"

Cole's chest heaved. He snaked his trembling arms around my waist and pulled me tighter against his frame.

"You're scaring me. What happened?"

"She's pregnant," he said to my feet.

"Who?" I asked, although the answer was obvious.

"Victoria. She's been calling all weekend. I called her back this morning. She's pregnant."

"But." I shoved away, stumbling backward. "How? I mean"—my stomach churned—"you said you hadn't been with her in months."

Face pale, gaze vacant, he whispered, "Vegas. She said we fucked in Vegas. When I was drunk. I don't fucking remember doing it, but I remember the next morning, and she was pissed, had bruises on her arms. Said I got rough with her." Worried eyes lifted to mine. "I've never been rough with any woman, Natalie. I've never been too drunk to remember fucking either."

My body deflated, a slow, pathetic leak, my future, my happy, my Cole, slipping away with every thump of my groggy heart.

"So that's it." I didn't recognize my voice. "I got you for a weekend. One perfect, beautiful weekend." I fell into the chair behind me.

"Natalie." Cole shook his head, his voice weak, strained, lacking fight. "Natalie, I don't..." He dropped his head. Tugged on his hair. "I don't fucking know what to do."

"You go to her. She's having your baby. You go to her. Marry her. Be a family." Impressive, the calm in my voice. "There's no other way to do this, Cole. You were in love with her. You don't just shut that off. You still love her, or you wouldn't be struggling right now."

"But the things she did to you. How can...?" His voice broke.

Oh, God. The pain in my chest. I was seconds from crumbling under the hurt and anger. The vile rage. If he came close, I would hurt him with fists, teeth, and razor blades if I had them.

He was torn. I was one solid piece of fleshy resolve. Even if Cole chose me, I refused to live a life—share a life or a child—with Victoria. She'd ruined me for the last time.

I couldn't hurt Cole with my fists, so I used words. "This weekend was great, Cole, but let's be honest. That's all it was. Great sex. You sowed your wild oats, and now you can go settle down with the love of your life."

The broken man opened his mouth to speak. Looked over my shoulder. Scratched the stubble on his jaw. Steely eyes met mine. He nodded. Pushed to stand. "You don't mean that."

"Get out." I couldn't look at him. I'd break. I'd beg him to choose me. I stared out the window, teeth grinding. Letting him go was the right thing to do, no matter how painful.

"I need to talk to her. I'll be back."

"No, you won't." She'll win. She always wins, I left unsaid. "I'm not the right decision, and you know that."

Cole stormed to my bedroom. Came out minutes later, fully dressed, though still disheveled. I hadn't moved.

He stood in front of me. I stared at his stomach.

Cole dropped to his knees and cupped my wet cheeks. When I was brave enough to meet his eyes, they were liquid, too.

"Before I go, you need to hear this one thing, and know that I mean it from the depths of my soul."

I couldn't speak, or nod, or breathe.

"You are, and always will be, the love of my life." He dropped a kiss to my forehead. Stepped away. "I'm going to talk to Victoria. Then I'm coming back."

He wouldn't return. He would do the right thing for his family. For their future. He was that kind of man. Who was I to stand in the way?

"Go home," I mumbled to the floor, setting him free. "Don't come back."

A heavy sigh. "Natalie."

I was seconds from shattering. "Get out!" I yelled, my outburst cowardly, my intentions self-preserving.

I sat paralyzed while Cole let himself out. Prisoner to the devastating pain, my soul wept on that godforsaken chair while shadows moved across the room, time moving on as if my hopes hadn't been crushed by wretched sorrow. Two boxes of tissues later, I made the biggest decision of my life.

Cole

Ten minutes into the reception, and Martin was drunk. No surprise. He'd been an ass since the moment Victoria and I announced our impromptu wedding. He'd arrived fucked out of his brains to the bachelor party and had refused to stand at my side during the ceremony.

"Congratulations, brother." A heavy hand clapped my back. A sloppy voice mumbled in my ear, "You landed a queen, didn't you?"

I watched Victoria sway across the dance floor in the arms of my father, a regal beauty in her white gown. She caught my eyes and flashed me a knee-buckling smile. Dad had never looked so proud.

I wondered what Natalie was doing at that moment. I wondered if she regretted not taking my calls or answering her door.

Then I envied Martin his ability to drown his bullshit with a bottle of bourbon.

"Where's the honeymoon?" he asked, using my shoulder to hold himself upright.

"Why don't you slow down on the Pappy's." I reached for his glass.

He dodged, holding the glass out of reach. "Can't."

"What's with you?"

He pounded his chest. Once. Twice. Gaze unfocused, he confessed, "Broken heart."

Martin hadn't dated anyone since Natalie. Hell, he hadn't bragged about banging anyone since Natalie had given him the boot. Obviously, her rejection had hurt more than he'd let on.

I could relate and, damn, I couldn't allow that pain any real estate on my wedding day. "Wanna talk about it?"

"No. No. This is your moment, my friend. Glad you came to your senses and made an honest woman of Vic. You got your girl, man. You always get the girl, don't you?"

Jesus. Fuck. His breath reeked of stale alcohol, the dark skin under his eyes boasting a three-day bender.

"Yeah. Yeah, sure." I gestured to Ellis, who stood by the bar. He came our way. "Martin needs a coffee."

No explanation necessary. With one beefy arm, Ellis guided our inebriated friend toward the back deck.

Lacey, looking lovelier and rounder by the day, hooked my elbow and stole me to the dance floor.

Dad winked and twirled Victoria while Ed Sheeran sang about dancing barefoot in the grass.

"You did the right thing, you know." Lacey stared up at me, eyes hard and motherly.

I moved her into the crowd with measured steps. "What do you mean?"

She waited until we were clear of earshot. "Natalie told me. Everything. I can't believe she kept her feelings for you a secret for all those months."

I swallowed, unsure how to proceed, unable to meet her piercing, probing glare. I searched for my wife and found her beaming and laughing at something my father must've said. She was undeniably beautiful. But even though she was legally mine, I couldn't shake the feeling I didn't fully belong to her.

Lacey followed my stare. "If you had chosen Natalie, the two of you never would've lasted. Not with the past she shares with Victoria."

I met her exotic eyes, and there wasn't a hint of malice or bitterness toward Victoria despite their history. Lacey was a pure soul, a light that warmed even the coldest hearts.

I knew our conversation would stay between the two of us, and my confession spilled. "I know I made the right decision." Not that Natalie had given me a choice. "I can't fathom raising a child in a broken home. I'm not built that way. But there's this heavy weight in my gut that won't go away, like everything is unsteady. Like the rug is gonna be pulled out from under me any moment."

"That's guilt. Nothing more. It'll fade. Especially when you hold your child for the first time. You'll know then, without a doubt, that you did the right thing."

"I need to talk to her. I left so much unsaid."

"Not a good idea." Lacey picked at a fuzz on my shoulder. "Clean breaks are best. You talk to Natalie, that'll only stir up feelings that don't belong in your marriage."

The truth was a bitter pill. "I know. You're right."

"Besides, she's gone," she whispered, her voice breaking.

I swore something broke in my chest, too. "Gone?"

"Took a job out of state."

"Where?" The question came out desperate, betraying my undue concern.

"I promised not to tell a soul." Eyes closed, she shook her head. "Not even Ellis."

"Because of me?"

"Because leaving was the right thing for her to do. Just like you marrying Victoria was the right thing to do."

Lacey's round belly bumped against mine, and I looked down between us, my heart swelling. Soon Victoria would be round and swollen and, *dear God*, I couldn't wait to feel my child move inside my wife.

Natalie had been mine for a short time, and for that blessing, I'd be forever grateful.

Choosing Vic, I'd done right by my child. I vowed then and there to be the best fucking husband and father despite the hole in my chest.

I bent to kiss Lacey's cheek. "You're right, Lacey. You're right. Thank you."

Dad and Victoria came our way again. He took Lacey's hand, and I swept my bride into my arms. I'd never seen her so damn happy.

"How are you feeling?" I asked, bending to taste her mouth.

Morning sickness had stifled the "making up" part of our making up. We'd come close a couple of times, but then she'd make a mad dash to the bathroom, and the romance had fizzled.

She turned her head and laughed. "Don't smudge my lipstick."

I kissed her anyway. She let me. A chaste exchange.

"I can't wait to get you alone," I whispered in her ear.

She lifted her chin, bringing our mouths a breath apart. "Do you forgive me, Cole?"

"For what?"

L.O.V.E.

"For walking out on you." She lifted a delicate finger to wipe the color from my lip. "For the person I was back then. The things I did to Natalie."

Truth be told, I'd been disgusted when she'd admitted the depth and depravity of her past obsession with Natalie. The bullying. Especially the bullying. A gnawing ache settled in my gut. Like Natalie, I'd been on the shit end of that scenario. Coming to terms with Vic's transgressions would pose a challenge. And still, when I looked at my wife, I couldn't see that girl full of hate, hurt, and evil intent. I only saw the woman with the big heart who loved her family, fiercely protected her friendships, and gave her free time to children's charities.

Before I could answer her question, she looked around the room, then asked, "Where's Martin? He was sloshed. Should we keep an eye on him? I don't want him to ruin our night."

"I think he's pouting over Natalie. He hasn't been the same since they broke up." Natalie's name tasted too damn sweet, but I tamped that shit down deep, hardening those feelings to lifeless, colorless clay. "Ellis has it handled."

Victoria's cheeks reddened. "You think Martin still has a thing for her?"

"I don't want to talk about them. This is our day." I stole another kiss and twirled my bride through the crowd. The DJ announced a break. I escorted Victoria to our table. The evening moved on. We laughed and mingled. Guests dwindled. Martin never returned.

Victoria excused herself to the restroom. She returned smelling of cigarettes, igniting our first fight as a married couple.

Before the reception ended, Victoria had canceled the honeymoon.

"What did you find out?"

I swung the door wider, allowing my friend, Detective Waters inside.

Dark bags nested his sullen gaze. "You need to have a seat, Cole."

"I'll stand." Arms crossed, I braced for what was sure to be bad news. "You found her?"

Waters scrubbed a hand over his face. "If you don't wanna sit, can I?"

Fuck.

The sofa was a mere ten steps away. My legs grew heavier with each lift and drop, but I managed to sit, and Waters followed suit.

"Martin's car was found at the bottom of a cliff in Monterey County a couple hours ago."

"California?" I asked.

Staring at the floor, he nodded.

"What does Martin have to do with my missing wife?" Victoria had lied about a weekend trip with her girlfriends while Martin had ghosted days after the wedding. I hadn't seen or heard from him in the two weeks since.

He nodded. Swallowed. Gave me a hard look.

"No. Don't say it."

Again he nodded, his jaw tensing before he forced the words through gritted teeth. "Martin's body washed up on shore about a half mile down. They recovered Vic's ID and a suitcase full of women's clothing. Her body hasn't been found, but that's not uncommon in these types of accidents."

The room blurred. Truths speared my chest, razor-sharp puzzle pieces slicing me wide open. Vic and Martin.

Jesus fucking Christ, what a fool I'd been.

L.O.V.E.

Veins ice cold, I stared at the wall above his head, unnamable emotions rolling through me. "She emptied our joint bank account twenty-four hours ago."

"I'm sorry."

"They'll keep looking for her, right?"

"Of course." He ran a hand through his graying hair. "Most likely, though, the ocean claimed her body."

"Understood," I managed to say, though I would never fully comprehend. My best friend. My wife. My child. *Fuck. Was the child even mine*? Had there even been a child?

I stood and gestured to the door. "Thanks for coming by, but I...I um..." I couldn't form a thought, my mind and body numb.

"Can I call anyone for you?"

"No. No, I just need a..." I couldn't finish. My fists curled, the urge to strike someone overwhelming.

He came to my side, braced my shoulder. "We'll talk tomorrow. I'll be back around nine. I called your pops. He's on his way."

"Appreciate that," I choked out. And before he stepped outside, I warned, "We need to keep this out of the press."

"I'll do my best," he said.

I closed the door and fell to the floor.

Father Christianson gave his final blessing, and the mass of mourners slowly rose and made their way toward the exit, leaving the gloom of the church behind, the procession mostly silent save a few sniffles.

My body, a thousand pounds of rage, remained glued to the pew. I stared ahead at nothing in particular, the room around me shrouded in a red haze, the pulpit, the cross, the flowers, colorless, lifeless, dead. Like my wife and my best friend.

"Son." Dad wrapped an arm around my shoulder.

I shrugged him off.

"We'll give you a few minutes," he rasped before escorting my mother toward the aisle.

Seething and broken, I had watched Martin's ceremony from the shadows. Victoria's service, however, demanded my presence, and despite her betrayal, I set my mask firmly in place and played the grief-stricken widower while burning and churning and boiling over with ugly, vile hatred.

Maybe that hatred would eat me alive. Maybe I could join my friend and lover in Hell. I would enjoy watching them burn.

"Cole." Natalie's voice, a lowly whisper, cut through the dark, pernicious haze and sliced me open, demonic fury spilling from the wound.

"Get the fuck out." My words echoed off the stained-glass windows.

A sharp breath, then silence. Soft footfalls retreated.

Finally, a target for my rage. I rose from the cursed bench and stalked behind, ignoring every well-meaning soul I passed. When Natalie reached her car, I growled, "Why the hell are you here?"

Shoulders bunched, she turned to face me. A black dress covered her body from neck to knees, hiding the seductive curves underneath. Her hair was pulled into a tight knot, not a fucking strand out of place.

Natalie met my eyes. Cleared her throat. "I'm not sure. I just... I...um...I just needed to come."

She was beauty. I was spite. "To gloat?"

"What?" She hugged her handbag like the black leather would protect her. "No."

185

"You hated her."

"She hated me."

"Why did you come?" Why did she ever let me go?

"I don't know. It felt like it was the right thing to do."

"Fuck the right thing." I moved closer, craving her pain. "Look what doing the right thing has cost me."

"Cole, I'm sorry."

The sincerity in her voice broke me all over again. Sorry didn't mean shit. Sorry wouldn't right any of the wrongs. I'd chosen the devil. I'd suffer the consequences. "Sorry? Sorry for what? Sorry she'd been fucking my best friend? Sorry they'd stolen from me? Sorry Martin had gambled his way into a debt he'd never get out of, and used my wife, my fucking money, to run? I'll never—" Anger clogged my throat. "I'll never know if that baby was even mine. She lied so I would marry her. So she would have access to everything I owned. What the fuck? Who does that shit?"

"Victoria." Natalie found her voice, her spine straightening. "Victoria does that shit."

"You knew, didn't you? You knew all this time that she'd ruin me."

"I hoped she wouldn't."

"You knew her soul was poisoned, and you stood by and watched. Waited."

"Cole, no. That's not what—"

"Shut up. Just shut the fuck up."

Cheeks crimson, her eyes liquified. I hated her in that moment. Hated that I wanted her, wanted her tears, wanted her sympathy. Hated that I needed to break her so I could feel better.

"I'm such a fucking fool."

With a trembling hand, Natalie reached behind and gripped the door handle, seeking escape.

I couldn't let her off that easy.

"Victoria wouldn't fuck me. Even on our wedding day, she wouldn't fuck me. At first I thought she knew I'd been with you and was punishing me."

Natalie stood speechless, half turned away from me.

"You know what's most fucked up about this whole scenario? She started fucking Martin only after you came into our lives. I found her journal. She kept a goddam record of her infidelity." I moved closer, towering over her trembling form, hating myself but unable to stop the purge. "You had Martin. She wanted him to spite you. So really, this is your fucking fault, isn't it?"

"Cole, stop," came from her trembling lips.

"I was perfectly, cluelessly happy. Until you."

"That's enough."

"No. Not enough. It'll never be enough. I don't have my wife. I don't have a child." I sucked in a jagged breath, whispered in her ear, "I don't have you."

Natalie broke, choking on a sob. She shoved me away, curled into her SUV, and locked herself up tight.

Hands pressed to the window, I watched her cry and fed off her pain.

When she drove away, I stared at the empty space, the black asphalt dark and dirty as the tar in my heart. I hated Martin. Hated Victoria. But most of all, I hated myself.

Cole

I got the call at 1:36 AM. The baby was on his way two weeks early.

I arrived in time to catch Ellis when he turned green and made like a falling tree.

Lacey was a champ. They shooed me out of the birthing suite when it came time to push.

Three hours later, I met Leon Matias Chambers.

I excused myself when Natalie's parents stormed into the room, giving them privacy to fawn over Lacey and the dark-haired angel.

A haggard Ellis found me in the cafeteria, getting my caffeine fix. He fell into the chair next to me, eyes heavy with fatigue, smile wide and proud.

"He's perfect." I shoved my cup of Joe his way. "Just perfect."

"I can't believe this is my life." The exhausted pallor of his skin blended with the dull peach walls. His hair stood straight up on one side. But that grin on his face? Priceless.

"Believe it, buddy. You've got a beautiful baby boy. An amazing wife. You deserve this. All of it."

Ellis stared into the dark liquid, then pinned me with a hard glare. "You deserve the same, Cole."

I deserved exactly what had transpired. I'd been unfaithful. For that, I lost everything.

I'd refused to discuss Victoria and Martin's affair with anyone, unable to acknowledge a deception I'd yet to wrap my head around.

"I miss Martin," Ellis said to his coffee.

"Me, too." I forced the lie through clenched teeth. Truth was, the hatred had taken root and spread. A rampant plague. But that was my burden to bear. My disease to carry.

I refused to tarnish Ellis's memories of our best friend.

"I'd like you to be Leon's godfather. We're baptizing him in two weeks. But if you're not feeling up to it, I understand."

"I'd be honored," I said, autopilot engaged. "Wouldn't miss it for the world."

"Natalie will be his godmother, of course," he added, clueless to the tempest he'd conjured with the mention of her name.

Natalie. Of course. *Fuck.* I nodded, unable to look Ellis in the eye, instead focusing my attention on an elderly couple two tables away.

I became hyper aware of the Barry Manilow Muzak playing in the background. The man sitting behind me started to sing along.

Every nerve in my body zinged, itching for a fight, an outlet, a damn receptacle to vomit my inexhaustible anger.

"Mind if I join you boys?" When the deep voice came over my shoulder, the mounting pressure eased. "Thought I'd give the ladies some alone time."

189

L.O.V.E.

Ellis pushed to stand, but the man patted his shoulder and offered his hand to me. "Charles King."

Natalie's father. Tall. Well built. Silver hair. Blue, wise eyes, framed in well-earned wrinkles. I liked him. I didn't want to like him.

"Cole Adams."

His grin faded, but that grip strengthened, a show of support. "Cole. I'm so sorry about your wife."

"Thank you, sir." I managed to hold his knowing gaze, despite wanting to bow under the weight of undeserved compassion. The man wouldn't be friendly if he knew what I'd done to his daughter.

Settled in his chair, he clapped Ellis's shoulder again. "Congratulations, son. He's a beautiful boy. Beautiful."

"Any advice for a new dad?" Ellis asked, beaming.

"Take care of that lady of yours," he advised, crossing strong arms over a thick chest. "That's number one. You take care of Lacey, set a good example for your son, the rest will fall into place."

"That I can do."

We BS'd about the weather, the Seahawks, the stock market. Ellis couldn't stand another second away from his new family and practically danced out of the cafeteria, leaving me alone with Charles, a lukewarm coffee, and ice cold agitation poisoning my veins.

I stared at the man whose daughter had spun my world out of orbit.

"Must be rough, being here after losing your wife and child."

The guy didn't beat around the bush. Respect.

"Not sure the baby was mine," I blurted.

Charles didn't flinch. Like me, like Natalie, he knew the truth about my deceased wife, had witnessed her trail of destruction firsthand.

"She lied to everyone." Like he'd pierced my bubble with a pin, the words burst out on a rush of air, the truth leaking. "She didn't want me at all, you see? She wanted my money and my best friend." God damn, what a relief to say those words out loud, to unburden the weight I'd carried.

"Doesn't make it any easier. You loved her. I suspect you loved that unborn child, too. The loss is real."

I slumped, no longer able to hold up the facade. I was not okay. I hadn't been okay for a long time. And the man staring back at me, the stranger with familiar eyes, was one of only a handful of people who might understand the level of psychological damage Victoria had inflicted.

"I loved her, true. But was it Vic I loved or someone else? Was it all an act?"

He released a heavy breath. Shook his head. "I can't answer that question, son."

"Funny thing? She ran away with my best friend. And I should be angry with him. But I can't. He—"

Charles interrupted, "She was a master manipulator."

I nodded.

"You feel like she deceived him, too."

"Yes." Jesus, the man got it.

"And you're struggling because you're angry with her and not him."

"I hate Martin. Hate that he's not here. That I can't tell him how I feel or beat him to a bloody pulp."

"That's understandable."

"I shouldn't be talking to you about this."

"No?" he asked, leaning forward, arms crossed on the table.

"What she did to your daughter was far worse than what she put me through. And I hurt Natalie, too. More than once."

"Natalie." He nodded, knowingly, then hit me with a hard glare. "My girl's a fighter. Back then, Linda and I offered to move her to another school time and time again, but she wouldn't leave Lacey behind. She put up with years of torment so she could stay with her best friend."

Torment. That word struck hard, wrapping around me like a scratchy blanket, then settling, softening, cocooning my soul.

My pain had a name. My illness diagnosed.

"She didn't have to put up with the harassment this time," he continued.

"Because she was able to leave," I concurred, bruised by the brutal honesty of the conversation.

"She had no choice really."

That statement, paired with his glower, held more meaning than I was able to stomach. Did he know about Natalie and me? Our sinful attraction? Our brief affair?

She'd had a choice. She could have stayed and fought for us. Maybe I had needed her to fight for *me*. God, was that the root of my anger? If so, that made me a fucking selfish prick.

"Listen, Charles. I said some horrible things to Natalie at Victoria's funeral, and I need to apologize—"

"I can't help you, son," he interrupted before I had the chance to beg.

"Sure. Sure, of course." Anger rushed through me, and I choked down a slew of profanities. The guy was only protecting his daughter.

Charles studied me, my heated face, my ticking jaw. He knew. A father always knows.

Natalie wanted nothing to do with me. For now, I'd let her believe she was safely hidden away. Because, for the time being, distance was the safer option.

He pushed to stand. "I should head back upstairs."

I rose, too, and shook his hand with more vigor than necessary. "Great to meet you, Charles."

"You too, Cole." His smile was genuine, though cautious. "You coming with?"

"No. No. Would you give my love to Lacey? Let Ellis know I'll call him later?"

"Sure." He turned to leave.

My feet rooted.

Five paces away, he turned. "Word of advice?"

I nodded, gnawing my bottom lip.

"Get your heart and head in the right place before you try to see my daughter again. She's tough, but she loves deep. That means she hurts deep." He huffed, straightening his shoulders. "I don't like to see her in pain."

With that, he left, leaving me with his unspoken threat.

The pastor's words fell victim to the deafening thump-thump, thump-thump pounding between my ears, the crowded pews a blur of color in my periphery. I focused on the sleepy baby boy and willed my body to stay upright. Unless in the ring, I wasn't a fan of center stage.

Natalie stood at my side, a fucking statue wearing a painted smile, mile-high nude heels, and black and pink glasses that matched her pretty rose-colored dress.

We hadn't spoken a word; we'd scarcely exchanged glances. She'd stayed ten feet away from me until we were forced to stand side by side in front of the congregation.

I deserved as much.

When the baptism was over, Ellis and Lacey headed to their seats next to Ellis's parents to enjoy the rest of the church service. Natalie, I assumed, claimed her spot next to her mother as I fled, leaving the congregation behind, shoving through the back door, where I beelined for my waiting vehicle. Only then did I draw steady breaths. Only then did my racing pulse slow.

Fuck. I wouldn't make it through lunch. I'd have to bail. Come up with a pathetic excuse.

I wasn't strong enough to celebrate the happy couple and their newborn. I wasn't man enough to face Natalie.

A tap, tap on my passenger window pulled me from my harsh introspect.

Natalie offered a shy smile, eyes glistening, so fucking beautiful my chest crumpled.

Shit.

I stared, scrambling for an excuse to bolt.

She held up a glittery pink flask, an icebreaker, a peace offering.

I hit *Unlock.* She settled into my passenger seat.

The vehicle shrunk around me.

"You ditching the rest of the service?" she asked, breathy and conspiratorial.

Shame choked me, suppressing any response.

Natalie worked off the lid, then passed the bottle my way. "You looked ready to faint in there. Thought this might help." Her tone held no anger, no bitterness.

"You've had this on you the whole time?"

She answered with a wide smile, an enthusiastic nod, and a tap to her oversized handbag.

"You're drinking..." I sniffed the opening. "Rum. At nine in the morning."

"I was nervous about seeing you." She snatched the bottle, downed a swig, then shoved it back into my hand. "It's the good stuff. And clearly, I'm not the only one who's a wreck."

"Was I that obvious?"

She laughed, then sighed and turned to face me, resting her temple against the headrest. "I'm probably the last person you want to talk to right now, but I'm here. I'm a good listener."

Natalie King was the only person I ever wanted to talk to, and that was a problem because my head was a mess. My ticker? That vile thing was torn in two, one half black and decayed, the other shredded, but thumping back to life in her presence.

"I'd love a drink, but"—I tapped a thumb on the steering wheel—"I have to drive."

"So drive to Ellis and Lacey's house. Park down the street. We'll drink. We'll talk. We'll join the party when we're good and ready."

Not what I had in mind, but at least we had a plan. I nodded, fired up the engine, and pulled into the Sunday morning traffic before confessing, "Before you accosted me, I was figuring out how to ditch lunch."

"I don't blame you." Natalie fiddled with the hem of her skirt. "I can't imagine how hard this is after losing Victoria and the baby."

I forced my anger into the steering wheel, squeezing hard, and ground my teeth together to keep from screaming. Natalie didn't deserve my rage. After two measured breaths, I said, "I owe you an apology for the things I said at the funeral. I was in a dark place, needed someone to dump on."

She nodded in acceptance, curled her lips between her teeth, and stared at her hands. Then her watery eyes met mine. "For what it's worth, I am sorry for your loss."

"I know."

Two blocks from Ellis's place, I parked under the shade of a tall maple, then turned to face the gorgeous girl with rosy cheeks, dark blond hair, and a smile that reminded me I was flesh and blood human, not a hollow shell. "I'm so angry all the time. So goddamn angry. I look in the mirror and I see me, but my skin doesn't fit right, like there's a slithering, vile, black entity underneath this mask I wear."

"That's some heavy shit to carry around, Cole." Natalie again twisted the top off her ridiculous flask, took a swig, then offered me a drink.

I didn't refuse and reveled in the burn as the liquid hit my throat. "Shit. That *is* the good stuff." I took another shot, my chest feeling a hundred pounds lighter.

Then the beauty laughed and said, "Only the best for my friends."

Goddamn, she looked gorgeous in my Roadster. My chest cracked, my stomach knotted, and that bitter, nasty being under my skin shivered. "Is that what we are, Natalie, friends?"

"Well"—she smirked—"we're something, Cole Adams, aren't we?"

I couldn't help my grin. "A hot mess."

Again with the laugh, and I wanted nothing more than to turn those giggles into moans.

Instead, I laid my heart at her feet and my palm on her cheek. "I miss this face."

"Cole." She blew a long, slow breath, leaned into my touch, conviction hardening her features. Bile rose in my throat. I knew what was coming. Bullshit in the form of *you're grieving*, or *you had to choose Victoria*.

Nobody understood what I suffered. Nobody could comprehend the war of conscience I battled every waking moment of every miserable day.

I pressed a finger to her lips because I didn't want her response, good or bad. "You don't have to say anything.

I just wanted you to know." I landed a soft kiss on her forehead and said, "I'm glad you're here," then pulled away and settled into my seat, putting distance between us and shielding my black heart. "Tell me about your job."

Her eyes lit, those gray irises sparkling. "I got promoted to the Corporate Accounts team. Worked my ass off to get there." Her gaze darkened, and she seemed lost in thought, staring over my shoulder. "I suppose, in a way, I have Victoria to thank. She always told me I'd be a nobody. That I was no prettier or smarter than"—she held up her free hand, making air quotes—"an ugly cow in a field of ugly cows."

I refrained from punching the dash.

Natalie slumped, then continued. "I never loved school, but I was dead set on proving her wrong, so I graduated top of my class."

She was a fighter, like her father had said, and she'd fought her way to the top, overcoming the bully.

"Why banking?" I asked, plucking the flask from her hand and downing a shot.

She laughed, shaking her head. "It's silly, really. When I was little, I loved going to the bank with Mom. They always had lollipops for the kids, and the people were so nice. I thought it was cool they got to work behind those giant glass walls. Started out as a cashier, worked my way up."

That wasn't silly. That was Natalie.

For the next half hour, we made small talk. She told me about her promotion. I told her about the new development projects Dad and I had in the works and my plans for expanding CFC.

I got a text from Ellis at the same time Natalie's phone chimed.

"We better head in," I grumbled, not ready to leave our safe place, not ready to let her go.

Natalie offered a shy smile that pummeled all my vulnerable places. I held her hand. We walked in silence. Instead of begging her to keep in touch, I kissed her cheek, said, "It was good to see you," and opened the door, following her inside.

We parted ways. The hole in my heart grew wider but somehow hurt a little less.

Natalie

I found Lacy in the nursery, babe at her breast, lids heavy, cheeks flushed.

"There you are," she whispered, swinging her free arm wide for a hug.

Our embrace was sloppy but vital, the child our new reality. I kissed Leon's fuzzy head, that heavenly baby scent eliciting bittersweet emotions.

"Please tell me you were with Cole," she said, a hint of intrigue in her tone. "He looked like he was going to faint."

I planted my butt on the fuzzy blue rug next to the rocking chair. "Are you mad I left early?"

"Of course not." She shifted the baby to the other breast. "Ellis is worried. We've hardly seen Cole since the accident." She winced, adjusted her boob, then continued, "He disappears every night after work, doesn't return calls." Lacey's eyes turned liquid.

Grief and Lacey were well acquainted.

"He's hurting," I whispered, my body aching with sadness, though I wasn't sure why. I studied the wall behind mother and son. Gold stars scattered across a midnight blue wall, the pattern erratic but inspiring infinite hope and wonder.

The baby made a squeak and released his mom's boob.

"He done?" I said, fighting tears.

Lacey nodded.

Hopping to my feet, I ordered, "Hand him over." I scooped that little bundle of joy into my arms. I burped him like a pro, then smothered him with kisses.

Holding him warmed me deep, soul deep.

"You can lay him in the crib." Lacey nodded to the white wooden bed and yawned.

"I don't want to let go." Tears trickled, catching on my lip and chin. I had no free hands to wipe them away.

"Look at my little boy, collecting his jar of hearts already." Lacey rose from the chair and used her sleeve to dry my face. "Sit." She nudged me toward the rocking chair.

I lowered myself into the cushion, and she tucked a pillow under my arm.

"He's so perfect. So beautiful and perfect."

"I know, right. I did good, didn't I?" Lacey yawned, stretched, then righted her shirt, adjusting her plump breasts in her nursing bra.

"Head downstairs and join the party. I need some bonding time with my godson."

"You sure?"

"Definitely. Go." I shooed her away.

"Love you, Nat Brat." She stared for a long spell before heading toward the door.

"Love you, too, Lulu." I blew her a kiss and watched her retreat, admiring the new roundness to her hips before giving the baby my full attention.

I studied the chubby little face, his thick dark lashes, that pink little mouth, and dusted a finger over the silky black fuzz on his head. "You're going to be a lady killer, aren't you, little guy?"

He stretched, squeaked, pursed his lips. My vision blurred. God, such beauty.

"Someday, I hope I can give you cousins to play with. I don't see that happening anytime soon, though. You see, I don't have the best of luck in the love department. I'll probably grow old alone. Turn into a crazy cat lady. On the bright side, you'll always have cute little kitties to play with. No, that could never work. I don't like cats so much. Anyway, point is, I'll always be here for you, no matter what. Okay? Don't ever forget that. I got you, little guy." I dotted his face with kisses, and when he started to fuss, I rocked to my feet and made my way to the window, swaying and humming, holding him cheek to cheek.

He fussed, body coiling, so I rubbed his back and started to hum the tune I loved most, "Someone to Watch Over Me."

Outside, the sky was bright and clear, and the trees boasted beautiful shades of red and orange. I caught sight of a reflection in the window. I turned to find Cole, arms crossed, leaned against the doorjamb, eyes dark and liquid and aimed at the baby. The man was painfully beautiful, his grief a pulsing entity.

My chest caved. *God, how he must hurt.*

That invisible string between us tightened, and I moved in his direction. The broken man dropped his gaze to the floor, then disappeared.

Cole manned the grill, can of Bodhizafa in one hand, tongs in the other. Dad stood at the far edge of the deck, deep in conversation with Ellis's father, staring and pointing sporadically across the property. Ellis wrestled with a garden hose halfway across the lawn.

"This house is gorgeous, isn't it?" Mom said from behind, her arms coming around my middle, her chin resting on my shoulder.

I nodded, unable to stray my focus from the sight outside. Cole poked and prodded the sizzling meat, feet set at a comfortable stance, his shoulders bunching and rolling under his dress shirt, his tight ass putting on a fine show in his navy slacks.

"Lacey is so happy and loved," I whispered.

Cole turned to say something to Ellis, then lifted the beer to his lips, revealing in profile his square jaw, that straight nose, and thick, luscious, talented lips.

He was overdue for a haircut, not that the shaggy locks hurt his image by any means. Not even the grief haunting his eyes could mar his beauty.

Mom sighed in my ear. I sighed, too, folding my arms over hers and breathing through the bone-deep ache.

Cole turned to toss his can in the trash. Our eyes met through the window, freezing time and space. His dimple made an appearance, brief and unsure, but aimed my way regardless, stealing my breath, my wits, my heart and soul.

A nod our way, and then he severed our connection, turning his back to me once again.

Mom's arms tightened against my full-body shiver. "How long have you been in love with Cole?"

A simple question. No appropriate answer. "How did you know?" My voice broke.

"Oh, baby." Soft lips landed on my cheek. "Any fool can see."

"Dad told you."

She straightened. "Your dad knows?"

"He didn't tell you?" I turned, bracing her shoulders. "Am I that transparent?"

"I'm your mother. I can read you like an open book."

Blinking back tears, I confessed, "I couldn't share my feelings with anyone, Mom. Cole wasn't mine to covet. And I struggled every day with the guilt of wanting a taken man."

Knowing eyes pierced my soul, and she sucked in a breath before cupping my face. "He's the reason you took the job in Whisper Springs."

"Yes."

"Oh, sweetheart." Mom wrapped me in a tight embrace, and I melted into her soft curves with a sigh. Mom hugs had magical healing powers, and I absorbed that shit like a shriveled sponge.

"I had to get far away," I mumbled into her hair, fighting tears.

There was no disappointment in her tone, only concern. "Because he was taken."

"I had no right wanting him. I never should have befriended him. I told myself I was doing it for Lacey. But that was a lie."

"Why then? Because of Victoria?"

"No. Oh, God, no. Because I loved him. I fell head over heels the first time he looked at me. Before I knew he belonged to her. He was a stranger, and I thought I'd never see him again, but it didn't matter. He looked at me, and I fell." I pulled away, shaking my head. "I know that sounds ridiculous."

"Why? Why is it ridiculous? The first time I laid eyes on your dad, I knew he was the one. I saw our future laid out. Sure, details were foggy, but our fate was there, certain as the rising sun."

"Dad wasn't engaged or unavailable when you met him."

"True." She wiped a tear off my cheek, her lips quirking. "So you fell in love, and the timing was terrible. But you didn't act on that attraction, right?"

I shook my head.

"Good. But—"

"Cole." Ellis walked through the back door. "Need help with that?"

My guts twisted. Mom gasped. We turned our heads at the same time, and thank the good Lord for Mom's arms because my knees buckled at the sight.

Cole stood against the kitchen island, gripping the over-stuffed platter of meat, brows pinched, eyes dark, a thousand turbulent emotions encased in those golden globes.

Clueless, Ellis slapped his shoulder.

Still as a statue, he stood, holding me prisoner with the weight of that glare.

Lacey walked into the room, clapped her hands together, and said, "Oh, good. Steaks are done. I'm starving. Nat Brat, grab the salad out of the fridge." She snatched a stack of plates off the counter. "It's a beautiful day. Let's eat on the deck."

Mom gave my fingers a squeeze, cleared her throat, then breezed past me and the men, as if Cole hadn't just maybe, possibly—oh God, who was I kidding? He'd heard every word. Every crazy stupid syllable that came out of my mouth.

With a muttered, "Fuck," Cole pinched his eyes closed, shook his head, and turned to follow Lacey.

Three deep breaths, and I made my way to the bathroom to splash cold water on my face before joining the others. We sat around the large round wrought iron table, Cole two bodies down.

We ate and laughed, and I pretended like my heart wasn't breaking, or that my nerves weren't shredded, and I avoided looking to my right at all costs.

Until Lacey said, "So, what are your plans tonight, Nat Brat?"

"Oh." I shot a quick glance her way, Cole in my periphery. "I'm joining Finn and Mona for dinner before her show."

Lacey's smile fell, but she quickly recovered.

"Don't worry. I'll be by first thing in the morning to say goodbye. And I'll be back for Thanksgiving."

"And Christmas, too," Dad interjected, brows raised as if I'd dare to challenge him.

"Of course."

Leon's wails brought all of our attention to the little white monitor at Ellis's side. I pushed from the table, shouted, "He's mine!" then dashed away before anyone could beat me to the baby.

When I returned, Cole was gone.

"Tonight I'm going to do something I rarely do on stage. But a new, and very dear friend of mine, made a special request. When I asked him why, and why this song, he simply said, "She's home." Mona dropped her head, took a measured breath, and cleared her throat, collectively enthralling the crowd.

"His cryptic response was so full of heartache and regret," she continued. "I didn't question further. So, my dear friend who wished to remain anonymous, this one's for you."

The spotlight changed from white to blue, then followed Mona to the piano. She sat. The room fell eerily silent.

Mona hit the keys at the same time her husky rasp hit the mic. She crooned the lyrics to "Wicked Game" by Chris Isaak.

Riveted to my chair at the small table in front of the stage, I fell victim to the haunting melody. I thought of Cole and our one weekend together. I'd been so desperately, selflessly, irrepressibly in love.

I still was hopelessly, foolishly, obsessively in love.

Mona continued.

I blinked back tears, the lyrics flooding my veins with grief for the man I'd had for one perfect weekend.

Next to me, a chair scraped. A thigh bumped into mine, then settled warm against my leg, but I didn't care. I couldn't tear my gaze from the stage or my attention from the message. Whoever the song was for, I wanted to know their story. I'd have to torture the truth from Mona after her set.

A hand landed on my thigh, then moved to grab my arm, sliding down to entwine our fingers, stealing my breath and my wits. I knew those fingers, that strong grip, the scent of him intimately. Tears fell harder. If I looked his way, I'd shatter.

Seconds passed before I was composed enough to whisper, "What are you doing here?"

"You know what I'm doing here."

Though I focused my blurry stare on Mona, the weight of Cole's gaze heated me head to toe.

"Torturing me?"

His breath warmed my cheek. "You like the song?"

"Was it you?" I asked, turning, bringing our mouths painfully close.

"Fitting, don't you think?"

The song was perfect if his intention was to slice me open.

"Tell me something, Natalie." He let go of my hand, then settled his arm around my shoulder, cocooning me, caging me. "Do you miss me?"

A loaded question. "Cole, please. Don't do this."

Somewhere around us, applause, though the room stayed dark.

"Because I miss you. Every second of every goddamned day." His chest rose and fell. "Do you know what it did to me, seeing you with that baby in your arms?" He pulled a strand of my hair through his fingers, toyed with the end. "Do you have any idea how you broke me, hearing you tell your mother that you loved me?"

Oh, God.

He cupped my face, his fingers trembling. "I needed those words from you, Natalie. You should have said them to me, not her."

I managed to speak over the ferocious boom in my chest. "I couldn't."

"I know." He dropped his forehead to mine. "You're leaving tomorrow."

"Yes."

"Stay with me tonight," he pleaded.

"That's not a good idea." He had my heart, he had my love, all of it. But what did I have other than a man torn apart, split down the middle, one half fueled by lust, the other drowning in grief?

His whole body vibrated. Heat and frustration and unbridled energy. "Stay with me tonight."

"Cole."

"I fucking need you, Natalie." His voice broke. "Give me this one night." His lips dusted mine, soft and unsure.

"Why?"

"You know why."

I knew. Because whatever cruel twist of fate we'd befallen, he was cursed, the same as I. Our connection, the attraction, made no sense. The timing was always off. The pull, though, that was undeniable, otherworldly, and yes, at times sinful. But I knew, the same as Cole, that we were something, and our relationship, whether good or bad, friend or foe, hot or cold, was very extraordinary.

One more night would break my heart a thousand times over.

One more night might be all I'd ever get of Cole Adams.

I rose from my chair, took his hand, and led him to my car.

Cole slammed the SUV into park. Ran to my side, opened the door, and helped me out, his grip tight, as if afraid I would run.

I stared at the CFC painted on the window. "You're staying in the gym?"

"I have an apartment above the gym." Cole pushed open the door, waited for me to enter, then locked up behind us. "Can't stand being in that house," he mumbled before leading me upstairs, then past his office to a small apartment.

His living space was small but clean. Too sterile. Exposed brick and beams. A small, open kitchen was tucked in the corner. Large arch windows. One small couch and a large screen television. To my left, an open barn door exposed a small room, the unmade bed the only clue that someone lived there. No art, no life, only empty space full of potential.

L.O.V.E.

Silence stretched, anticipation and hesitation crackling the air between us, my fingers itching to touch, my body primed. My heart guarded.

"Mona said on stage that you were a new, but dear, friend."

"True." He loosened his tie. Tugged the silk off his neck.

"When did that happen?" I stood still, waiting for his cue.

"When you left," he said, dropping his tie, wetting his lips.

"I don't understand."

"I don't either." He stepped close enough to kiss me. "All I know is that when I'm there, I feel closer to you."

"Why can't you go home?" I asked, lifting my face to study his sad expression.

"Too many memories."

I nodded.

"Not just of *her*, but Martin, too. He helped me buy that house. We remodeled the kitchen together. Now, when I'm there, I want to take a bat to the place."

"I get it."

"I don't think you do."

"Maybe I shouldn't be here. God, you're still grieving. I should've known better."

A huff. "Don't leave."

"Cole, I—"

Warm hands cupped my cheeks. Cole stared down at me, heated and pleading. "No more. I don't want them in my head when you're here."

He claimed my mouth in a kiss both punishing and desperate, his full body trembling against mine. Finally.

His fingers tangled in my hair. I gripped his shirt in tight fists, my body heating and softening, aching for his possession.

Fucking my mouth with his tongue, he lifted the hem of my skirt, grabbed my ass, and yanked me tighter against his erection.

I moaned.

Cole shivered.

My back hit the wall. He slapped a hand above my head and rolled his hips, grinding against me, adding fuel to the flame and, *oh, God,* I was lit. Fire in my belly. Skin fevered. Heart burned to ash.

"Jesus. Fuck," he mumbled into my mouth.

A grunt, and he was on his knees. My panties were gone, and my skirt was bunched around my waist. Rushed kisses peppered my abdomen before he moved lower, digging fingers into my thighs and going straight for the kill, sucking my clit like his life depended on making me come. Like he didn't have time for any other nonsense, his sole purpose to kneel at my feet and worship my body. He sucked and licked and sucked again before plunging a finger between my folds. I came hard, grinding against his face, my back scraping against the brick wall.

Before I could recover, he rushed me to the bed. A mad scramble to remove our clothes. A frantic rush to roll on a condom.

Too damn long before he filled me, hot, hard, perfect. Sweet Lord, the man was everything.

He moved, I moaned. He kissed, I cried. He pounded me into the mattress, and I clung tight, absorbing his anger, his pain, his grief, his feral energy.

He growled his release into my neck, then collapsed at my side, caging me with heavy limbs.

L.O.V.E.

My body was spent. My heart demanded *more, more, more.*

We fucked again in the shower.

By the third time, my body ached and my heart bled. We hadn't made love. Cole had purged while I had comforted.

Sad thing? I wasn't upset. He needed release. I needed...him. Any broken, bloody part he offered.

Cole tucked a leg between mine and buried his face in my hair, his arm draping over my ribs, his cock thickening against my backside.

"Don't leave, Natalie."

"I'll be back for Thanksgiving."

"Tell me where you live." He laced our fingers and squeezed. "I'll visit on the weekends."

"Cole. Listen."

"Don't." He rolled to his back, leaving me cold. "Don't give me the fucking speech."

I stared at the empty brick wall, hating what came next. "You're grieving. You're unsettled. I've just started a new job in a different state."

"I've lost you, haven't I?" Such venom in his voice.

I rolled over but didn't touch. I couldn't touch and hold my ground. "I don't want that. I don't want us to be strangers, but I don't see how we can be more than... God, I don't even know what we are."

"A hot fucking mess." Cole shoved the sheet off his body and sat up, dropping his feet to the floor. "Doomed from day one."

Our time had come to an end. I slid out of bed, hunted for my clothes. "I'll be home for the holidays. Can I see you then?" Bra and panties. Check. Dress. Check.

"I hate that idea." He stood, came toe to toe, then spun me around, closing my zipper. He kissed my shoulder. "That's months away."

"I know."

And then he broke me, growling, "You'll be fucking other men by then."

I turned and slapped the sneer off his face. "That was cruel."

He didn't flinch.

He wanted me to hurt him. He wanted me to hurt.

I snatched my shoes off the floor. Found my handbag by the front door.

Cole stood behind me, his heat no longer soothing. "The only good thing in my life is walking out the door, and there isn't a damn thing I can do about it."

"You're hurting and lashing out at me," I said to the door, my hand on the knob. "For your information, you've ruined me for any other man. Once you've digested that fact, get some help. You need to work through your grief with a professional. At the very least, direct your anger elsewhere, but I won't stay here and be your goddamned punching bag."

I slipped out the door and dashed toward the stairs, biting my lip to keep the tears at bay.

Heavy footsteps came behind me.

"Don't follow me."

I hit the stairwell, Cole hot on my heels.

"I mean it. Don't follow me," I yelled, jogging down the cement steps.

I made it to the exit before he caged me against the heavy metal door. His chest heaved against my back. God, how I wanted to stay. Fall into his arms and promise my love and devotion for all eternity. But there were awful, unrelenting obstacles standing between us. His dead wife. My new job. His grief. My fear.

He reached around me, inserted a key into the lock. More angry than apologetic, he rasped, "For the record, you've ruined me, too."

Cole

"What the hell, bro?" I peeled my face off the mat and rolled to my back, a furnace boiling just below my skin. I didn't bother testing my left eye. The swelling would seal my lid shut in a matter of minutes anyway.

Ellis dropped to his knees and tossed his gloves. "You're off your game." Leaning over me, he inspected my face. "Sorry, dude. Shit."

He poked. I swatted his hand away.

In the two and a half decades I'd known Ellis, he'd only landed one punch to my mug, and that was the night of Prom, eleven years and hundreds of fights ago, and only then because I'd been shitfaced and jumped naked into the wrong bed, with the wrong girlfriend, while Ellis had been showing her the wonders of oral.

Good times.

I rolled to a sitting position, and the room took on a life of its own, swirling and distorting. Yeah. Horizontal was the better option.

L.O.V.E.

My head hit the mat. Ellis jumped to his feet, jogged out of sight, then came back with an ice pack and played doting mom while I breathed through the wave of nausea.

"I knew you were in no condition, man. What the fuck was I thinking?" He squatted next to me. "We should get you to the doc, get that eye checked out."

"I'm fine."

"Head injuries are nothing to—"

"Jesus, you didn't hit me that hard!" I laughed. Couldn't help myself. God, I loved this guy. "And what the hell do you mean I'm in no condition?"

With a huff, he dropped his head, roughed a hand through his sweaty hair, then lifted worried eyes. "You haven't been yourself for a long time, dude. That's all I'm saying."

Truth. Couldn't argue. So I didn't.

"I miss him." Ellis scratched his chin.

I hated him. "So do I."

"We haven't talked about the accident."

And we never would because I hated lying to anyone, especially Ellis. Martin had betrayed me in the worst way, but that would remain between me and God. Ellis deserved to have nothing but good memories of our longtime best friend.

"Cole." He blinked, shoulders slumped. "I love and respect the hell out of you, so I'm not gonna beat around the bush."

Aw, fuck. I threw an arm over my throbbing face. I couldn't take that look. I couldn't take seeing him distraught. Not for me.

"He was our friend. Our brother. But he was a bastard eighty percent of the time. And if he and Vic were…" He cleared his throat. "If they were…"

Jesus. Fuck. He knew. "Yes! Yes! They were!" My guts coiled. I was not ready for this conversation. I rolled to hands and knees. Pushed to a stand. "I miss them. I really fucking miss them. But, God, I fucking hate them." The ice pack hit the wall with a disappointing thud. "They were fucking behind my back. Now they're dead. End of story."

"Cole."

I made for the locker room.

"Wait, goddammit!"

A heavy hand landed on my shoulder, and everything inside of me turned red hot, molten, boiling over. I twisted free of his grip. Turned. Landed one on his jaw.

My beast of a best friend barely flinched, and I hadn't held back.

Eyes liquid and red, he growled, "Do it again."

So I did. I gave him everything I had. A left jab. A straight right to the gut.

Ellis stumbled back but didn't bow. "Again!"

"No!" Came an angry voice from behind. "Ellis Keaton Chambers. Go get yourself cleaned up right this second," Lacey whisper-yelled, holding the baby tight to her chest.

The change was comical—beast to teddy bear in a blink.

Shaking his head, he shoved past me, grumbled, "You're gonna have to talk to me eventually," and disappeared.

"And you." Lacey aimed a pointed finger my way. "Get your shit together. He's given you time to grieve, but he's hurting, too. He lost someone, too." She stepped closer, smelling sweet but sounding bitter. "You still have each other, so help each other."

The firecracker dropped a blue bag at my feet, mumbling under her breath. "*Puta madre.* Acting like stupid little boys." Again with a finger in my face. "I'm late

215

to pick up Natalie, and you're in here fighting like scrapyard dogs." More words in Spanish.

Slowly, I registered that she'd mentioned Natalie's name. Like a scolded child, I stood absorbing her ire. Then, she shoved the chubby, bundled baby into my sweaty arms. "Linda is waiting for me in the car. I have to go. Tell Ellis I'll be home in a couple of hours. There are bottles in the diaper bag." She turned to leave, then turned back, kissed her son on the forehead. More Spanish. A glare. "If I come home and my husband's face looks anything like yours does right now, I'm going to hurt you, Cole Adams."

With that, she stormed out the front door.

Leon's face scrunched, then he let out a mighty wail. I got busy with the hush, hush, rock, rock. When that didn't work, I hollered for Ellis. He didn't come. I remembered finding Natalie singing to him on the day of the baptism. She'd looked every bit the goddess, and a natural. I'd stood in the doorway, imagined her singing to our baby, and that thought had damn near killed me.

Leon continued to cry. When Ellis finally came out from the locker room, showered and dressed, he found me, ass to the floor, crying right along with his son.

There were no words for the loss we both suffered. Regardless, I confessed. "I'm so fucking tired of hating them."

Ellis took his son. I couldn't look him in the eye, but I clapped his shoulder and made my way upstairs.

Under the heavy spray of hot water, I cussed and screamed and yelled. Then, I fell to my knees and gave every vile, hateful thought to God because I wasn't strong enough to hold them anymore.

"You're coming by later, right?" Ellis asked, his voice hopeful but unsteady over the phone.

What Ellis asked seemed impossible, but I wanted nothing more than to get away from the barrage of condolences. *How are you holding up, son? I'm sorry for your loss. Holidays are always the hardest.*

I'd heard them all fucking day.

"I'm not sure."

He released a breath. "Listen. Got a bottle of whiskey from Dad. Cards are ready."

That was the kicker. Thanksgiving tradition dictated we ended our evenings with Cubans, whiskey, and a game of poker. Me, Ellis, and Martin. For the past six years.

I stuck my fork into my second slice of apple pie.

As if reading my mind, he said, "C'mon, man. Don't make me do this alone."

"Yeah. Right. Sorry. I'll be there."

I finished my dessert, then made my way to the kitchen, kissed Mom on the cheek, and snatched the dirty platter from her fingers. "I'll finish up here. Go join the others."

"You wash, I'll dry." She moved away, shaking her head, and pulled a towel out of the drawer. "I can't listen to another one of your uncle's dirty holiday jokes. Who're you hiding from?"

Everyone. "If I have to hear about Auntie Dot's diverticulitis again, I might shoot myself."

Mom bent over in laughter. "I know. I know. Bless her heart."

God, that smile. Precious. After Cadence passed, Dad and I feared we'd never see her face light up again. We survived that death. I could survive another.

Sharing small talk, we finished the dishes. When the last of the holiday china was put away, she pulled me into a tight embrace. "You did good tonight."

I hated every second. "I wash a mean pan."

"Sweetie." Mom pushed away but held my arms in a firm grip. "This is your first holiday after the accident. I know it has to be hard."

Defenses up, I snapped, "You didn't even like Victoria, Mom."

Her eyes glistened, but she mirrored my glare. "I loved her because you loved her."

"But you didn't like her."

"Honey." Mom backed away and leaned against the counter, arms crossed. "We don't have to talk about this now."

"I need to talk about it." I needed Mom's grace.

She nodded. Sniffed. Straightened her spine. "Your dad and I never thought she was the right fit. There isn't much more to it than that."

"Bullshit."

"Okay, fine." With a huff, she turned to ready the Keurig. "You doted over her. Gave her everything she wanted. You were always trying to please her, and that's a wonderful quality, sweetheart. It is, but..." Silence. A deep inhale.

"But what?" I stood at her side, snagged two holiday mugs off the high shelf.

"Do you remember what you told me when you first met Victoria?"

"No."

"You told me you'd tried to turn down her advances, let her down gently, but then she'd told you about her abuse. Do you remember?"

Fuck. I remembered. First her uncle, then her last two boyfriends before me.

Mom continued. "After that, you never left her side."

"What does that have to do with anything?"

"Your girlfriend before Vic, what was her name?" Mom lifted a finger to her mouth, stared out the window, and then said, "Jocelyn."

Jocelyn Garcia. We'd lasted nine months before she'd dumped me with no explanation. "I don't understand where you're going with this, Mom."

She rolled her gorgeous eyes, grabbed a mug out of my hand, smirked. "She'd lost her mother a week before you met her, right?"

"Yes." I headed to the fridge to grab creamer.

"And the girlfriend before her?"

"Had a broken leg when we met," I answered, my nerves shot. "Are you saying I'm attracted to damaged women?" I shut the door too hard, bottles and jars clinking.

"Oh, God, no." She waved her hand in the air, then rested it over her heart. "You wanted to save them." She dropped her gaze to the tile floor, swallowed, met my eyes again. "You couldn't save your sister, honey. You tried to make up for that loss by helping those women."

Mom wasn't entirely off the mark. Wasn't easy to admit, though. I was about to tell her so, but she continued.

"You rarely smiled or laughed with Victoria. You were always so serious and focused. Too worried about keeping her happy."

"That a bad thing?"

"No." Mom reached up to cup my face. "You've got a beautiful spirit, my boy, and a smile that brightens everyone's day. And it killed me to watch that brilliant light of yours dim."

L.O.V.E.

Mom wouldn't talk ill of my dead wife, and she'd said too much already, guilt evident in the quiver of her lips and the shimmer in her eyes.

"I want you to be happy. To be with someone who makes you happy without having to work at it." She shoved a hot mug of coffee my way. "You're going to have an epic love story. I've known that since before you were born."

Cue the eye roll. "No, Mom. Not with that story again."

"Fine." She laughed, poured a hearty dose of Baileys into her coffee, then mine. "But it's true. Your grandfather knew it. I know it. Your soulmate is out there, and when the time is right, you'll know."

Relieving mom of her drink and anymore uncomfortable truths, I pulled her into a hug and whispered into her hair, "Thanks, Mom. I love you."

"Love you more."

"I'm gonna say my goodbyes and head to Ellis and Lacey's."

A full glass of Glenfiddich sat untouched in Martin's empty spot at the table.

Cigar smoke poisoned the air.

Unwanted memories stifled the mood.

Ellis, unusually quiet, couldn't keep his eyes off the door.

Upstairs, Natalie and Lacey laughed, and danced by the sounds of their footsteps and the low bass thumping through the floorboards overhead. I envied their joy.

Martin wasn't at the table, but his presence was stifling, choking all pleasure from the game.

Ellis was the first to state the obvious. "This feels like a betrayal. Playing without him."

"Betrayal?" I huffed. "Shitty choice of words."

"Sorry." He slammed his cards on the table. Scraped his fingers over his scalp. "Fuck."

"I think we should bury this tradition along with Martin." The words tasted sour. So I snatched the tumbler we'd filled for our dead friend, downed half the glass, the burn exquisite, then shoved the remainder Ellis's way.

Eyes liquid, he stared at the whiskey. His throat moved. He took the drink, his glare dark and tortured, swallowed the rest of the amber liquid, and then threw the glass against the wall, the shatter unsatisfying.

Ellis pushed from the table and paced the small room, hands to hips.

One by one, carefully constructed walls of ice shielded my battered psyche.

"I loved him. But he doesn't deserve to be here. Doesn't deserve a place of honor at our table. Not after what he did to you."

Stone still, guarded, I allowed Ellis his release.

"I was stupid to think we could do this." He stopped in front of me. Crossed his arms. "I'm sorry, brother."

My chest caved, but through that wall of ice, I mumbled, "Me, too." And I meant those words. "I've been caught up in my own shit. I haven't considered your suffering. I've been a shitty friend, and I'm sorry."

He moved around the table, poured two more shots. "To new traditions?"

We raised our glasses.

It hit me then that any new traditions would include Lacey. As they should. Envy embittered my already sour mood. I wanted what they had. "New traditions," I acquiesced, downing my drink in one swallow. Fighting the urge to hit something, I said, "Besides, you suck at poker anyway."

L.O.V.E.

Ellis only laughed. "Maybe we should join the ladies."

The ladies. God, I'd been itching to see Natalie's sweet face all night.

We headed upstairs, leaving the smoky basement and Martin's ghost behind.

Natalie and Lacey sat on the floor on opposite sides of the coffee table, a display of ridiculously large cards on the table between them. The baby slept bundled in a Seahawks blanket on the couch, down for the count.

"Go fish!" Natalie threw her arms up and then pointed at Lacey, wiggling in a happy dance, her red glasses falling down her nose. The air seemed thinner, and I forced slow breaths. In—one, two, three, four. Out—one, two, three, four. I reached into my pocket for the gold that was no longer there, my agitation rising again. But I focused on Natalie, the silver in her eyes more precious than the metal I'd lost. The shy smile she flashed before looking away more soothing than my missing charm.

"What's going on up here?" Ellis asked, curling up behind his wife.

"Go Fish," Lacey said, arching her neck to kiss Ellis.

"It's our Thanksgiving tradition," Natalie threw in, righting her glasses. She scooted to the left. "Want to join us?"

Ellis and I exchanged glances. He shrugged, shooting me a *why not?* gesture.

"Sure," I mumbled, thankful for the alcohol in my veins. I wouldn't survive the evening without liquid aid to dull the jagged edges.

"Perfect." Natalie clapped her hands together and hopped to her feet, snatching her wine glass. "I need a refill. Anyone else?"

"One more for me," Lacey sang.

Ellis hugged his wife. "Water for me, please."

"Cole?" she asked over her shoulder on her way to the kitchen.

"Yeah," I answered on reflex, "I'll have a drink."

That cursed, invisible string between us tensed, drawing me closer, and I followed behind, focused on the sway of her hips. My balls tightened. Chest constricted. Hands curled into fists.

Unsettling how much I wanted this woman.

She stopped at the counter. Lifted a bottle to fill her glass.

Mind numb, body reacting to her witchery, I closed the distance between us and lifted the Barolo from her fingers, placing it out of reach.

Natalie turned.

I pinned her to the counter, my loafers bracing her bare feet. Hands to her cheeks, I ducked, claiming that sinful mouth, stealing her precious breath. Sweet and fruity. God, she tasted too good.

Her tense body softened. Her tongue met mine and, sweet hell, she kissed me back with all the softness I lacked.

My life hung in the balance. Natalie held the string.

Cold fingers found their way under my shirt, dancing along my heated skin before digging grooves down my ribcage. She rose on her toes like she wanted to climb my body.

Cupping her ass, I pulled her closer, ground my hips, and sucked on her tongue.

Natalie whimpered, fucking whimpered, going boneless in my arms, and I lost control, instinct taking over. My only conscious thought—burying myself in Natalie King.

My cell rang. I ignored the wretched tone.

Natalie pulled away. I gripped the back of her head and brought her back to my mouth.

The ringing continued.

Natalie brought her palms to my chest and pushed.

"No," I growled, holding her steady.

"Cole," she protested into my mouth.

That fucking incessant ringing.

Natalie pushed again, her rejection crushing.

I bit her bottom lip, pinching her flesh between my teeth, ensuring she couldn't pull away. Couldn't leave me.

But she did.

"Goddammit, Cole. Stop," she said, slapping my chest and jerking back.

Her chest rose and fell. Worried eyes met mine. Her tongue made a slow drag across her bottom lip, and she winced.

Good. I wanted her pain. Wanted to kiss her better. I wanted everything.

The ringing stopped, then started again.

"Fuck," I mumbled, yanking the cell from my pocket. I looked at the screen. Guilt washed clean my lust haze.

"Everly, hi."

Natalie's head whipped up, her blush darkening.

"Cole? Honey?" Sobs came across the line.

Victoria's mother hadn't reached out to me once since the funeral, despite my calls and frequent attempts at visiting.

"Everything okay?" Agitation balled in my gut.

"I can't. I can't. Oh, God. I miss my baby so much."

"Yeah. Yeah, me, too," I said out of habit.

Natalie pushed me away, much harder than before, and I stumbled back, catching my balance too late to grab her before she fled.

"Cole. I'm sorry. I'm a mess and I just..." Everly continued, but I couldn't hear a word.

Natalie shoved her feet into her boots and before I reached her, she was shrugging into her jacket.

Lacey asked, "What happened?"

Ellis stood, arms crossed, glaring my direction.

Sobs and a shrill voice pierced my ear.

Natalie turned to her friend, ignoring me. "I need to go. I'll call you in the morning."

She couldn't leave. "Natalie, wait!"

"Natalie? Who's Natalie?" came through the speaker, loud enough for everyone to hear.

"Everly. Give me a moment."

"Everly?" Lacey clapped a hand to her chest. "Oh, Nat Brat."

I shoved the phone back into my pocket. "Natalie, what happened?" I reached for my girl, my saving grace.

She dodged my hand.

"Please don't go."

"I have to."

"Why?"

"Because." She pointed to my pocket. "Even from her grave, she's trying to ruin me." One tear let loose, and she quickly swiped it away.

I wasn't sure how to process her comment. Conscience had dictated I take the call from my dead wife's mother. "That's not fair."

"I can't do this, Cole. I'm sorry."

She was leaving. Again. Rage erupted so fast and furious I didn't have a chance to keep it in check. My fist met the wall. An ungodly pain shot up my wrist. Natalie screamed. Ellis braced his arms around me and twisted, forcing me away from the women.

L.O.V.E.

A strange noise filled the vast room, long and loud and full of anguish. It was my voice, my lungs straining, my soul releasing months of poisonous fury.

Ellis held tight, not letting me fall.

When the storm cleared and my head stopped buzzing, Natalie was gone.

15

Natalie

I lay between Mom and Dad, my head on Mom's lap, my feet tucked under Dad's thigh. We'd spent the morning drinking too much coffee and eating too many Christmas cookies. It was good to be home, but I missed my Lacey Lu something fierce. I couldn't remember the last Christmas I'd spent without her.

We stared at the big screen. Watched Will Ferrell pour syrup on spaghetti and laughed until our stomachs hurt.

When the movie was over, Mom gave my hip a slap. "What time are you heading to Lacey's house?"

"I'm not going to their dinner party," I said, pulling the blanket tighter under my chin.

"What?" Mom squeaked.

Dad snorted, then shifted, leaving my feet exposed and cold. "What's the matter? You not feeling well?"

"I feel fine." I shrugged. "I would rather hang out with you guys today."

L.O.V.E.

Cold fingers clamped over my forehead. "You don't feel hot. Is it your period?"

"Mom!" I swatted her hand away, then swung my feet to the floor. "No. I just don't want to be around a bunch of people today."

"Cole won't be there," Dad said, pointing the remote at the television.

"Dad!"

"Just sayin'. If he's the reason you're not going to see your very best friend and your godson, then you're staying home for no reason."

I turned to face my father, but he didn't return the courtesy. "How do you know Cole won't be there?"

"He's in New York."

"How do you know that?"

Click. Click. He raced through channels. "We bump into each other now and then."

"So you're buddies now?"

"I wouldn't say that." He smiled. "But the kid has one helluva golf swing."

Unbelievable.

"Ugh. Dad. What are you doing?" I threw my arms over my face.

"He's your best friend's husband's best friend. That makes him your friend-in-law. He's practically family." Dad huffed and finally turned my way, his brows knitted. "I thought you loved the guy."

"I fell in love with him on accident."

"Nothing is an accident," Mom piped in.

"And then I moved away. To get away from him. Because he was getting married!"

"He isn't married anymore," Dad said, looking truly perplexed.

"Because his wife is dead. And might I remind you, she was my mortal enemy."

Mom's turn again. "Might I remind you that if it weren't for Victoria, Cole wouldn't have come back to Seattle."

"That's true." Dad gave Mom a high five over my head. "You never would have met him."

"Oh. My. God. Why am I having this conversation with you guys right now?" I stood, aimed my ire at Mom. "And why are you on his side? What happened with the Caleb lore and all that destiny mumbo jumbo?"

"Oh, my God, honey. I just remembered something." Mom sprinted up the stairs.

Dad eased off the couch, groaning louder than usual, and turned off the television. He limped to the stereo and pressed *Play*.

Adding salt to my wound, Nat King Cole's version of "The Christmas Song" played in surround sound.

I dropped my head back in surrender. Dad came my way, wrapped me in his arms, and sung along while he spun me around the living room, paper crinkling under our feet.

"Nat King Cole." He laughed. "Natalie King and Cole. What are the odds?"

I only refrained from smacking my dad because he was the freakin' bomb. And even grown up girls needed their father's arms once in a while. I missed our impromptu dances and his incessant teasing.

When Mom returned, panting and wild-eyed, she slapped a photo into my hand. "Fate!"

"What?"

I looked down at the fading image. Mom was holding a brand spanking new baby—me, obviously. Next to her sat a woman, also holding a brand spanking new baby. Both women were smiling. I slept, my lips pursed, and the other baby's face was hidden in the mother's chest.

L.O.V.E.

"Who is that?"

"That's him." She pointed at the baby as if that would answer my question.

"Him, who?"

"Caleb. Your soulmate. I found the picture when I was rummaging through the attic the other day."

Mom studied the photo, wonder and tears filling her hazel eyes. "Her father-in-law was so happy to be a grandfather. So happy. That man whistled or sang every time he walked through the hospital." She looked at Dad with a twisted grin. "Tell your Nugget what song that was, honey."

Dad chuckled, his arms still around me. "Nat King Cole's 'L-O-V-E.'"

Of course, it was.

I was done. Rising to my toes, I landed a kiss on Dad's cheek, then Mom's, then headed toward my room.

"Where are you going?"

"I'm going to Lacey's."

"Take one of those pies with you," Mom shouted, though I was only down the short hall. "I baked too many pies."

"Not the apple pie," Dad yelled. "That's mine."

"Oh, and some of that—" The slamming bedroom door cut off their teasing.

My room hadn't changed much since I'd moved out five years ago. Still the same bright turquoise bed frame. Patchwork quilt. Too many bed pillows. Pink and fuchsia striped walls. My Maroon 5 and Nick Jonas posters had been swapped out for antiqued, white trellis mirrors in different shapes and sizes and my Ikea dresser and nightstand had been upgraded to Pottery Barn sophistication.

Off with the candy cane leggings and baggy sweater, on with the sweater dress, tights, and boots.

Mascara. Lip gloss. Hair fluff. Good to go.

Mom swayed in Dad's arms when I came back out, her cheek to his chest, his lips in her hair. "Baby It's Cold Outside" playing on the stereo.

For a moment, I watched in awe and wonder of their connection, my heart aching for the same. Then I snapped a pic.

My phone buzzed. A text from the one and only Caleb, my new ridiculously handsome and sweet supervisor, whom I hadn't mentioned to my parents for obvious reasons.

Merry Christmas. Enjoy UR family. Get some rest. I need my star player on the field to start our new year with a bang.

I liked that Caleb texted me. But his communications didn't give me tingles.

I scrolled through my contacts and pulled up all the texts Cole had sent me since Thanksgiving. One a day, at least, apologizing. All of them short and sweet. Not once, though, had he asked me to answer his calls or call him back. He gave but asked for nothing in return.

On my way out the door, Dad shouted, "Hey, did you get the invite to your uncle's retirement party next month?"

"I did."

"Will you be able to make it?"

I looked over my shoulder. "Of course, I will."

"Good. You're his favorite niece. It'd break his heart if you couldn't come."

"I'm his only niece," I shouted, closing the door before they could continue.

"Oh, Nat Brat." Lacey threw her arms around me. "I'm so happy you came."

L.O.V.E.

"I made it."

"Hey, Beautiful." Ellis strolled out of the kitchen and planted a kiss on my head.

"Merry Christmas." I handed Lacey the pies, then snatched the baby out of Ellis's arms and slapped my keys in his palm.

"Presents are in the trunk. Do you mind?"

His deep chuckle was intoxicating. "Of course." He gave Lacey's ass a squeeze before jogging out the door.

I sighed, their affection swoon-worthy, then settled onto the sofa for cuddle time. The large Craftsman style home looked like a horde of drunk elves had thrown a rave. Every wall, window, and shelf was adorned with twinkling lights, garland, and Christmas cheer. Atop the tree sat an angel dressed in white. Lacey's prized possession, passed down from her grandmother, to her mother, and then to Lacey.

"It smells like cinnamon rolls in here."

"Been baking all day." Lacey fell into the cushion next to me and brushed soft strokes over Leon's head. "Dinner's almost ready. Ellis's parents will be here in a bit."

"He's perfect," I said, staring at the gorgeous baby. "Absolute perfection."

"I know." She swiped a tear from my cheek. "How are you doing? We've hardly talked since Thanksgiving."

"Been busy. My boss handed me the lead on two major accounts."

"That's great, but you know I don't want to hear about work. What's up with the men in that town? I heard Idaho breeds some of the prettiest people in the Northwest."

"It's true." I winked. "Must be all the fresh air."

The baby smiled up at me and, oh, sweet Lord, my heart. "You keep that up, little lady-killer, I might marry the next man I see just so I can make babies of my own."

232

Lacey laughed. Leon cooed.

"So? No mountain men banging down your door?"

"Absolutely no banging whatsoever." I refrained from mentioning all the dates I'd turned down. That was between me and my broken heart.

"I don't believe you for a second." Lacey leaned closer, gripped my wrist. "Is it Cole? Is that why you're not dating?"

Scary how well she knew me.

"Just been busy, Lulu," I sighed. "Trying to rule the world."

Wise, brown eyes searched mine, unconvinced. "What about that boss of yours?"

"He's remained strictly professional. Though I have caught him staring at me on more than one occasion." And he had a killer dimple, I left unsaid. Every damn time he grinned, I was reminded of Cole. "Not that it matters. I would never date someone I work with, especially a supervisor."

The door swung open, the bang echoing through their massive home. Ellis stumbled in under a mountain of shopping bags overstuffed with pretty packages.

"Oh, honey." Lacey pushed from the couch, laughing. "Let me help."

"We got it, sweetheart." He nodded over his shoulder. "Look who came home early."

Behind Ellis came another tumbling display of bright presents donned with ribbons and bows. A stuffed bear fell out of one bag, and a denim clad leg lifted to catch the toy on the top of his booted foot. He balanced. Hobbled. Caught his balance again.

"Cole!" Lacey ran to the rescue and snatched the toy, then one bag from his arms before rising on her toes to kiss his cheek.

L.O.V.E.

My skin prickled, and I lifted the baby to my shoulder, certain the chubby little angel could shield me from such cruel beauty.

Cole stood, arms full, face red from the cold, taller and broader than when I'd seen him last. He smirked at something Ellis said and scanned the room, his mirth faltering when he spotted me on the sofa.

"Natalie." His gaze softened, a slow melt like brown sugar stirred into warm butter, sweet and decadent, and making my mouth water.

"Hey," I managed, though casual seemed an insult. He'd been inside me. He'd held my heart in his fist and squeezed the bloody thing dry before I'd snatched it back. Yet, when he looked at me that way, there wasn't a thing in the world I wouldn't lay at his feet, my battered heart included.

What a dangerous predicament. The man only lost his wife a few months ago. His emotions couldn't be trusted any more than mine.

Ellis dropped his load of bags by the Christmas tree, then relieved Cole of his bundles.

"I thought you weren't coming home until after New Year's," Lacey said, pushing Cole to the left so she could close the door.

He grunted a response that I couldn't make out, and Lacey's eyes widened. She shot me a glance, then shared a conspiratorial, wordless communication with Ellis.

Cole hadn't stopped staring, our gazes locked in a painful, yet necessary, exchange. Certain that everyone could hear the thump, thump, thump in my chest, and afraid of giving away my unstable state of emotions, I blurted, "I think the little guy needs a new diaper," and made a mad dash for the nursery.

Leon's diaper wasn't soiled, but I changed him anyway, stalling. Searching for my backbone. Cole was downstairs.

Cole had trimmed his hair and shaved, and the dark ghosts no longer haunted his eyes.

Cole still had the power to break me.

My godson started to cry. I swaddled him and moved to the window. Lacey's view was almost as nice as mine. Where she had the city skyline in the distance, my condo boasted a view of Lake Willow and the surrounding mountains.

Leon fussed, so I bounced and hummed while watching the rain fall from dark clouds, and soon the little angel was sound asleep, his weight heavy and fulfilling in my arms.

The door opened and closed behind me. No need to look. Soul deep, I recognized his aura, my body buzzing, coming alive.

"Merry Christmas, Natalie." Cold fingers brushed the hair from my neck. Warm lips grazed the sensitive spot below my ear, melting me skin to bone, leaving me warm and gooey, and wanting.

"Cole," left my lips on a soft plea when I should've moved away or told him not to touch me that way. He had no right, yet nothing had ever felt so damn right.

He moved around me and stole the infant from my arms, his dimples popping as he took a good look at the boy, *and oh, God*, my legs turned to wet noodles at the sight. He cradled Leon like he was the most precious gift. When he kissed the little button nose, I almost fainted, the rush of hormones maddening and flooding my body with heat.

Before the moment passed, I slipped my phone out of my bra and snapped a pic.

"What's with you and the pictures?" he asked, his focus still on Leon. "You don't post on social media. I checked."

Tucking my cell away, I admitted, "I take one a day of something that makes me happy."

L.O.V.E.

His broad shoulders stretched under his black sweater as he laid the baby in the crib, drawing my attention to his slim waist and round, tight ass.

Was there anything more appealing than a man caring for a child?

Dimples. Dimples were better, especially the two aimed my way. Cole turned on the baby monitor, grabbed my hand, and pulled me into the hallway. The second the door closed, Cole spun me until my back was to the wall. He captured my face in both palms, and his tongue darted out to wet his lips before he hit me with a toe-curling kiss.

There was not one single moment when I hesitated, or questioned, or recoiled. When we were joined, there wasn't room for wariness, there was just us, heart and soul, the rest of the world a canvas for us to paint our future.

Cole pulled away, panting, and adjusted his crotch. I was thankful for the solid wall to hold me steady.

The doorbell rang. Guests were arriving.

"I missed you," he rasped, devouring me with a heated gaze.

"Me, too," I whispered.

"Stay with me tonight."

"I can't," I said, though my words held no conviction.

"Why?" The bastard smirked. He knew he had me.

So many reasons. I hadn't shaved. My Jockey undergarments were made for comfort, not sexy time. I hadn't found a gym since moving to Whisper Springs, and I'd had a torrid affair with the buffalo burgers at my favorite diner. Cole wouldn't care what I wore. The ten pounds I'd gained wouldn't matter. But having him and leaving him again would destroy me. I could have given him any excuse. Instead, I whispered, "You know why."

To which he responded, "Only thing I know is that the world feels right when you're with me."

Oh, my heart. I was doomed. "One night," I conceded, then to shield my battered soul said, "Our last night. We can't keep doing this."

"Yes, we can."

"Cole, please. Stop."

"Stop what?" He planted his palms on either side of my head, leaning close, brushing his nose over mine. "Stop wanting you? Impossible." A soft kiss to my cheek. "Stop dreaming about you?" Another kiss, another cheek. "Missing you?" He bit my earlobe, his breaths heavy. "Hearing your voice, seeing your face every night when I close my eyes?" He kissed my neck, my chin, my nose, everywhere but my lips, driving me mad. "Stop feeling ill with regret? 'Cause that will never happen."

"There you are." Ellis stood at the top of the stairs, trying and failing to hide his amusement. "I'm ready to crack open that bottle of Blue. Can't toast without you guys."

"Blue?" I asked, still clinging to the wall, thankful for a change in conversation.

"Johnnie Walker Blue. A wedding gift from Cole. Been waiting for the right time." He shrugged. "No better time than now. My best friend is here. Lacey's best friend is here." Ellis came between us, hooked a beefy arm around each of our shoulders and guided us back down to the party.

We toasted. We ate a delicious dinner and too much dessert. We said our goodnights hours later, and I followed Cole home.

Cole's small apartment was dark, the streetlight outside offering enough of a warm glow to navigate the sparsely furnished room.

He tossed his keys onto a small table near the door and shrugged out of his coat before helping me out of mine.

I moved deeper inside his home, made my way to the large window. Traffic was light on the street below, but I could feel the rumble, hear the buzz. "I miss the city noise sometimes."

When he said nothing, I turned to find him standing across the room, hands in his pockets, head tilted in contemplation.

He dropped his gaze to the floor, kicked at something on the hardwood. "Why didn't you return my calls or texts?"

There was no room for lies. "It's too easy to loose myself in you, Cole. I can't afford to do that right now."

Chin down, he raised his gaze. "I can find a million things wrong with that statement."

"And I was embarrassed by the way I left on Thanksgiving."

"You did the right thing." He raked both hands through his hair, then clasped his fingers behind his head. "I wasn't in a good place."

"I heard Everly's name, and I panicked. All those horrible memories came rushing back, and I..." God, I'd used Victoria's mother as an excuse to bolt. Truth was, I'd been terrified. Of my feelings. Of feeling *more*. Worried that I'd made the wrong decision to move away. Scared that moving away had been the right choice and maybe Mom was right, that I had a soulmate named Caleb out in the world somewhere, waiting for me, and that Cole, and all the vast, ridiculous feels I had for him, were just a chapter in my life, a stepping stone, a soon-to-be fond memory.

What a terrifying thought. I wanted to voice my concerns, but the words wouldn't form.

With a huff, he dropped his arms and stepped closer. "Tell me there's still hope for us. That we can be something other than nothing."

He should've been my everything.

I had no answer. None that would change our immediate circumstances.

Cole nodded as if he understood my silence. "Well, then. We better not waste this night." One deep breath. Three long strides. Two strong hands tilted my face to meet his mouth in a crushing kiss that broke too soon.

He knelt, and one by one, helped me out of my boots.

While still on the floor, he gripped my thighs, and with heavy breaths, slid his hands under my dress to the top of my tights, then rolled them down. My panties came next while I stood shivering under his touch.

He raised my hem higher, laid kisses on my belly, my hips, and then between my legs, where I needed his kiss the most.

Deft fingers. Talented tongue. Ravenous lips. I fisted his hair and held tight, his moans erotic, his ministrations devout, my pleasure swirling, swelling, consuming. When he nipped my clit, my knees buckled.

Cole laughed, easing the tension, then rose, hoisting me over his shoulder, my bare ass in the air. Before I caught my breath, he tossed me onto the bed.

Before I could ditch my dress, he was over me, then inside me, his clothes still on.

I didn't care.

Frantic worked.

Heavy breathing. Hard pounding. Teeth clashing. Dirty declarations. We were desperate; we were crazed. *We* worked. My orgasm was fast and furious, but that didn't matter because before the tremors subsided, Cole was stripping off his clothes and then my dress.

With maddening leisure, he tasted every inch of my skin. I touched him everywhere I could reach, trembling and panting and coiling tight. Cole was on my skin and in my lungs, the drum in every heartbeat, and I wanted more, more, more... *Oh, God.*

I wanted not to crave him. I wanted not to love him. Not to ache so desperately for his smile. I wanted to fuck him out of my system. Slow and steady was for long-time lovers. We were part-time fuck buddies at best.

I pushed Cole and ordered him to lie on his back.

His skin was hot, his face flushed, his lips swollen, and I claimed that sinful mouth while I mounted him, and then bit his lip as I sank down over his thick erection.

Oh fuck, the way he filled me. Too much. Never enough. I rolled my hips, clawed his chest. I rose and fell, kissed and bit and ground against him. Cole tried to ease my pace. Fuck slow. Slow allowed room for emotions.

Selfishly, I rode the man. When I came again and collapsed onto his chest, he held me, stroked my back, kissed my head, rolled me over.

Cole then broke my heart, making love to me, taking me tender and slow.

He kissed my tears away. He brought me to the peak again, that time coming with me, and we lay tangled, talking and laughing and pretending tomorrow would not bring another goodbye.

"Spend a few days with me," he whispered, stroking my thigh.

"No," came my knee-jerk response. "We can't keep doing this."

His lips landed on my forehead, warming my soul. "We can do whatever we want, sunshine."

I couldn't respond. Leaving hurt too much.

"We're supposed to be together. Haven't you figured that out by now?" He pulled me closer. "It's fate," he mumbled, voice sleepy.

I was beginning to hate that word. "Fate is bullshit," I whispered into the dark.

He chuckled, his chest vibrating.

A wave of anger crashed over me. "It's not funny, Cole." I rolled to face him. "It's bullshit. All of it. If fate was on our side, we would've met before *her*. If fate was on our side, I wouldn't live in another state. I wouldn't get to touch you only once every couple of months. Don't you get it? All the shit that's happened since we met? Fate is cruel, vindictive. She's punishing us for what we did."

With a curse, he was over me, his hips between my thighs. He cupped my face with trembling fingers. "What did we do, Natalie? Tell me, what did we do but try to fight this thing between us?"

"I wanted you when it was wrong." Guilt spilled down my cheeks, wetting his fingers.

"We fought it. You moved away. I married the monster. We did the right thing. We fought. So what does fate have to punish us for?"

I shook my head. Against his reason. Against the emotion. Against the unbearable, biting pain in my chest.

Cole rose from the bed and headed to the bathroom. I rolled over, contemplating an escape. On his nightstand sat a short crystal vase stuffed with red peonies. Heart meet steamroller.

Footsteps. The mattress sank behind me.

L.O.V.E.

I couldn't hide the tremble in my voice when I asked, "Why do you have peonies?"

With one strong arm, he pulled me flush against his body. "You know why."

I didn't. Nothing made sense. "I don't understand."

"They're your favorite. And they bring life to this dull home."

My favorite. How did he know? Wiggling free of his heavy arm, I flipped to face him again. "You have to order them weeks in advance this time of year."

Oh, sweet Jesus, his dimples close up were mind numbing. "I have a standing order."

What man did such things? "Since when?"

He traced the curve of my hip with his fingers, glanced at the flowers, then back to me. "Since Leon's Baptism."

"Why?"

"Because I thought I'd never see the sun again, but there you stood, bright and feminine as a goddamn peony. My fucking sunshine." He laughed, licked his lips, then his smile disappeared. "They remind me to breathe when my chest gets too heavy. Help me remember the sun is still shining when I'm lost in the dark."

I stared at his lips, his gaze too potent, his confession breaking me in two.

Forehead to mine, he begged, "Please, stay until morning. I'll make you breakfast. We'll talk."

No hung on the tip of my tongue.

I hadn't the will to deny him, lacked the strength to say goodbye again.

I snuggled into his naked warmth.

When his body softened, melting into the mattress, I kissed his cheek and slipped out of bed. Before leaving, I dug the small wrapped box out of my handbag and placed it next to the vase on his nightstand.

"Merry Christmas," I whispered, then made my way home.

16

Natalie

No expense had been spared for my uncle's retirement party. The ballroom took my breath away. Square four-tiered crystal chandeliers dangled from the ceiling. Bronze paneled walls hid blue mood lights. Four mirrored columns framed the pristine white marble dance floor. I stood on the edge, watching guests sway and twirl to the live orchestra tucked in the corner of the massive room.

"Natalie." An arm came around my waist. "My favorite niece. How's the new job?" He dipped to accept a kiss on the cheek.

"Uncle Joe." I leaned into his embrace. "Love the job. Kicking ass and taking names."

"That's my girl." He looked out into the sea of moving bodies. "I'm so glad you're here."

A photographer floated around the ballroom, recording the festivities.

"Wouldn't have missed it for the—wait." My heart dropped three inches. "Why is Cole Adams here, and who is he dancing with?"

I studied the tall, curvy beauty in his arms. Dark hair fell in soft waves down her back. Small waist, ample bottom, long, toned legs. She moved effortlessly in a pair of—I ducked to get a better look—yep, Louboutin.

Cole held her intimately but not too close. But his smile. That rare, beautiful smile was all for her.

"Cole Adams?" Joe asked, his thick, white brows rising. "You know him?"

"Yes. We're friends-in-law," I said.

"What?"

"Never mind." I grabbed my uncle's wrist and begged, "Who's the woman?"

"Oh. That's—"

"Joe King," came a deep voice from a short man wearing too many gold rings and one infectious grin.

Joe laughed. Then men embraced. Introductions were made.

And just like that, my uncle left me standing like a jolly green jerk, elated to see the man I'd walked away from, deflated by the stunning woman in his arms, and so shamefully envious that she brought his dimples out to play.

"Here ya go sweetie. Barolo." Dad stood next to me, wine glass in one hand, whiskey neat in the other, looking sharp as ever in his new suit. "Who ya staring at?"

"Thanks." I retrieved my liquid courage from his hand, then pointed to the crowded dance floor.

"Oh great! Cole's here," Dad shouted. He slapped my back. "Small world, huh?"

I lifted the glass to my lips. I hadn't seen Cole since Christmas. Four weeks had passed since I'd left him sleeping in his bed. We'd texted. He'd called me at the stroke of midnight for New Year's. He'd kept the conversations short

L.O.V.E.

and sweet. *How was your day? I bought a new building yesterday. Your dad kicked my ass at squash. Leon puked all over my Brioni suit.*

Not once did he ask where I lived, or worked, or if I missed him. We never broached the subject of dating or when I'd be back in town. He never mentioned the gift. Every night, I fell asleep browsing the pictures of him on my phone.

"Who's here?" Mom cozied up to my left, the hem of her full skirt brushing against my bare leg.

"Cole Adams," Dad said, pointing, and then...*oh, shit.* Waving.

Yes. Waving.

We'd been spotted.

I had no choice but to stand wedged between my parents with a fake smile pasted on my face, choking on the bile rising in my throat while Cole came our way, his hand on the back of the woman at his side.

I studied the grooves in the white marble. How did they keep the floor so clean?

"Natalie."

Oh, God. That voice. Thick and warm, like melted caramel. I was toast. I couldn't look. I couldn't let them witness my crumbling dignity.

"Linda. Charles." Cole cleared his throat. "I'd like you to meet my mother, Felicia."

"Oh," I whispered, smiling, feeling ten thousand pounds lighter and one hundred percent the fool.

A horrid gasp came from my mother, so loud I jumped, spilling wine over my fingers, but not on my new Armani dress, thank you Jesus.

"Felicia?" Mom shoved her glass of wine into my free hand and threw her arms around Cole's mom.

246

Felicia laughed, then bellowed, "Linda? Is it really you?"

I met Cole's beautiful, dreamy eyes, all the more spellbinding under the blue lighting, and I knew I needed to fight the hypnotic pull, but I couldn't remember why.

Before I could say hi, or apologize for my mom's behavior, or peel the two women apart, Cole snatched the drinks from my hand, set them on the table behind him, and caught me in his arms, sweeping me back to the dance floor.

An old, airy tune played, and he pulled me close, cinching my waist with one arm, securing my hand with his other. He'd clearly had lessons because we swayed and twirled through the crowd, and even with my two left feet, we didn't so much as brush against another couple.

"What are you doing here?" I asked, breathless and so turned on by the friction between our bodies I could barely feel my legs.

"My dad and your uncle go way back. Remember?"

Oh, yes. I'd met his father on the street all those months ago.

His lips grazed my ear, eliciting a shiver. "And I knew you'd be here."

Heaven help me. I tripped, his voice, his confession making me dizzy. That strong arm of his held my weight, then tightened, securing our bodies.

On a twirl, I caught sight of our moms, now sitting at a table with their arms around each other, each of them dabbing tissues under their eyes.

"What do you suppose is happening between our mothers right now?"

"No clue," he said, his lips dangerously close to mine. "How have you been?"

I dodged, avoiding any accidental lips-locks. "Do you think we should find out how they know each other?"

"I don't want to talk about my mom while you're in my arms."

"Aren't you worried?" I stretched my neck to see over his shoulder. "What could they be talking about?"

He had the audacity to laugh. "They're planning our wedding. Plotting grandchildren."

"But they're—"

His lips covered mine in a hard, no-holds-barred kiss, those strong hands holding me rock solid against his steel frame in the middle of the dance floor in front of my uncle's family, friends, and colleagues.

Was everyone staring? *Oh, God*. I couldn't open my eyes. I couldn't move, breathe, or think straight because Cole held me like he owned me, claiming me in public for the world to see.

He broke the kiss. Solemn eyes met mine. "You're not kissing me back."

"I can't," I said, staring at his full lips.

"You want to."

God, those dimples. "It hurts too much when I have to stop."

"Because you want us as much as I do."

"Let's not talk about this right now. Not here." I pulled free and skirted through the crowd toward our mothers.

Mom's head was down, her face pressed close to Felicia's. When she saw me, she jumped to her feet. "Natalie."

Hiding my ebbing tears, I dodged the table. "Be right back, Mom." Like a coward—a lovesick coward—I headed toward the ladies room but instead smacked nose to chest into my Dad.

"Natalie," he said, voice stern, grip steady. "You need to hear this." He turned me to face Mom, and by the look on her face, I knew, undoubtably, that my life was about to take a major turn.

Cole now stood behind his mother, hand on her shoulder but all of his attention on me.

Mom and Felicia held hands. "Felicia is the woman from the hospital." Mom wiggled in her stilettos like an excited child. "From the day you were born. The photo. This is her."

"No."

Felicia nodded.

"No." I looked between the two women, then to Cole, then to my mother. "Mom. You said his name was Caleb."

"I got it wrong. I was in labor you know, then on pain pills, sleep deprived, and well...Cole. Caleb. Close enough."

I shot a questioning glance Cole's way. Dad squeezed my shoulders and whispered, "What do you know? Soulmates," before letting go.

The room faded into millions of blurry raindrops, the only clear point Cole's gorgeous face. "When is your birthday?"

"March first."

Same as mine.

"Where were you born?"

Brows pinched, he said, "Seattle."

"What hospital?"

"Seattle Memorial." He stepped closer. "Why?"

"I have to go."

"Wait. What's happening right now?"

I turned to flee but heard Felicia say, "Natalie is the baby I always told you about. From the day you were born."

L.O.V.E.

Cole

Natalie was the one.

My grandfather had told me so.

My mother had told me so.

The fates had just slapped me upside the head with that brilliant, well-timed gift.

She was the one, and she was running away.

Not again. Never again.

"Natalie, wait." I followed behind, far enough to give her space, close enough to keep her from disappearing. "Just wait a minute. Where the hell are you going?"

Slowing her pace, she said over her shoulder, "I need to think."

"What's there to think about?" She was mine. She'd always been mine.

She stopped so fast I damn near plowed her over. When she turned, we were toe to toe, and, fuck, if her aura didn't knock me off balance and rob my breath.

"What isn't there to think about?" She adjusted her glasses.

God, there was nothing cuter. The red frames matched her dress and her lipstick.

We stood impossibly close, but I shoved my hands into my pockets to refrain from touching. "How about for one goddamn minute we stop thinking about everything and enjoy this huge fucking revelation dropped into our laps? You know how many times I heard that story growing up? Told my mom she was crazy? Laughed it off?"

Natalie stared, long and hard, studying my features, then slumped. She took one step back, then another.

"You are not walking away from me again." I followed, matching her stride for stride. My guts knotted. Unnerving, that invisible string between us. "Don't run from this."

Still inching away, but letting me gain ground, she whispered, "This is crazy, Cole."

"Crazy or fate?"

"I can't leave my job," she whispered, her argument lackluster at best.

"I can't either."

She pursed her dewy red lips. Nodded. "So there we have it. What's the point of pursuing a relationship when we live in different states?"

"The point is...the point is..." The truth I'd buried deep rose from the depths of my sheltered spirit, a confession given wings. A deliverance. "I love you, Natalie King." I grabbed her shoulders, not to keep her from running, but to ground myself before I spiraled out of orbit. "I fell head over heels that day in the coffee shop. One look. One fucking look, and I fell. We connected. There was something there. Something greater than you and me, or Victoria, or Holden Oswald Travers the Third."

"God, I always hated that name," came a gruff voice from my left. Natalie's uncle landed a firm pat on my shoulder as he passed, drink in hand, swagger unsteady, his timing pretty damn spot on.

Natalie took advantage of the interruption, turning her face and swiping her cheek.

I ducked to catch her gaze, missing that connection. Her eyes on me? Fuck. Better than any drug.

A tear rolled down her cheek, and I lifted my hand to catch the moisture, but she caught my fingers in her own.

"Say it again." Her voice broke.

My chest cracked open, spilling confetti hearts, bright flowers, puppies and kittens and, fuck, a rainbow, too.

L.O.V.E.

I'd give her those words a thousand times. Every day. For eternity. "I love you."

"Again." She lifted her eyes to mine.

"I love you," I repeated, my throat thick with emotion. "I've loved you since the day you were born."

My beautiful Natalie nodded, sucking her lips between her teeth, face scrunching.

I owned those tears.

Tucking her safely to my chest, I escorted her around the corner and down a long hallway, away from prying eyes.

Cupping those drenched, rosy cheeks, I lifted her face and drank the salt from her lips, our kiss slow and tender.

A familiar tune floated down the hallway. Only the piano at first, then a sultry voice, belting the lyrics to "My Way."

Mona King.

Natalie dropped her head to my shoulder, her breath warming my neck. "My cousins have arrived. We should join the party."

"I'm not ready to share you." I assumed the position, her left hand in my right, my left hand at her waist, and twirled my girl around the empty space.

"How'd you learn to dance?"

"Mom insisted. If I was going to be a fighter, I needed the grace of a dancer."

"Remind me to thank her later."

God, she killed me. I'd dropped my bleeding heart at her feet, and she wanted small talk. Whatever. I'd give her anything.

"Can you believe this shit with our mothers?"

Natalie didn't answer, instead studying my face, her eyes liquid and worried.

I spun, once, twice, until her back hit the wall. Loved her that way, safe between my arms, breathing hard and blushing. "Whatever doubts you have floating around that head of yours, stop. I've got this. I've got us. We'll figure this out."

She opened her mouth to argue. I silenced her with a kiss.

God, the way she kissed, taking all that I gave, giving it back tenfold, her entire body getting involved, melding to mine.

I had no plan other than holding her and taking my fill, but then she coiled her arms around my neck, hopped up, and hooked those sexy legs around my waist, and my sole purpose became making that woman shatter in all the best possible ways.

"Fuck. I need you. Right now."

The vixen moaned, grinding against my erection, and...*Jesus...fuck*. My knees buckled.

"Good God!" A sultry cry bounced off the marbled walls. "Sorry. So sorry to—Natalie?"

"Shit." I laughed. What else could I do?

"Oh, God." Natalie dropped her feet to the floor, and I held her steady and close, blocking her from view until she righted her skirt.

She looked up at me, biting her lip and laughing, too.

"Hi, Angelique," Natalie said, clutching my shirt and turning her head to face the intruder.

Angelique. Finn's mother. They had the same exotic eyes

"Sorry, Natalie." The statuesque woman clutched a small silver purse to her clingy black dress. "I was looking for the ladies' room."

"It's on the other side of the bar."

Cheeks crimson, Angelique raised an eyebrow at me, smiled, then said to Natalie, "Oh, my sweet child. I'm so

L.O.V.E.

glad you moved on from that oversized doofus. You know, the one with the funny name." Then, she shot me a wink, turned, and made her way back into the ballroom, her red heels perpetuating a killer hip swing that only a well-seasoned lady could pull off.

"I like Angelique." I lifted Natalie's arms back around my neck.

"She's a character. And one of the smartest women I know."

"Can we get back to kissing?" I pinned her against the wall once again.

"Nats! There you are." Finn's voice boomed our way.

Jesus. Fuck. Enough with the interruptions.

With a heavy sigh, Natalie pried her body from mine and fell into her cousin's arms. Their embrace was short and sweet, but long enough for me to wipe the lipstick off my mouth and straighten my tie.

Finn looked my way. "Dad's about to give his speech. Come on."

Arm around Natalie's shoulder, he offered his hand. We shook. He guided my girl back into the ballroom. I followed and joined my parents while Natalie joined her family.

Joe King gave a heartfelt, funny speech, waxing poetic about hard work, integrity, and the love and support of his wife.

Coworkers took their turns at the mic, and accolades turned into heartwarming stories, then raunchy jabs at the guest of honor, and soon the entire audience was in tears. Drinks were had. The dance floor abused. And when I couldn't stand another second away from a happy, smiling Natalie, I bid my parents and her parents goodnight and stole her from the party.

The little firecracker wiggled between me and the front door, kicking off her heels, her delicate fingers raking over my chest, working my buttons. "I need you naked. Now."

I fumbled with her zipper, tugged. Tugged again. "Fuck. It's stuck."

"No," she half laughed, half cried, turning in my arms and pulling her hair off her back. "Try now."

I pulled. Pulled again. Wiggled. Yanked. The damn thing wouldn't budge.

The dress was gorgeous. On her, a work of art. Tight red bodice that hugged and lifted her tits. A short, full skirt that highlighted her toned legs. Too bad I would have to shred the damn thing.

Natalie turned to face me again, cheeks flushed, lips parted, eyes wild with need. Again she worked at my shirt buttons and nipped at my chin. Fevered. Desperate.

When she tugged at my belt and her fingers grazed my cock, my vision blurred.

"Fuck. Fuck!" I cupped her breasts, claimed her mouth, and then with one hard tug, tore that damn fabric down her chest, exposing her hard, pink buds.

Natalie gasped. I ducked, catching her perfect flesh in my mouth, nipping, sucking, teasing with soft licks.

Her fingers curled into my hair, holding me tight to her chest, like she wanted more but couldn't ask.

I pulled her harder into my mouth and sucked. *Good fucking God.* Salty and sweet. Heavy and soft. Perfect. And mine. Thank fuck, they were mine.

I slid a hand between her legs, under her panties, and over that smooth flesh, finding her swollen and hot. My head spun, all the blood in my body rushing to my cock.

L.O.V.E.

Fuck the bed. To hell with taking it slow. Natalie was finally in my arms, and I would take her in every goddamn square foot of my home, starting with the floor.

When her back hit the cold hardwood, she didn't complain, only begged for more with a heated gaze and clutching hands. I shoved that skirt up to her waist, grabbed her panties in my fist and pulled them aside, diving in for a taste of that sweet pussy. God, I'd missed her tang, the way she writhed and moaned.

My cock begged for mercy, trapped between me and the hard floor, but I didn't care because, sweet Jesus, the noises she made. She came fast and hard, ripping at my hair. The woman could have every strand, tear it all from the roots. She could rip me to shreds, and I'd bleed dry for her with a smile on my face.

Golden hair formed a halo around her head. Her chest rose and fell. I freed my cock and drove deep, grunting, "Fuck!" incapable of anything other than profanity.

When the stars cleared from my vision, I found her arched beneath me, panting, her neck exposed, her tits shoved against my chest.

A perfect moment I'd forever treasure.

"Fuck me," she purred. "Hard."

And I did. I fucked her halfway across the floor because I couldn't get deep enough, drive hard enough, come fast enough.

And shit, I'd wanted her so desperately I hadn't grabbed a condom, but I wasn't about to pause, so instead of coming inside her like instinct dictated, I pulled out and came all over that gorgeous red dress.

Fuck it. I'd buy her a new one. I'd buy her a thousand dresses just so I could replay that moment, over and over.

A phone chimed somewhere in the dark. Not mine.

I sat back on my heels. Natalie leaned up on her elbows. Hair a gorgeous mess. Tits on display. Killer grin.

Another chime.

"Ignore it," she said.

Not a problem. I wasn't about to share her with anyone.

She sucked me off in the shower.

I ate her out on my couch.

She passed out in my bed after round five. Her phone continued to chime, and I loved that she didn't check it once, giving me one hundred percent of her attention.

But the incessant ding drove me mad. I found her handbag in the dark and dug out her cell, my intention only to power the damn thing down.

Her screen was full of texts, all of them reading the same.

I found you.

You can't hide.

You're dead.

Mother fuck.

I dialed Detective Waters before considering the time.

A groggy voice answered, "Yeah?"

"If there's even the slightest chance she could have survived that accident, I need to know."

Soft breasts pressed against my chest. A bare pussy nestled against my thigh. Warm breaths hit my neck. Good God, waking to such bliss could ruin a man.

I wasn't ready for the day. Dreaded goodbye. The sharp stab in my gut every time she left. My chest ached despite the way she clung to me.

Cupping her ass, I ground my erection against her belly. My beauty stirred but continued with the deep breathing, her faint snore the sexiest melody.

I brushed her hair away from her face to reveal two scars, almost identical in size and shape, but on opposite sides of her forehead.

One of which Victoria had caused.

Fuck. I had married, then buried, a monster, and seeing evidence of the hell she'd put Natalie through filled me with vile hatred. Anger welled, heating my core, but I refused to allow my rage in the same bed as my angel.

Slow and steady, I inched my way off the mattress, leaving my sleeping beauty to dream. I threw on my workout gear and made my way downstairs to the gym.

Early morning hours were my time to purge. Me and the heavy bag. And, fuck, how I needed a good cleansing.

Blood. Sweat. Pain. Release. Release.

Release.

One strike for every memory.

Martin's betrayal. Jab. Cross.

Victoria's deceit. Jab. Cross. Uppercut.

My naive ass. Jab. Cross. Hook. Cross.

Those fucking texts.

Strike after strike, I expelled the demons. Cleansed my murderous urges. Purified my soul of the humiliation.

Only when I couldn't draw steady breath or lift my arms for another blow, I headed for the treadmill, ditching my gloves on a nearby bench.

"It's six in the morning."

Her sleepy voice hit me like a freight train full of happy juice.

"On a Sunday," she added.

I turned to find Natalie in the doorway, feet bare, wearing my plaid pajama bottoms rolled tight at the ankles and a black T-shirt that hung halfway down her hips. Hair a mess. Still the sexiest damn woman I'd ever seen.

"Morning, sunshine." For a long moment, I stood stone still, unsteady emotions rolling through me. Guilt a ball and chain holding me captive in the pits of my despair.

Mere months ago, I'd sworn to forever love another woman. Yet when I shared space with Natalie King, thoughts of my dead wife were nothing more than smudges on the window of my past, too easily disregarded, too hastily wiped away.

Then, Natalie flashed that gorgeous smile and came my way. I met her halfway, and we collided, arms cinching, lips crashing, bodies melding, and she didn't give a fuck that I was drenched in sweat. She didn't care that someone might see her in baggy clothes, messy hair, or no makeup. She was there for me and only me, and somehow that mattered more than pride, grief, self-pity, or the guilt I carried for loving one woman while violently mourning another.

I kissed her dizzy. Urged her legs around my waist, then walked to the mirrored wall and pinned her against the glass.

"Why are you down here and not in bed with me?" she asked, her voice the sweetest aphrodisiac.

Because my maybe dead wife might be sending her messages. God, had Natalie even looked at her phone yet?

"You see a therapist. I beat a heavy bag."

Sad eyes studied me. "You can talk about them, you know. To me. If you need to."

Fuck. She was everything. "How long do I need to mourn before its appropriate to make you mine?"

Natalie raised a finger to my forehead, traced my eyebrows and the slope of my nose. "Is that something we have to worry about right now? We have this morning, then I have to go home."

"God. I don't want to let you go," I growled into her neck before taking a nibble.

Natalie's finger dropped from my jaw to the gold chain around my neck, her silver eyes shimmering with questions. I'd never thanked her for returning the pendant, or for the chain that was far to masculine for the small cross but paired perfectly regardless. *Thank you* never had seemed sufficient.

I choked down a thick ball of emotion and managed to mumble, "It was my sister's."

"You carried it around in your pocket," she whispered, then tapped on my chest. "You should keep it closer to your heart."

She decimated me. Tore me to shreds, then stitched me back together, a better, stronger version. Where she'd found that cross, or how she'd known I'd carried it in my pocket, didn't fucking matter. The fact that she knew and cared? *Fuck.* Words fell weak.

Instead, I poured all my passion and gratitude into a kiss, everything inside me spilling over. Natalie took and gave back tenfold, writhing and moaning in my arms, and I fell into a heavy fog of love and lust.

Natalie pulled away first, her cheeks rosy, her gaze feral. "Take me back upstairs."

"I need to show you something first." I dropped my arms, and Natalie lowered her feet to the ground, claiming my left hand, entwining our fingers. So trusting.

I locked up the gym. Hand in hand, we ascended the stairs. We bypassed my office, then my apartment, and I took her to the security elevator and punched the code.

One floor up, I kissed her hard before the doors slid open.

Fresh paint stifled the air. That smell meant progress.

Natalie spun a three-sixty, taking in the reception desk, the office doors, the security cameras. Down at the far end of the hall, plastic sheeting hung floor to ceiling and a ladder lay folded on the floor.

"What is this?"

We couldn't go any farther since construction was still underway.

"You already know my sister died."

Natalie grabbed my hands and nodded, giving me her full attention.

"What I never told you was that she'd died at the hands of her boyfriend. She was a freshman at UW. I was still in high school. I fucking idolized her. She was so goddamn smart. Wanted to be a pediatrician." I blinked against the moisture in my eyes. "We knew she had a boyfriend, though she never brought him home. She was fucking good at hiding the bruises. None of us had a clue. She'd withdrawn from the family, but I assumed that was because of her workload at school.

"The first time he put her in the hospital, she told us she'd tripped down the stairs at his apartment. I don't remember her excuse the second time, but when he'd insisted she recover at his home, rather than with her family, we knew."

"I dragged Martin and Ellis to his place. Practically knocked his goddamn door down. He came home while I was packing her things. The fucker insisted we were wrong. Cadence backed him up. They threw us out. I called Dad. Dad called the police. They couldn't do a goddamn thing.

"A month later, he ran her down with his Impala. She was in a coma for two weeks before she passed."

"You blame yourself," she said, swallowing hard.

"I should've tried harder."

Natalie stared at me, lips pursed, a thousand questions in her eyes, but she didn't downplay my guilt. "So what's all this then?"

L.O.V.E.

"When it's finished? A safe place for victims. Any resource they need, they'll have, right here. Doctors. Counseling. Child Care. Lawyers. Detectives. Food. Clothing. Online schooling. Upstairs? Apartments, rent free, for as long as they need. A day. A week. Months. Doesn't fucking matter."

"You're a good man, Cole Adams."

"My mother says I have a Savior's complex. Maybe she's right. I don't know. When Cadence died, I blamed myself. Shut down for a while. Hid in the gym. Training was my only outlet, the easiest way to exhaust the anger and guilt. The only other thing that helped me out of my funk was helping people."

"All those charities you support," she whispered, wrapping her arms around my waist, laying her cheek against my sweaty chest. "You tried to save me, didn't you? When you'd insisted I take those self-defense classes."

She was right. Still, I said, "You've never needed saving."

"I need saving right now, Cole."

"That so?" I chuckled, turning her toward the elevator. "From what?"

"Take me back to bed, and I'll tell you."

Heavy-lidded eyes met mine and, with a sweet smile, Natalie grabbed my hand and tugged, urging me toward the bed. She smelled like sex and tasted like toothpaste. When I pulled her toward the shower, she dug in her heels and shook her head no.

"I'm a sweaty mess," I argued.

"I want you dirty, Cole," she said, her voice dripping with need.

The hounds of Hell could've dragged me kicking and screaming to the fiery pits, and I would've fought my way back, picking my teeth with their bones. *Fuuck*. She wanted me dirty. Sweeter words? Not in my lifetime.

I gave her dirty. I gave her deep. I gave her hard. I gave her bites and licks and moans and every filthy thought that came to mind.

And when I came inside her, I gave her all of me, holding her tight, panting, "I love you. God, I fucking love you."

We lay silent and still, only our breaths between us. I was exhausted and sated and so damn happy, and I couldn't let her walk out of my life again.

Dropping a kiss to her nose, I whispered, "Tell me where you live." I already knew. Did that make me a jackass? Too fucking bad.

"Why?" she asked, eyes bright and hopeful.

"You know why."

"Because our mothers believe we're soulmates?" she teased, snuggling closer, her heated skin melting into all of my empty spaces.

"We are." I smoothed a hand over her naked ass, then gave her a hard slap, her squeal an angel's song. "Why can't you admit they're right?"

"If it's true, if you're my destiny, then it won't matter if you know where I live. We'll find our way back to each other."

She wanted to play. I wanted to beg her to stay.

"You little devil."

"What do you say?" She pushed away from me, planting a palm on my chest. "Shall we test the theory?"

I'd play along. Anything to keep that smile on her face. And hell, I could use her game to my advantage. "On two conditions."

"What conditions?"

"I get you every night on the phone, and I get you at least two weekends of every month. You can fly home on my dime."

She rolled to her back. "I can come home on my own dime."

"Fine." I climbed on top of her, caging the spirited, quirky beauty. I'd lock her in a tower if I could. "But I get you every night on the phone."

"That won't be a problem, but I have a condition as well."

"What's that?"

Her soft fingers grazed my cheek. "You find someone to talk to. You can't let everything they did to you fester."

I hated the idea of talking to a shrink, but not as much as I loved making her smile, or laugh, or moan, or fuck—not as much as I loved her. "Agreed."

Shimmering eyes held my gaze. "This is crazy."

"This is us." I kissed her nose.

"How long you think we can do this?"

I'd give her a couple of months, tops. My sunshine wasn't just a city girl; she was a Seattle girl. From those stormy silver eyes plucked from the clouds, to the vibrancy that flowed through her veins, drawn straight from the pulse of our colorful metropolis. I nudged her knees apart and nestled between her thighs. "For however long it takes you to realize you can't live without me."

PART FOUR

Even More Than Barolo

Natalie

My thumbnail was chewed to the quick. My stomach twisted in knots, and I'd squirted ketchup on my favorite green sweater. And the cherry on top of my morbid Sunday? Three new texts.

I found u

Bitch

You tried to hide

That last message was new. The past few days they'd read *U can't hide.*

Now, *You tried to hide* blared like a bad omen on my screen. I was done. I'd head home, change my clothes, and visit Whisper Spring's Police Department.

"Where's Caleb?" I asked, shoving my phone into my handbag.

Monica peeked around her cubby. "He's following up on the proposal you put together."

"Good job, by the way," Brandon added from the other

side of the wall. "Not sure how you came up with those numbers, but Caleb was impressed."

I didn't mention that I knew the owner of Rossi Enterprises. That I'd had coffee with his wife at their diner at least once a week. It wouldn't matter, anyway. As far as Rossi Enterprises was concerned, the proposal came from Pacific Regional Bank. My name was nowhere on the documentation.

"Thanks guys. But it was a team effort." With a smile on my face and a ball of nerves in my gut, I said goodnight to my coworkers and headed for my car.

Wind whipped my hair, and I pulled my coat tight around my middle to ward off the chill. January was in a foul mood. Ominous clouds hung heavy in the sky. The waterlogged earth gave under my weight, soaking my boots with muddy slush from the melting snow.

My focus was not on my surroundings as Dad had drilled into my brain. Instead, I focused on dodging puddles.

Two steps from my vehicle, a hand lay on my shoulder.

I screamed.

My boss dodged a strike aimed at his throat.

"Caleb!" I stabbed his chest with my finger. "You scared the shit out of me."

"I was calling for you." He wore a cheesy grin that made him look ten years younger.

"Shit. Sorry. The wind." I realized I was still yelling, pulled a chunk of hair out of my lipstick, and asked, "What's up?"

A hearty gust knocked me sideways. Caleb grabbed my arm to hold me steady.

Hair tangled in my glasses, and I pushed them on top of my head to help tame the strands.

He leaned closer, his grin smug. "We got the meeting."

"What?"

"First thing tomorrow. Carlos Rossi was impressed."

"Oh, my God. That's great!" Inside, I squealed like a little girl. Outside I was... Oh, who was I kidding? I clapped my hands together and hopped on my toes. "This is great, right?"

"This is better than great, King. We land Rossi Enterprises, we quadruple our numbers for the year." Hands to my shoulders, he laughed. "You'll be head of your own division in no time."

I could've floated away with the winter storm. Unable to contain my joy, I threw my arms around my boss and gave him a celebratory squeeze.

His reciprocation was quick and innocent, and before letting me go, he whispered in my ear, "Now go home and rest up. Big things happening tomorrow. Big things."

His hands slid to my waist, brief and more fatherly than affectionate, blue eyes beaming. "Glad you're on our team, King."

He reached around me, opened my door, and waited for me to settle in the seat.

"See ya' tomorrow," I yelled, watching him retreat.

God, I'd never sleep. The Rossi account was huge. I couldn't wait to tell Cole.

I fired up the engine and cranked the heat. Movement caught my eye, and I glanced at the rearview. A blurry figure passed behind my car, but a head of blond hair was unmistakable.

I turned in my seat and righted my glasses to get a better look, but whomever I'd seen was gone.

Halfway home, my phone chimed with incoming texts.

Not until I was safely locked in my condo did I check my messages.

The first was a pic of Caleb and me mid-embrace.

Then another of Caleb looking down at me, his hands on my hips.

To any outsider, we could've been mistaken for lovers.

Gotcha, whore

Oh, God. Somebody had been at the bank. Watching. Taking photos. Close. Too close.

My doorbell chimed, announcing a visitor. I dashed to the small screen. A hooded figure stood outside, their back to the camera.

My heart thundered, my chest constricting. I was safe. Four stories up. My caller was outside with no way in unless I wanted them in, but I'd never felt more exposed. I pressed a trembling finger to the speaker button. "Who is it?"

The dark visitor didn't move.

"Hey. Hi. You buzzed?"

Silence.

I waited, gaze glued to the small screen.

The person moved out of sight, but not before a wind gust blew a lock of blond hair over the top of the hood.

My cell chimed in my hand. I jumped. Screamed. Dropped the phone. The cursed thing taunted me from the floor.

New toy?

Not for long

The room spun. She was dead. Someone was playing a cruel joke. *Oh, God. They never found her body.* Had she even been in the car?

Victoria was dead.

She had to be dead.

Curled in a ball, phone to my ear, I waited, every ring a reminder of the distance, every second ticking another chink in my armor.

Four painfully long rings before he answered.

"Gorgeous. You're early." Heavy breaths blew through the speaker, traffic noise in the background.

"I couldn't wait," I said, my voice not my own and inaudible through the heavy rap in my chest.

"I know the feeling." He laughed. "Been a crazy day, and I can't stop thinking about seeing you next weekend."

"Cole?" My voice quivered, and I forced a deep and slow inhale, exhale.

"Natalie. What's wrong?"

"I...um." I considered spilling my guts. But at what cost? Those texts couldn't have come from Victoria. She was dead, right? God, what if I was wrong? I refused to drag Cole through that hell. Not without knowing for sure. He'd suffered her cruelty too much already.

No denying, though, I was shaken. My heart and head were a bloody mess of warring emotions. Cole would come to the rescue, I had no doubt. My white knight. My dimpled hero. A simple, "I need you," and he'd come running.

But girl power and all that jazz. "Nothing. I'm fine. Just feels good to hear your voice."

"You sound upset."

"You sound busy." I shouldn't have called.

"On my way to a meeting."

"I won't keep you. Call me tonight. Our scheduled time."

A door slammed, and the street noise disappeared. "Talk to me."

"Really, I'm a thousand times better now that I've heard your voice."

A huff. "This won't work if we aren't honest with each other."

"I possibly landed a stellar account today," I blurted, hoping to divert the conversation. "We're meeting with the clients tomorrow. If they like my proposal, it would be a game changer for our division."

"That's great, sunshine. I'm proud of you. But you didn't answer my question."

"Really, I'm fine. I don't want to make you late for—"

"Goddamn, Natalie!" A hard slam. "Don't do that." Weighted silence. A deep inhale, loud exhale. "Fuck. I'm sorry I yelled. But I'm going out of my fucking mind here, okay? It's hard enough trusting someone again. I need transparency. All the time. I can't do this if... I can't live like..." The phone crackled like he was changing hands. "You're far away, and I need to know you're okay."

He wasn't asking too much. Honestly, I loved that he worried. Worry meant he cared, right? Or maybe it wasn't worry for my wellbeing but for his own piece of mind. We were hundreds of miles apart, and I could betray him in countless ways if I were so inclined.

Victoria's infidelity had done a number, the wound still raw. Cole wanted to trust in us, in me, but he couldn't and, yes, that truth hurt, but I understood the root of his misgivings.

"Okay. You're right. Something happened today. But I'm safe, in one piece, and I'll tell you, but not while you're at work. Full disclosure tonight. I promise."

Foreboding silence ticked like a doomsday countdown. The organ in my chest boom-boom-boomed to the grim rhythm.

Cole was my one. Extraordinary circumstances brought us together. If my fears were confirmed, if Victoria was alive, a thousand and one horrible things could tear us apart. My time with Cole was possibly limited, and I couldn't end our conversation on a negative note. "Are we having our first fight, Cole?" Dreadful silence. My heart beat faster, louder. "Because if we are, I can't wait for the makeup sex."

A huff, followed by a chuckle. I pictured his dimples and sighed, my muscles uncoiling.

"Jesus, Natalie. I'm sorry."

"Forgiven."

An engine roared to life, loud music blared then diminished. Cole huffed. "I really have to go. Need to be across town in twenty minutes. I'll call you as soon as I get home."

"I like fighting with you, Cole Adams. Talk to you soon."

"Natalie?"

"Yes."

"Be naked when I call."

Another sigh, and I hit *End*, curling deeper into my down comforter.

I must've nodded off because I woke myself up screaming when my nightmare hit too close to home, a hooded figure with blond hair, long sharp nails, and a distorted face dragging me through a dusky, wet forest.

My room was dark, the windows offering no illumination. I fumbled for my phone, searching the rumpled bedding. It buzzed at the same time my fingers came in contact with the cold metal.

"Cole," came out more a plea than a greeting.

"You naked?"

L.O.V.E.

Shaken by my dream, overwhelmed with need, and desperate to keep Cole as long as possible, I blurted, "I live in Whisper Springs, Idaho in a secure building, but I don't feel safe, and I don't wanna play this game with you anymore. Testing fate was a stupid idea."

No hesitation. "You've been crying."

Fuck fate and fuck Victoria, and girl power could suck it for a while. "Yes. And I—"

"Natalie." A dark voice cut me off. "I'll be there in six hours."

The call ended.

"You're here." I jumped, knowing he'd catch me and curled around his big strong body, hooking my ankles behind his perfect ass.

"I'm here." Cole kissed me long and hard, then spun, backing through my door, one hand supporting my butt, the other pulling his suitcase inside.

God, I loved his strength.

"Did you drive all night?"

"Yes," was his simple reply.

I peppered his face with kisses of gratitude and didn't let go until he'd walked me through the hallway, past the kitchen, and into my living room where he sat on the couch with me in his lap, then gave me a lip-lock for the ages, full of heat and tongue and teeth and groans of appreciation.

Deft fingers made their way under my sleep shirt and worked my nipples to tight peaks.

I rolled my hips, his erection nestled in the sweet spot, rubbing the ache, erasing the fear.

Cole cupped my cheeks, gold eyes assessing. "I've missed you more than you can imagine."

That perfect face, those sleepy eyes, that lazy grin. Heaven help me.

"I didn't text you my address." I pushed off his lap and took a step back. "How did you know where I live?"

He leaned back, stretching his arms across the back of my sofa, his gray wool coat pulling open to reveal a black thermal that fit like body paint over his well sculpted torso. "I have my ways."

God, that smirk.

I ditched my shirt and tossed it his way. Another step back, and I stepped out of my pajama pants. "How'd you get past security?"

Cole stared from his seated position, my top hanging half off his shoulder, his bottom lip caught between his teeth. "Can we talk about all of that later?"

I shimmied out of my panties. Those, too, landed in his lap. "Let's go to bed." I turned and sauntered toward the hallway. "No sex, but we're sleeping naked."

"Is there any other way?" Footsteps fell behind me, and by the time he caught up, he was nothing but skin and sexy grin.

I hit the lights and slid under my sheets. Cole snuggled behind me, melding our bodies, and whispered, "We have so much to talk about."

"Tomorrow," I answered, bringing his knuckles to my lips.

He pulled me tighter, and three heartbeats later, soft snores filled my room.

Mr. Sandman must've skipped over me entirely because my clock read 5:06 AM, and I still lay awake, tuned in to every creek and groan of the quiet building.

I slipped out of bed and fired up my computer. I hadn't ruled out Holden as my stalker, though I doubted he would

275

dedicate enough time to finding where I lived. He loved his work, mostly the attention his online presence garnered, but still, I was compelled to check.

Ten minutes into my search, I'd confirmed that Holden was attending a fitness expo in Salt Lake City.

The revelation both relieved and terrified me.

If Holden was not taunting me, then that left one other option.

The worse of the two options.

I crawled back into bed and curled around my sleeping man. The man who would do the right thing and take care of his possibly resurrected wife.

He hadn't asked me what was wrong, thank you, Jesus, because the truth I had to tell would kill him.

Our view was perfect, the mood somber, my nerves shot.

I hunched over the red Formica table, pretending to read the menu, scrambling for the right words, the correct way to share my suspicions with Cole and possibly slit my own throat.

But I was a coward and selfish, so instead asked, "How is it you're so put together and on top of things after three hours of sleep?"

He winked at me over the laminated cardboard. "I'm trying real hard to impress a girl."

"Lucky lady."

"Morning, kids. You ready to order?" came a big voice from a small human.

Cole didn't miss a beat, laying his menu down and facing the child. "What's good here?"

"Special today is..." The boy with jet black hair and exotic green eyes looked over his shoulder, then back to Cole and leaned close. "Rocky's triple chocolate peanut butter milkshake. Mom says milkshakes aren't for breakfast, but I say they're better than oatmeal."

"We'll have two."

The kid grinned wider than a pancake. The eight-year-old was the spitting image of his father, who happened to own The Truck Stop Diner, and who also happened to own the condo I lived in, along with Rossi Enterprises, the very company I was scheduled to woo in a few short hours.

"I'll also have the veggie omelet, and my beautiful lady will have..." Brows raised, Cole shot me an endearing look.

"I'll have my usual, Rocky."

"Okay, beautiful lady." Rocky winked, then pulled his lower lip between his teeth and scribbled on the pad.

"Rocky. Cool name." Cole offered his hand. "I'm Cole."

Rocky tucked the notepad under his arm and gripped Cole's fingers, giving him a hard shake. "Rocky James Mason Rossi."

"Rossi, huh? Are you the boss around here?" Cole scratched the stubble on his chin.

"No, my dad is." Rocky leaned close, lowered his voice. "At least that's what he says. But he pretty much does whatever Mom tells him."

Cole laughed and, sweet Lord, there was no better sound.

"Your dad happen to be here?"

"He's in the office with Mom. They're probably kissing and stuff." Rocky scowled. "Nasty."

"Gross." Cole scrunched his nose.

Seriously. That man. What was he up to?

"Yesterday they forgot to lock the door and I—"

"Rockster, did you steal your mom's notepad again?" came a booming voice from the kitchen.

"Uh. Oh." Rocky dashed away, ducking behind the counter.

The double doors in the back of the dining room swung open, and a tall drink of water barreled through, scanned the area, then stopped cold, a bright smiling lighting his handsome features. "Jesus H Christ. Cole Adams. In the flesh. I thought we weren't meeting until noon."

I looked at Cole, who was already on his feet.

"Tango Rossi." The men embraced with hard slaps to the back.

Cole turned to face me. "Tango, this is my girlfriend—"

"Natalie." Tango cut him off and came my way, offering his hand. "Good morning."

"Morning, Tango."

Brows pinched, Cole's gaze bounced between me and Tango. "How do you know each other?"

"I eat breakfast here at least twice a week," I said, then added, "and I'm good friends with his wife."

"Small fucking world." Tango's smile was infectious.

"I'd say it was fate," Cole teased, shooting me a wink.

My brain reeled. "How do you two know each other?" I asked, pointing between the two large, blindingly beautiful men.

"Went to school together, back East." Cole clapped Tango's shoulder. "This guy kicked my ass in the ring more than once."

"Our fathers have partnered on a few projects," Tango threw in.

Missing pieces clicked into place. "Rossi Enterprises owns my building. That's how you found me, isn't it?"

They exchanged glances.

"And that's how you got past security."

Cole cleared his throat.

"I gotta run." Wearing a boyish grin, Tango clocked Cole in the arm, then nodded at me. "See you soon, Natalie." He took a step backward, then pointed at Cole. "We're still on for lunch, yeah?"

"Wouldn't miss it for the world."

With that, Tango turned and sauntered away.

Cole fell into his seat and grabbed my hand across the table. "I've known where you were the whole time."

"What?"

He didn't even have the courtesy to feign remorse.

"Oh, come on, Natalie. What man worth anything would let the love of his life out of his sights for one single heartbeat?"

Love of his life. I tucked that statement away for later processing. "You weren't supposed to cheat."

"I knew where you lived before we made that deal." He dropped his chin, fiddled with a napkin, and said, "I've known for months."

"That's still cheating."

"You're right. I lied by omission. I'm sorry, but you were so damn cute and determined to make this difficult. You wanted to play. I needed to make you happy."

"I'm too tired to be mad at you right now. Maybe after another coffee."

As if on cue, a waitress I didn't recognize brought refills. "Your breakfast'll be right out."

"Thank you," Cole said, sitting straighter in his chair, turning his attention to the blue sky outside.

Early morning sun rays beamed through the window, lighting him in a dusty glow. I slipped my cell out of my bag and took a series of pics before he aimed his gaze my way again.

Oh, God. My heart.

The way he drank me in, those golden eyes dreamy and wanting and sleepy and grateful.

My phone chimed. I ignored the incoming text.

The waitress brought our plates. I used a fork and knife. Cole dug in with just his fork, his fingers long and graceful gripping the metal utensil. Thick veins mapped his hands, and dear God, I wanted those fingers on my skin. I wanted to spend the rest of the day in bed with that body and those dimples.

My phone chimed again. I shoved the annoyance away.

Cole stiffened. "What time's your meeting this morning?"

"Nine sharp. I need to be at the office by eight fifteen so we have time to prepare."

The third chime would come in three...two...one.

Yep. There it was.

Cole shot a glance at my cell, then back to me. "Don't you need to get that? What if it's work?"

"It's not," I mumbled before considering the consequences.

Faster than I could backtrack, he snatched the device off the table and read the screen.

Had I not been exhausted, I would've put up a fight.

The room heated. Cole stared at the words, his eyes going dark and liquid, his hands trembling.

"I've been getting them every day since Joe's retirement party," I confessed. "The exact same texts every day. Until yesterday."

Cole's chest rose and fell. He studied me like I was a mystery to solve.

I shrunk into my seat. "I had every intention of going to the police last night, but then I fell asleep and—"

"It's not her," he growled, slamming the phone down. "It's not fucking her," he said again to his plate.

God, how I wanted his words to be true. "What if it is?"

His fists clenched on the table. Jaw tight, he drew a deep breath, then shook his head, eyes seemingly unfocused.

The excruciating silence lasted an eternity.

He fixed his gaze on me once again. "Do you trust me?"

No hesitation. "Yes."

"Let me take your phone today."

Cole

Our table sat in the corner of the dining room, eight stories above Lake Willow. The five-star restaurant occupied the eighth floor of Whisper Springs Resort—one of many hotels Rossi Enterprises owned—and boasted a million-dollar view. Mountains, lake, blue sky. Fine china and French crystal. Two men in crisp white shirts and black ties stood in wait far enough away to offer privacy but close enough to assist at a moment's notice.

"I was sorry to hear about your wife." Tango spread his white napkin over his lap.

He'd taken a while to broach the subject. For that, I was thankful. "Victoria is why I wanted to meet with you privately."

"What's up?"

I offered my old friend the grim details of my short marriage. My suspicions about the car wreck, the texts. Tango listened, not a lick of judgment.

"Thing is, they never found her body. State patrol says that's common for those types of accidents. Still, something's not kosher."

He leaned closer. "How can I help?"

"You still tight with Moretti?"

A smirk. "Why you asking about Moretti?"

Tango and his cousin, Tito Moretti, had been inseparable back in our college days. Tito had allegedly helped run underground fights for the infamous mob boss, Luciano Voltolini. His true skills, however, were behind the scenes, his weapons not fists but a keyboard. Wasn't a system he couldn't hack or a file he couldn't manipulate.

"He helped me out once before, but he's off the grid. I was hoping you could get in touch. Anyone can find the truth, it's Moretti."

Tango considered me for a moment. Shifted to grab his cell from his pocket. Typed a message. Shot me a sinister grin. "Yeah, I know how to reach Moretti."

Our server arrived with the first course. When out of earshot, Tango asked with one brow raised. "So, you and Natalie King?"

Fuck, I loved the sound of her name. I nodded. "She's it for me."

Tango stared, assessing.

"You're wondering how I can be with someone else so soon after Vic?"

"There's no timeline for grief, my friend." He lifted his hands. "Not judging. I've got mad respect for Natalie. Did she tell you we had a meeting today?"

"No." The little shit. She didn't want my help.

"Her boss didn't show. Pops was ready to walk, but that girl of yours took the reins. Impressed the shit out of both of us."

Not a surprise. Bewitching. Best word to describe my girl. "She's got a way about her."

"How's that gonna work, you living in Seattle, her in Whisper Springs?"

"Fuck. I don't know how this'll play out." I stabbed my salad, chewed. Swallowed. "I can't relocate right now. Opening three more gyms this year. Dad's not planning to retire any time soon, but he's slowing down. I'll be stepping up as CEO in a couple of years. But I can't ask her to leave her job. She loves it here."

"She's only an hour and a half away by jet." He rapped his knuckles on the table like he'd settled the matter. "That's no longer than a rush hour commute."

"True." Seattle traffic was horrendous. "All I know is I don't want a future without her. No choice but to make things work."

Tango nodded, leaned back, crossed his arms. "And if your suspicions about Victoria are true?"

Wasn't that the million dollar question?

"No easy answer," was all I could manage. I'd driven myself mad with what-ifs.

Tango glanced over my shoulder, then smiled wide. "Look who the cat dragged in."

Before I could turn, Tito Moretti planted his ass in the chair next to mine. "Fuckin' hell. Cole Adams."

The guy was imposing, from his head-to-toe black garbs, to the scowl, to the new scar on the side of his face. I knew better than to ask.

He offered his hand. The wedding ring took me by surprise.

We made small talk. We ate. I filled them in on my suspicions.

"You've checked out her ex?"

"First thing." I nodded. "He's in Salt Lake. He could be the one sending the messages, but someone took photos of her with her boss yesterday and possibly followed her home last night." The thought soured my stomach.

"Can you get me her phone?" Moretti asked.

I slapped her cell on the table. The guy cracked a rare smile. He stood, said, "Give me a day," and left without so much as a nod.

Tango laughed. I released my frustration on a long exhale.

Brow quirked, Tango asked, "You sure you're ready for whatever he digs up?"

Was I? Whatever the outcome, Natalie's safety was my only concern. "Can you two thugs help me hide a body?"

Pacific National Bank stood tall amidst a riverbank forest of pines with mountains and a snowy sky the backdrop. Post Malone played on the radio.

I watched the front door through darkened windows. At 5:11, Natalie exited the building. She paused, bringing a hand to her face to shield the sun, and scanned the parking lot. I tapped the horn. She looked my way, smiled that killer smile, and waved before stepping in my direction.

I'd every intention of meeting her halfway, but stalled, enthralled by the swing of her hips, the sway of her hair, the way that blue blouse clung to her breasts. I was helpless to do anything but drink her in, so damn grateful to be free to ogle the woman without one lick of guilt.

My pulse quickened. Soon she'd be in my arms.

Jesus. Damn. My chest. I offered the good Lord a quick prayer of gratitude, then hopped out of the SUV.

L.O.V.E.

The squeal of tires registered before I'd closed my door. Natalie's head snapped in the direction of the sound, and before I could set my feet pounding, a black Escalade barreled straight toward my girl.

The horrifying scene played out frame by agonizing frame.

Natalie twisted to avoid the vehicle, and before impact, her arms flew out, then up over her head, and her eyes, *goddamn*, they squeezed shut as if bracing for impact. Then she was out of sight.

Her handbag hit the windshield, blowing apart, its contents erupting like confetti.

No squealing tires. No crunch of metal. No sickening thud. The SUV sped off.

By the time I reached her, Natalie lay twisted on the pavement, hair tangled around her face, a pool of blood under her head.

I fell to my knees at her side, desperate to hold her, screaming for help. I fumbled for my phone and dialed 911.

A male voice answered. I couldn't form a coherent word.

People surrounded us.

A man dropped to his knees near her head.

"Don't fucking touch her." I shoved him away. "I don't know if she was hit or not."

The 911 operator continued talking. I shoved my phone into the guy's hand. "Give them the address."

My vision blurred, heat prickling my eyes. I crawled over her body, shielding, assessing. "Baby. Natalie. Sweetheart."

Her chest rose and fell.

"I'm here. I'm right here. Don't try to move." If I lost her, I'd rip everyone in that goddamn town to shreds.

"Please, baby. Please be okay. I love you. I love you so goddamn much. Please be okay," I pleaded, my knees, my hands, stained with her blood.

"What the fuck happened?" the man at my side asked.

I watched her chest for signs of distress. Her breaths were steady.

"Oh, God!" A woman screamed, "Is that Natalie?"

Natalie's chest continued to rise and fall. In. Out. In. Out. In. Out.

"Good girl. Keep breathing. Please be okay."

"Cole?" A moan escaped her lips.

A sob escaped mine.

I pressed a soft kiss to her forehead. "I'm right here. Don't try to move. Wait for the ambulance."

"My head hurts," she mumbled, her speech slurred.

"You're bleeding a little bit. Don't move."

"What happened?"

"Some fucker tried to run you down."

"Oh," she whispered, her voice weak.

Light as I could manage, I brushed hair off her face, away from her eyes and mouth. Her lips were bloody, and my stomach revolted at what that could mean.

"You're gonna be fine, though. Don't worry. I've got you."

"Cole?" She coughed, more blood trickling from her mouth.

I pinched my eyes tight, fighting the emotion, then met her sleepy gaze. "Yeah, baby?"

"Will you marry me?"

Never in my life had I cried in public. Rarely in private. But there on the dirty ground, surrounded by complete strangers, I cried and half laughed at her ridiculous timing.

"It's not funny. I'm serious. Will you marry me?" She smiled a morbid, bloody smile.

Sirens wailed.

Her lids fluttered shut, then lifted slow. "I'm tired."

"Try to stay awake, please? I need you to do that for me."

"You're crying." She gagged, then turned her head to spit blood.

I could only nod.

Her lids fell again and didn't open.

"Cole. Son." My body shook, and I bolted upright, blinking the room into focus.

Natalie lay in the same spot, eyes closed, monitors whirring. Her mother stood over the bed, her father stood over me, a hand on my shoulder, his eyes dark, sunken.

"You made it." My dry throat cracked.

"Thanks for calling." He stepped back and cleared his throat.

I pushed to stand, and the moment I was upright, Charles pulled me into a tight embrace. "Thank God you were here for her."

"Thank God is right," Linda whispered.

"Any word from the police?" Charles asked.

"Not yet. But the security cameras caught everything. They're trying to pull a license plate number."

Linda squeezed her daughter's hand. "Doctors said she'll be fine. Six stitches on the back of her head. No concussion, by some miracle. Twisted ankle. Bit her tongue pretty hard."

I laughed. Fucking twisted ankle saved her life.

Charles and Linda looked at me like I was crazy.

I explained. "If she hadn't caught her heel in that damn crack, that Cadillac would've hit her."

"Fate," Linda whispered, eyes welling.

I scrubbed at my facial hair. "They wanna keep her for twenty-four hours, keep an eye on her."

"That's good." Charles studied my rumpled, soiled clothes. "Why don't you go clean up. Come back after you get some rest and a good meal in you."

Hell no. I wasn't leaving her side.

"We won't let her out of our sight, Son. I promise." His patriarchal tone left no room for argument.

"Yeah," I conceded. "I'll do that."

"You staying at her place?"

Fuck. "Yeah. No worries, I can check into a hotel."

"Don't be silly," Linda said, waving her hand at me. "You have a key?"

If I wasn't mistaken, there was a twinkle in her eyes.

"She gave me her spare this morning."

I kissed Natalie's pale cheek and said my goodbyes. Darkness greeted me when I stepped outside. My cell said it was 1:27 AM. God, I needed sleep. The drive to Natalie's place passed in a blur. On autopilot, I showered, shaved, choked down a sandwich.

Will you marry me?

I laughed.

Crazy woman.

For the first time, I took time to study her place. The kitchen was clean, tidy. Simple. White granite counters. Stainless steel appliances. Turquoise tea kettle on the stove. Bright floral curtains on the window, a bright yellow dishtowel hanging on a hook near the sink.

Her living room was much the same. White walls, bright orange couch. Splashes of yellows and greens in the throw blankets, pillows, and artwork. A wall-to-wall window boasted a priceless view of the lake.

L.O.V.E.

The hallway leading to the bedrooms held framed photos of her family, candids of her and Lacey. At least ten of baby Leon. *And holy shit*, photos of me, too. Some blown up and framed. A few looked as if they'd been printed from home and tacked to the wall. Most of them taken when I wasn't looking. Some of me sleeping. One of me through the window of CFC, mid spar with Ellis.

Yeah. She was mine. But I'd been hers from day one.

I forced my feet forward when I wanted to fall to my knees in gratitude.

Natalie's bedroom showed a side of her I'd yet to fully explore. Shades of purples and grays and beige. Her bed was thick with pillows, soft and inviting. Sheer curtains gave the room a hazy glow, the scant moonlight encasing her bed.

Will you marry me?

I fell into her down comforter, pulled her pillow over my face, and breathed her in, my body and soul resting as if I'd returned home from a long journey.

I'd never be lonely sharing space with Natalie.

I'd never wake to cold, empty sheets.

Eventually, we'd have to exchange the queen-size bed for a king to fit children. Sundays would be lazy days, sleeping in, sipping coffee, reading. Chasing kids around the house.

Will you marry me?

I'd never wanted anything more.

"How's she doing?"

"Good. She's with her parents." I scooted to the chair closest the window, blinking against the glare from the lake. "What'd you find out?"

Tango and Tito settled into their chairs, Tango resting his elbows on the red Formica.

Tito dropped a manilla envelope between us and leaned back, arms crossed, dark eyes focused. "The car that ran down Natalie belongs to her boss, Caleb Griffin. Guy's in the hospital. His brother found him beaten to a pulp in his house. Broken arm, multiple facial fractures."

With one long finger, Tito pushed the envelope my way. Tango shifted in his seat. Cleared his throat.

"What is this?

"Open it."

The unsealed envelope looked safe enough, but the way my friends leaned closer, like shields, I knew my life was about to take a twisted turn.

I emptied the contents on the table. Photos. Gritty security camera footage. Some I recognized as the bank parking lot. Some were taken outside of Natalie's condo. All of them were of the same figure wearing dark clothes. Pale skin. Blond hair.

Not—*thank fucking God*—Victoria.

Tito then passed me Natalie's phone. "Fuckin' idiot thinks burner apps are untraceable." He pulled out his own cell and showed me an Instagram feed. @HOTraversFitness. "This guy is dumber than a bag of rocks."

Pics of Natalie littered his feed. In the gym, in the car. Various outdoor locations. Every single one of them recently posted, though it was obvious they were old photos by the cut of Natalie's hair.

The most recent post was uploaded two hours earlier and was of Natalie sleeping, half of one breast exposed, the light hitting her just right in a warm, erotic glow. It read: *To watch her sleep is the sweetest torture.*

Then the hashtags. #gettingmygirl #todaystheday #lovehurts #shesmine

"I gotta go." I slammed my palms on the table, my heart hammering, chest constricting. My only thought was getting to Natalie.

Footsteps tracked behind me. Heavy. Determined. I reached my car. Turned.

"You're not doing this alone." Tango walked around to the passenger seat.

"I can handle it," I argued, though I had no idea how.

"We know." Tito tucked into the back seat, filling half the space. "Don't wanna miss the fun." He was already on the phone. "Hey, Bunny, Aida still with you?" He paused, nodded, said, "Good. Listen. I need your help."

Sitting cool as a cucumber, Tango explained, "Tito owns the top floor of Natalie's apartment. She'll be fine."

19

Natalie

Children of all shapes and sizes littered the playground, their energy addicting, their giggles and squeals infectious as they enjoyed the first sunny day in months.

Cole's face lit up my screen, and I answered with a heady, "Hi."

"Hey, gorgeous. Where are you?"

"Sitting in the park. I sent Mom and Dad off, and it's so beautiful today I didn't want to go back inside yet."

"Do me a favor?"

"Sure." I snuggled into the collar of my coat. "What's up?"

"Head back. Lock up. I'm on my way. Should be there in fifteen or twenty minutes."

"Cole. Why do you sound upset?"

"I'll explain when I get there. Please. Just go back inside for me?"

"Okay." I looked around, worried. "You're scaring me a little bit."

A pause. A loud exhale. "Sorry, sunshine. Don't mean to scare you. Just got some information you need to hear."

"Okay."

"Call me when you're safe inside?"

"Sure." I tucked my phone into my back pocket, pushed off the bench, righted my crutches, and headed the half block toward home.

At the front entrance, my cell buzzed. I should've continued inside, but instead I read the screen.

Gotchu

Shit. Shit. Shit. I turned to look over my shoulder and dropped a crutch.

"Shit!" Hobbling on one foot, I bent to retrieve my fallen support.

"Let me get that," came the familiar voice.

I stilled, the chill permeating my bones.

Slowly, cautiously, head throbbing, chest pounding, I rose to face my greatest mistake.

"Holden." I scanned my surroundings. The street was busy, the sidewalk dotted with people. I was safe for the time being. "What are you doing here?"

"What do you think I'm doing?"

He reached for my cheek. I knocked his hand away.

His chest rose and fell. Once, twice, three times.

I feared my heart would detonate, the roar between my ears deafening. The man before me struggled for composure, and when he closed his eyes, took one long breath, then blew it out slow and steady, I knew I wouldn't like whatever came next.

"I'm here to fight for you, Nats." He scratched his head, messing his now shoulder-length blond hair. "I was such an idiot before. I never should've let you get away. I should've cherished you." His pale blue eyes darkened, filling my blood with adrenaline.

"Holden." I held up a hand and took a step back. "Stop right there."

"Let me speak," he said, his plea robotic, practiced. "Let me say what I need to say."

"No!" I didn't step away again, but instead hobbled closer and lifted my chin to make sure he heard me loud and clear. "Nothing you say will make me change my mind." I took a breath, measuring my words. "You have to stop. Creepy as this is, you stalking me to another state, deep down, I know you have a good heart—"

"I'm not a fucking stalker," he cut in, his glare darting toward the door, then landing back on me. He gripped my bicep, squeezing hard enough to let me know he wasn't messing around. "I'm not crazy."

Clearly, the man was unstable. Through the fear seizing my muscles, I said, "You're hurting me."

He blinked. Released my arm. Huffed. "You need me, baby. Look." He retrieved my crutch but held the metal aide with two hands. "Clearly, you're in need of help. It's fate, us bumping into each other. Let me help you to your apartment. We can talk."

"There's nothing to discuss."

Rolling his eyes, he hissed, "Our future."

"We don't have a future," I said, jerking the crutch from his hands.

The asshole laughed and stepped back, settling on his heels and crossing his arms. "We do now. I got rid of your boyfriend. He's not coming around anymore. I made it clear you belong to me."

"My boyfriend?" My veins went ice cold.

Leaning down, he hissed, "Don't play stupid. You got my texts and the photos. That guy outside the bank. The one who had his hands all over you."

Caleb. *Oh, God*. He hadn't shown up for our meeting with the Rossi Corporation. He wouldn't have missed that meeting by choice. "Got rid of?"

"I let him know I was back in your life. Gave him a taste of what would happen if he touched you again."

"How did you find me?"

"I'll always find you, Nats. Always. Because you're mine."

"Holden, this is…" I staggered back a step, then caught my balance. *Oh, God. What should I do?* Play on his emotions or scream for help? Surely, somebody would hear.

"I'm not feeling so well. Can we talk tomorrow?"

"You owe me one uninterrupted conversation, Nats. Let's go upstairs." Strong fingers cinched my arm. "Just hear me out, and you'll see. Everything will be fine."

The door behind me opened. "Hey, Natalie," came a soft voice. "Oh, no. What happened?" My neighbor, who also waitressed at The Truck Stop Diner, stepped between me and Holden, her blue eyes wide with worry, her breaths labored, like she'd sprinted down ten flights of stairs.

"Hey, Tuuli." I'd never been so happy to see another human being in my life. "Just a little fall. Twisted my ankle. I'm fine."

"Who's your friend?" she asked, her hand linking with mine and giving it a squeeze.

Strange.

We were friendly, but not holding hands friendly, and though she served me on more than one occasion at the diner, she was a woman of few words, and while I knew she lived in the penthouse of my building with her husband, we'd never bumped into each other outside of the restaurant.

"I'm her boyfriend," Holden announced, inching closer, offering his hand. "Holden Oswald Travers The Third."

Bile rose in my throat. But sweet Jesus, I was thankful for the petite body next to me, her size small but her presence mighty.

"Oh. Nice to meet you." Tuuli gave Holden a firm shake, then gasped and stepped back. "HOTraversFitness." She laughed, clutching her heart. "I follow you on Insta."

Holden smiled, his spine straightening.

My stomach twisted. What the actual F-word was happening?

"That's me," he said, chest expanding.

"My husband is a huge fan. That series you did on core health and sexual endurance." She ducked her head and laughed. "Life changing. You saved our relationship."

"Not surprised." Holden puffed like a peacock. "That's a popular series."

"He's upstairs," Tuuli continued. "He'd love to meet you." She grabbed my hand once again. "Maybe you've heard of him, Cole Adams." Squeeze. Squeeze. "He's famous in the fight world. Not as famous as you, though."

Cole was not upstairs. Only a few minutes had passed since he called. How Tuuli got involved, how she even knew Cole's name, I hadn't a clue, but what the heck did it matter?

The little actress had Holden. Hook. Line. Sinker.

Any chance for Holden to meet a celebrity, he was all in. Any opportunity to promote his brand, he was game.

"Yeah. Yeah. Sure." Holden cupped my face, rubbed my bottom lip with his thumb. "Nats and I were just heading up anyway."

Killed me, but I played along, allowing Holden to wrap his beefy arm around my shoulder and help me hobble inside and then to the penthouse private elevator.

L.O.V.E.

I tried and failed to speak on the ride up, which didn't matter because Tuuli and Holden rattled on about breathing techniques and stretching.

We were greeted inside the lavish home by a short and deadly gorgeous woman, a wiggling toddler in her arms. She looked vaguely familiar, but came at me like we were besties and hooked me in a tight, one arm hug, effectively freeing me from Holden's embrace. "Good God, Natalie. What happened? You shouldn't be on your feet." She landed a kiss on my cheek and whispered, "Play along," before shooing me to the other room, settling me on the couch, and shoving the child into my arms.

"Where's your husband?" Holden asked, his gaze sliding to me, then toward the stairs, then back to the two women at his side.

"He's in his office. I'll call him down." Tuuli moved around the kitchen island, grabbed her cell, and with thumbs moving across her phone screen, said, "Holden, this is Aida. Aida, Holden."

"Nice to meet you, Aida." His offered hand hung in the air for five heartbeats, his cheeks reddening. He finally cleared his throat and dropped his arm to his side, eyeing her warily.

I almost laughed. The two of them looked as though they'd planned their matching outfits, both donning black, zipped hoodies that stretched tight over fit bodies. While Aida wore leggings and Moto boots, Holden wore black jeans and Danners.

Aida, though small in stature, stood regal and commanding, sizing up Holden like they were opponents in the ring. "Damn, you're huge." She crossed her arms and started to circle. "What are you, one-eighty, one-eighty-five?"

Holden laughed, his chest swelling. "You're good. One-eighty-seven this morning."

"Hmm," she said, crossing her arms and planting her feet in front of his. "You a fighter?"

The baby fussed and wiggled in my arms, clearly not happy to be constrained by a stranger. I shifted her from my right thigh to my left and bounced my foot, my heartbeat a thunderous roar.

"No." He smirked, gave Aida his practiced smile, his gaze slicing to me once again before he said, "I'm a lover."

Cringeworthy? Oh, God, yes.

But Holden wasn't finished. He continued, "Isn't that right, Nats?"

Aida, bless her soul, didn't give me time to react. Dropping her hands to her sides, she shook her head. "That's not what I hear, big guy." She threw a wink at me over her shoulder.

Tuuli moved into the far corner of the kitchen, giving me a reassuring smile. Her eyes held wisdom far beyond her twenty-something years.

Aida stepped closer to Holden. "I hear you've been harassing my girl over there. Sending her vile messages."

Face a fiery shade, Holden ran a hand through his hair, shot me a glare. "Babe. Time for us to go."

"She isn't going anywhere, you big, ridiculous waste of space." Eye level with Holden's chest, Aida raised her chin.

Fists clenched, Holden stared down at the feisty warrior, the vein in his temple bulging, a warning.

My stomach lurched. What a fool I'd been, bringing Holden and his volatile temper into a stranger's home. I needed to get him far away from these women.

Lifting the child to my shoulder, I tried to stand on my one good leg. The baby squirmed and then pulled at my hair, giggling, and I fell back into the cushion at the same time Holden shouted, "Babe, let's—".

The floor shook with a loud boom. I looked up to find Holden on his knees. Aida moved fast, her arms a blur, striking Holden somewhere on his neck, once. twice. He fell face first on the hard, black tile.

Tuuli tossed Aida a rope. She bound Holden's hands, then his feet.

The child continued to squeal and yank on my hair.

As if she hadn't just taken down a man three times her size, Aida sauntered my way, untangled her daughter's fingers, then lifted her off my lap. "That was fun." She clicked her tongue. "Thought he'd put up more of a fight, though."

"Want coffee?" Tuuli asked from the kitchen.

"Ummmm." My head spun. Stomach protested.

"I'm Aida," the deadly bombshell said. "We needed to do this inside. No witnesses." She winked. Kissed her daughter on the head. "You look familiar. Have we met?"

Tuuli shouted, "You've seen her in the diner."

"Ah." Aida nodded. "That's it."

"I'm so confused."

"And you're trembling." Tuuli came my way and shoved a mug into my hand before pulling a soft knit blanket around my shoulders and said, "Aida's been studying martial arts since before she could walk." As if that explained everything.

The giant door slid open and a large, brooding man barreled through followed by Tango, and then, thank you Jesus, Cole.

Four long strides, and he knelt at my feet, inspecting, eyes frantic with worry. "Jesus. Fuck. Did he hurt you?"

I shook my head.

"Fuckin' hell, Aida. You left nothin' for us to do." That came from the man with the scar, Tuuli's husband.

"Really, Tits?" Aida smirked. "You would've made a mess. Lots of blood and broken dishes. I saved you the trouble."

Tango stood over Holden, phone in his hand, shit-eating grin on his face. "Natalie, how you wanna handle this? I can call the cops or we can make him disappear."

Hands trembling, I grabbed Cole's collar and pulled him closer. "He's kidding, right?"

Forehead to mine, he released a harsh breath and laughed. "He's kidding, sunshine. Cops are on their way."

I was reading the last twisted line of *The Wives*, half cringing, half cheering for Thursday when my front door opened then closed.

Cole toed off his shoes, then came my way, his gait heavy, face grim.

"So?"

"Holden's going away for a long time. His prints were all over Caleb's car and in his home. Long list of charges."

The past few days had worn Cole down, his burdens heavy judging by the slope of his shoulders and the dark circles around his eyes.

"What about Caleb?"

He stalked forward and sighed. "Beat to hell, but he'll survive."

"I need to talk to him. Explain." I fought a lip quiver. "Apologize."

"He knows it wasn't your fault." Cole dusted a finger over my forehead, then tucked a strand of hair behind my ear, eliciting a full body shiver.

He was so close, his breaths warming my cheeks. Whatever he'd eaten for lunch must've been loaded with garlic, but I didn't care. Cole was in my home, towering over me, and I was safe, warm, and wanted.

He pinched my glasses at the bridge, slid them off my face, and laid them on the coffee table. His dimples popped before he brushed soft kisses on the left corner of my mouth, then the right.

"How're you feeling?"

"My head hurts."

Weary eyes studied mine. "What can I do? How can I help?"

"Kiss me again?"

Cole pressed his forehead to mine. Sighed. Kissed my nose. "I don't want to hurt you."

"My tongue doesn't hurt so much anymore."

"That's good."

I urged him to sit next to me, then stood and made a show of shimmying out of my jeans.

"Sunshine, I don't think we should push it," he grumbled but made no move to stop me. He wore a scowl, his mood dark.

"I don't think I can wait another second." My shirt was next, then my bra. Then my panties.

Cole didn't move.

I pinched a nipple, rolling the hard flesh between my fingers. "Lose the shirt, Adams."

In one smooth motion, he removed his T-shirt and tossed it aside. I stepped between his knees, raked my nails down his stomach, then grabbed the hem of his pants. Still, he didn't move. I quirked a brow, waiting. With a huff, he lifted his hips and jerked his sweats down to his knees.

Commando. Jeez, what a turn on.

His swollen cock fell against his six pack, the sight so erotic my head buzzed. This man was mine. Mine. Mine.

Skin tingling, insides warm and aching, I gripped his shoulders, planted my knees in the cushions at his hips, and nestled my ass in his lap.

He hit me with a heated gaze full of unspoken promises, unnecessary apologies.

Lips parted, cheeks red, he slapped my ass with one hand, his grip tight and assuring. He stroked his cock with the other and lifted me high enough to position himself at my opening, sliding his head through the moisture before pushing inside.

I slammed down, knowing he'd take it slow.

"Jesus. Fuck." His head hit the back of the couch with a sharp inhale.

I smiled. Slow was not good. Slow would drive me mad, and I'd had enough crazy for one day.

I needed release. I needed lust and sweat and panting and mindless bliss, and I needed Cole out of his head, out of his mind.

Sweet lord, the stretch, the sweet sweet burn, the feral heat of those beautiful eyes, the rabid grip of his hands on my thighs. The rise and fall of that perfectly sculpted chest.

Neither of us stood a chance.

I leaned forward, close enough to taste his breath. "Say it," I said, almost a beg, mostly a soft plea. I rolled my hips, just a little. "Tell me what I need to hear."

Something akin to a growl rose in his throat.

I rolled my hips again, and his jaw clenched.

When he opened his mouth to speak, I silenced him with a kiss. "Say it, baby, please," I begged.

He opened his mouth again, and I swallowed his words, brushing my battered tongue against his.

His fingers dug deeper into my skin. They'd leave marks. Maybe that was his intention. I couldn't wait to see them in the mirror. "Say the words, Cole."

Again, he tried to speak, but I silenced him, pulling his bottom lip between my teeth, rising and falling on his cock, feeling every inch of his hard heat.

A curse escaped his lips.

But finally, finally, a small grin.

Good.

"There's my guy."

He huffed. Slapped my ass. "I love you."

"Yes, you do," I whispered. "And I love you. But you're too serious right now. I need your smile."

He sucked a nipple between his teeth. Licked. Nibbled. Drove me mad.

"I'll smile after you've come all over my dick."

"Deal."

His dimples popped, then disappeared, but the dark cloud hanging over us dissipated, and Cole took over, done with my teasing.

The man beneath me was hunger and heat, hard muscle and dirty words, tender touches and desperate thrusts.

He pumped into me, and I chased my release. When I came, my cries bounced off the walls. He grunted his release into my neck, holding me tightly, past the point of passion, our bodies close enough to fuse together.

Wrung dry, I collapsed, my head on his shoulder, his fingers tracing up and down my spine. My body hummed under his touch.

When our breathing slowed, he asked, "Is it bad that I couldn't wait for your parents to leave?"

"Is it bad that I kicked them out?"

His chest bounced. "You didn't."

"I did. They'd planned on staying the week. Mom pretended she was heartbroken, but really, she just wants grandchildren, and as far as she's concerned, you're the perfect baby daddy."

Cole stiffened under me, his warm hands leaving me cold. I sat back, searched his face. Cole looked right through me, lost in thought, and not a good one judging by the wrinkle between his brows.

I pressed a finger where his skin crinkled, rubbing a slow circle. "I didn't mean to insinuate..." God, did I? Had I assumed we were heading that direction without cause? He was my one. But we'd only started our long distance love affair, and the beginning had been bumpy to say the least, and though he never talked about the accident, he had lost the unborn child he'd believed to be his, and sometimes I forgot to consider his grief.

I had no idea how to rebound from my slip. To erase the pain off his face. "I need a shower."

Heart shriveling, naked and vulnerable, I headed toward the bathroom.

Three blissful days passed.

Mind-blowing sex. Deep conversations. Eating. More sex. The subject of children never came up. We never talked about the future, only the present, and select bits of the past, none of which included his time with Victoria.

On our last night together, we ventured out for dinner with the Rossis and their extended family. I made new friends. Cole caught up with old friends.

The day had come for Cole to leave. I woke to an empty bed, the ache in my chest already taking root. Music traveled down the hallway. I followed the tune, that invisible string tensing, drawing me closer to my destiny.

Cole wore a pair of running pants and nothing more. He stood at the coffee machine, tapping his fingers on the counter to the rhythm on the radio, a song I recognized but didn't know.

He belonged in my kitchen. My bed. My home.

God, how I wanted to keep him there forever, crawl on hands and knees and beg him to stay.

He sang along, messing up the lyrics. I laughed, making him jump.

The smile that greeted me was a heady mix of boyish charm, pure adoration, and a warning—full body collision in three, two, one. Oh, sweet Jesus, his hug was covetous, his kiss an awakening.

"One for the road?" His voice oozed sex.

"Please. Yes."

He fucked me on my kitchen counter, fast and furious, desperate and unrelenting.

We showered. We dressed. Cole packed his suitcase while I watched from my corner of the bed.

"You're going back to work tomorrow?" He smoothed his hands over the folded clothes, then turned face me.

I nodded.

"Against doctor's orders?"

"I can't stay on top of my game if I'm lounging around my damn apartment all day."

"I respect your drive, sunshine, but your health is more important than any job." He raked a hand through his hair and looked around the room. "I think that's everything."

The ache was bone deep. I hated goodbyes. "Truth?"

His gaze sliced to mine. "Always."

I picked at a thread on my bedspread. "I'd rather go to work than be here alone."

His chest sagged. He slammed the suitcase shut. "Natalie."

Shit. My lashes were wet.

"Look at me."

I did.

"We're gonna figure this out. I promise. There isn't another option right now. If I could stay, I'd stay. But I have a company to run. Soon, I'll have two companies to run. And I would never ask you to leave your job."

He didn't need to ask. I'd already chosen. I just had to get my ducks in a row before telling him so.

"I know," came out on a sob. "I love that about you."

"We'll work hard during the week. Fuck hard on the weekends. We'll have to get creative with the phone sex, but I love a challenge."

Oh, God. The dimples. "Me, too."

"Do me a favor?"

"Of course."

He smirked. "Take off your shirt."

I obeyed.

"Your pants, too."

Again, I obliged.

"Now sit there, just like that, and don't move."

"What are you up to?"

He pulled his suitcase to the door and stood, leaning against the jamb, arms crossed, taking me in, head to toe.

My room was warm, but I shivered, his assessment stripping me raw, and I wasn't even wearing my best underwear. "What are you doing, Cole Adams?"

"Committing you to memory. It's gonna be a long fucking week." He scratched at his chin, dropped his gaze to the floor, then broke my heart in all the right ways. "I was so fucking scared of losing you. When you were lying on the ground, bleeding, all I could think was, please, God, if you take her, take me, too. I've survived burying three loved ones, but you? My heart would've stopped on its own. I would've joined you in a matter of seconds."

His admission gutted me then filled me to overflowing with all the good things, those words better than a thousand I love yous. My eyes filled with liquid again. "Are you gonna kiss me goodbye?"

He shook his head, a slow *no*. "I won't have the strength to stop."

I watched him retreat. Waited for the ominous click of the door.

When it didn't come, I hobbled down the hallway.

Cole stood, hand on the knob, head down. He caught me in his arms. Kissed me hard and deep. And when he'd taken his fill, he cupped my cheeks and whispered, "For the record, when we get this figured out, I want to make a thousand babies with you."

"How about three?" I said, breath hitched.

"Deal."

He slipped out the door.

"You're okay?" Caleb slurred, his lips cut and bruised.

I limped his way, held his good hand, and studied his beaten face. "I'm sorry. So damn sorry. I had no idea he would..." The words caught in my throat, bitter and falling flat. "I don't even know what to say."

"Natalie. It wasn't your fault." He swallowed, coughed, then clutched his ribs, wincing. "Your boyfriend more than made up for it."

"What do you mean?"

"He took care of the hospital bill, the damage to my apartment, replaced my car. He didn't come to ask permission. Just to tell me he took care of everything."

"Why would he do that?"

His working eye blinked up at me. "Said you shouldn't have to worry. Said you'd feel like you owed me, and he wanted to carry that burden for you."

My knees could no longer hold my weight, so I perched my hip on Caleb's hospital bed.

"He's a good man." He coughed, winced. Breathed through the pain. "He's got it bad for you."

"I'm a little ruined for him, too."

Caleb shifted, adjusting his broken arm. "Can I ask you something?"

I reached across the bed to help him tuck a pillow under his cast. "Anything."

"Why are you here?"

"I don't understand that question."

"Why are you here and not with the man who clearly thinks you're the sun and stars and moon."

"Because my job. I'm a professional. I can't just up and leave." I was going to continue by giving him my two weeks' notice, but he was clearly on a mission and held up his good hand to keep me from speaking.

"Love is rare, Natalie. Bank jobs are plentiful."

A nervous laugh escaped. "Is this your polite way of asking me to leave after what happened? Oh, shit." I sat back, faking a gasp and clasping my chest. "Am I being fired?"

"God, no. You're an asset." He reached for my hand, squeezing gently. "Best job decision I ever made."

He was too easy. Clearly the guy was a romantic, and I couldn't wait to see how this played out. "Then why this conversation? I just got this promotion. This is a huge opportunity."

After a long pause and a deep breath, Caleb asked, "Do you love Cole?"

"Yes."

"Do you love him more than you love Whisper Springs?"

Silly question, but I'd humor my boss. I was the reason he'd been beaten half to death, after all. "Yes."

"Do you love him more than your apartment?"

"Of course." I refrained from rolling my eyes.

"Do you love him more than the thrill you get landing a client, surpassing your monthly goals, or being top dog at your job?"

"Yes." I bit my lip to contain a giggle.

Caleb's voice lowered to a scolding father level. "Would you love him if he lived in a cardboard box under a bridge?"

"I would." I crossed my arms, pinched my brows, and teased, "What's your point?"

With a huff, he growled, "Do you love him more than your pride, Natalie?"

"I can't imagine loving anyone or anything more than I love Cole." As the words left my lips, my pulse quickened. Saying those words out loud empowered me somehow. "I love him even more than I love Barolo."

"What?" He laughed, then winced.

Time to let him off the hook. "I appreciate your concern, Caleb. But honestly? I came here to ask a favor. Oh, and to give my notice."

Natalie

March 1st.
My birthday.

Our birthday.

Palms sweaty, gut churning, I re-read the string of texts.

Me: *I'm so sorry. I can't get out of this business trip. They threw it at me last minute.*

Cole: *Fuck, sunshine. It's our first birthday together.*

Me: *I tried to get out of it. You're mad. Please don't be mad. I'll make it up to you next weekend.*

Cole: *Where's the meeting? I'll come to you.*

Me: *I'd love that, but Caleb says it's a quick trip. We'll be in the air most of the time.*

Cole: *Caleb? You're traveling alone with Caleb?*

Me: *No. Mr. Sanchez, Caleb's boss, will be there, too.*

Cole: *Seriously? Traveling alone with two men?*

Me: *Hello...business trip!*

Cole: *...*

L.O.V.E.

Me: *You're mad.*

Cole: ...

Lying was not my forte. Nope. And I'd suffered for my deception—four weeks of no sleep. An ulcer-like pain in my gut. Zits. Found a gray hair two days ago.

But my dark days were over. In a few short minutes, I would be free of the fib.

I stood behind the heavy red curtain, the drone of conversations filtering through and adding to my racing pulse.

"You ready, doll?" Mona asked, squeezing my sweaty hand.

"Not even a little bit," I whispered. "Is he here? I'm too scared to look."

"Finn promised to have him here on time. Has to bring him in through the side door when the lights are down so he won't notice all the familiar faces. You won't be able to see him from the stage. But he'll be in the left corner if you want to look that direction."

"I can't believe I'm doing this."

"You'll be great." Mona kissed my cheek and then slipped away.

The spotlight fell on the stage, blinding me through the crack in the curtains. The dining room fell silent.

The bodice of my dress tightened, and I closed my eyes, drew in a slow, deep breath, then blew it out, releasing my nerves. The tiny box in my hand weighed a thousand pounds.

"Good evening," Mona rasped. "Tonight I have a very special guest. She's going to help me out with the first song. This is her first time on stage, so please make her feel welcome."

The piano started. My cue. One more deep inhale, exhale. As practiced, I slipped between the heavy fabric and into the spotlight next to Mona.

She sang the first line of "Someone To Watch Over Me", the part about love being blind.

I stood at her side, shaking harder than a chihuahua, fighting nervous tears. When it was my turn, I searched the dark to the left of the stage, hoping Cole would see on my face all that I was trying to tell him. When I sang about him being my big affair, my voice broke but, thank God, Mona stepped in until I gained my composure. She lowered her mic, and I struggled through the last verse, my chin quivering, but I managed to sing on key.

We finished the song to furious applause and whistles.

Mona stepped back into the dark, and I stood to the mic, trembling, squeezing the life out of that little box.

When the room fell silent once again, I cleared my throat and looked again to the left. "Cole Adams. According to our parents, you were the first man to ever make me smile. Apparently, I've loved you since the day we were born. We had a shaky start, to say the least, but..." I shook so hard my words faltered. "Oh, God." I scratched my head. Laughed. "I had a really good speech, but I can't remember a word. So bear with me."

Someone whistled. Someone shouted, "You got this, girl." More applause.

Clutching the box to my sternum, I drew a deep breath, then released my nerves in a long exhale. "Cole. You're my one. You've always been my one. I want you to watch over me every day until the day we die. And I want to be the one to watch over you, too. Happy Birthday, Cole." I held the box up in the direction where he was supposed to be seated and popped the lid. "Will you marry me?"

L.O.V.E.

The audience erupted. Whoops and hollers, whistles, thunderous applause.

No Cole.

Oh, God.

No Cole.

Cole

Jesus Christ, she was beautiful. A clingy black dress hugged her curves from breasts to wobbly ankles. Her hair was pinned up at the top, long loose waves falling over her bare back, and she wore a new pair of black glasses, glamorous cat-eye frames with touches of gold. I wanted nothing more than to get her alone and help her out of that gown.

It'd be a long time before that happened.

I slipped out of the shadows and took my seat. I hated leaving her there, alone on that stage, heart on her sleeve, vulnerable, waiting for me to come to her rescue. With everything in me, I hated leaving her there.

"Fuck, I'm a jackass," I whispered.

Finn gave my shoulder a squeeze. "You're doing the right thing."

Fate didn't play fair. She'd been downright nasty in my opinion. But there was no denying, my future with Natalie was well earned. The woman on that stage had been through hell and back to be with me. She deserved the world on a silver fucking platter. She deserved a proper fucking proposal.

I had no doubt I was doing the right thing.

But shit, I hated watching her shoulders slump when she realized I wasn't joining her.

The spotlight shut off with an audible click, leaving Natalie in total darkness. The entire house fell quiet, each and every one of our guests privy to the turn of events. All but Natalie.

When the blue light shone again on Mona, Natalie gasped.

I spread my fingers on the ivory and started to play.

Mona started the first line of "L-O-V-E" by Nat King Cole.

The crowd applauded.

Mona continued to croon while sauntering my way, until we were both encased by the only source of light in the room.

Natalie sobbed. Mona sat next to me and took over the keys.

Fuck, I was about to make a fool of myself, ruin a beloved song, in front of all our friends and family, and Ellis would undoubtedly record every second and use the footage to humiliate me for the rest of our lives. But goddamn, Natalie King was worth the sacrifice. My pride. My balls. Everything. Anything. Amen and thank you, Jesus.

I leaned into the mic and sang about the letter V, those five words spot-on because goddamn, our love affair was very fucking extraordinary.

My voice cracked. Singing was not my strong suit, but the evening wasn't about talent. The performance was about Natalie and doing right by my girl.

She hadn't moved from her spot center stage, so I joined her there, circling, throwing in a shuffle here and a sashay there, butchering the song. She laughed, though tears poured down her face.

On the last line I dropped to my knees, laid down the mic, and pulled the little blue box from my pocket.

I couldn't hear myself talk over the roar of the audience, all of them friends and family. Natalie joined me on the floor, her steepled hands pressed to her lips, those ridiculously adorable frames sliding down her nose.

Fuck, she was gorgeous. She was everything. I gripped the side of her glasses and slid them back into place.

The audience chanted, "Nat King Cole, Nat King Cole."

I'd practiced a speech as well.

Staring at my girl, my future, I couldn't remember a word.

I removed the ring from the box. Pulled her hand away from her face, then slid the gold band onto her finger. I leaned close, kissed her wet lips, then whispered, "Yes, I'll marry you. My heart is yours. Always has been. Please, please don't break it, baby."

Natalie

We celebrated into the early morning hours. Until I couldn't dance anymore, cry anymore, or hug, laugh, or see straight.

Cole drove me to his home above the gym. His one-bedroom apartment where a prince of the city lived like a commoner.

We made our way up the stairs. Cole carried my shoes and held me close. Inside the apartment, he helped me out of his suit jacket and then toed of his shoes.

"Still living above the gym," I teased, looking around the dark space.

"Got a problem with that, sunshine?" He pinned me to the door, his gaze fixed on my lips.

"I don't." I grazed his mouth, savoring the taste of tobacco, the Cuban he'd shared with my father. "In fact, I like it here."

"Yeah?" He dropped his head and nibbled the top of my breast.

"I do. I love the view."

He chuckled. "There is no view."

I wiggled free and escaped to the window, where he pinned me once again, my back to his front, my breasts smashed against the glass. Soft kisses dotted my shoulder, eliciting a shiver.

"The view is extraordinary." I tapped a finger on the window and pointed. "See that building?"

He lifted his head. "There's nothing out there but buildings."

"The silver one that's shorter than the others."

He slid his hands to my waist and rested his chin on my shoulder. "That's your old bank building."

Cole thought he'd had the last laugh, hijacking my proposal party. But that soiree wasn't my only birthday surprise. Swaying my hips against his erection, I whispered, "That's where I work."

His arms snaked around my waist. "Are you fucking with me right now?"

"I start next week."

With a grunt, he flipped me around to face him, then kissed me with all the grace of a drunk baboon. "You did that for me?"

"No. I did that because I love this apartment." I shoved him away and made for the bedroom, trusting he'd follow. "It's walking distance. And my favorite coffee shop is just around the corner."

L.O.V.E.

I stopped at the foot of the bed, then peeled the black, stretchy gown down, over my breasts, past my waist, my thighs, then let it fall to the floor. "I did it because there's this gym downstairs with a really hot owner. Nothing turns me on like sweaty men with muscles."

"Fuck, Natalie." He leaned against the dresser, drinking me in. "You were naked under that dress this whole time?"

I looked down at my naked body and shrugged. "No room for undergarments."

He unbuttoned his shirt cuffs. Then yanked at his tie and dropped it at his feet. "Had I known that, I would've thrown you over my shoulder hours ago and skipped to the end."

He removed his shirt while he stalked closer.

"But then I wouldn't have been able to hear you sing." I grabbed his belt and kissed his neck while I worked the buckle, my entire body tingling with need.

"So you're back home. For good?"

"No more long distance love affair." God, what a great feeling.

Impatient with my trembling fingers, Cole shoved his pants to the floor and kicked them out of the way. His boxers followed.

We stood toe to toe, skin to skin, my eyes level with the cross he wore around his neck.

His chest rose and fell twice before his lips landed on my forehead and he asked, "What did I do to deserve you?"

I lifted my chin to savor his golden gaze. "We didn't have to do anything, because you're my destiny, remember?"

"I'll never forget." Heat poured from his body. "Happy birthday, Natalie."

"Happy birthday, Cole."

He wrapped an arm around my waist, then took my left hand in his right, and we danced in the dark room, naked as the day we were born.

Free to laugh. Free to dance. Free to love.

The End

Thank you so much for reading L.O.V.E. Thank you for sticking through the ups and downs, the pretty parts and the frustrating situations. Like life, Cole and Natalie had tough decisions to make. They stuck to their guns, and chose the paths they believed right. And because this is romance, their integrity and faithfulness paid off in the end. My wish for you, my cherished readers, is your own personal happily ever after, no matter your journey.

Acknowledgements

SexyBoyfriend. Our love story isn't always pretty, but I've never doubted that you are my destiny. We have countless chapters to go and I can't wait to see how our journey plays out.

My babies. You are my everything, even when I'm locked in my office and begging you not to bother me.

Corinne. Thank you for your wisdom and guidance. I'm beyond grateful to work with you again. I hope there are many books in our future.

Lia. You are gracious and gorgeous and you always lift my spirits. Thank you so much for working on this book with me. Your kind words always come when I need them most.

Gloria. I love and respect the hell out of you. Thank you for being my cheerleader in both my careers.

Tyler, Jennifer, Hanna, and Gloria. Thank you so much for taking time to read L.O.V.E. in its early stages and giving me your thoughtful feedback.

Jessica and all the lovely ladies at InkSlinger PR. Thank you so much for all your hard work and helping me get this book into the hands of readers.

Other Books

The Truck Stop Series
Truck Stop Tango
Truck Stop Tryst
Truck Stop Tempest
Truck Stop Titan

Standalones
How To Kill Your Boss
L.O.V.E.

Apotheosis Series
Aflame
Aglow

Connect

Website
krissydaniels.com

Facebook
www.facebook.com/authorkrissydaniels/

Instagram
www.instagram.com/krissydanielsbooks/

Twitter
twitter.com/kdanielsbooks

BookBub
www.bookbub.com/profile/krissy-daniels

Newsletter
https://bit.ly/krissynews

Lightning Source UK Ltd.
Milton Keynes UK
UKHW011506070720
366156UK00003B/616

9 781733 615983